A dinner

"I loved this book."

"I felt I was part of New York society back in the good
old days of larger than life,
quirky, but always interesting characters.
I would have loved being at this dinner and reading this
book was a real treat."

Judy Osborne

"I really enjoyed the book,

and the way it is written. It was good to see some of the
most interesting people at that time, 1958, come alive again
for the book. Even though it is fictional,
I could see the interactions of them before me as the author is very good at telling the story and creating the dialogue
between the characters."

Zassi, Amazon.com review

Dinner at Mr. B's

Karen Hagestad Cacy

"A dinner invitation, once accepted, is a sacred obligation. If you die before the dinner takes place, your executor must attend."
Ward McAllister, New York socialite of the late 1800s.

ALSO BY KAREN HAGESTAD CACY

Fiction

Death by President
Return to Ismailia
Summer at Pebble Beach

Plays

"SAY UNCLE!"
Dinner at Mr. B's

This is a work of fiction.
Places and incidents are either the product of the author's imagination or are used fictitiously. Any resemblance to actual events is entirely coincidental.

However:
Mr. Balanchine's and his guests were celebrities, people who lived their lives in the public domain. Many conversations contained here are drawn from their actual pronouncements and may be found in various biographies and other non-fiction sources from the era.
(Please refer to notes at end of book, for annotated sources.)

Ballet lovers credit George Balanchine for revolutionizing the art form known as ballet by inventing new, transcendent life forms. Of one of his stars, Suzanne Farrell, the impresario said *"I call her 'pussy-cat fish,' because the cat was cheetah, for speed, and the fish was dolphin, for intelligence."*

Impresario: im.pre.sa.rio\n,
1: the promoter, manager or conductor of an opera or concert company
2: one who puts on or sponsors an entertainment.
Webster's Ninth New Collegiate Dictionary, Merriam-Webster, Inc., 1990.

George Balanchine, known as "Mr. B" to those closest to him, directed the New York City Ballet from 1948 to 1982. As America's premier dance impresario, Balanchine forged the traditions of the Russian ballet with the American Century, setting the standards and direction of ballet for years to come.

He might have agreed with one of his dancers, Gelsey Kirkland, who said, "Ballet is a riddle of means and ends . . . It is as if the performer and spectator come together to hold in their hands a bird with a broken wing. The creature can be felt to stir, to struggle for freedom. Its life responds to human warmth; its wing might brush your cheek as it flies away."

This book is dedicated to:

Four contemporary ballet choreographers:
Nacho Duato
Nicolo Fonte,C
Christopher Stowell
Christopher Wheeldon.

With energy and humor, they are building on the traditions of
Petipa, Diaghilev, and Balanchine.

The future of ballet is in good hands.

Preface

"Everyone is ga-ga on names today. That's why the paparazzi have taken over. People can't get over other people." **Diana Vreeland**

A voracious reader, Jacqueline Kennedy Onassis, once was asked if there were persons in history living or dead she would choose to dine with, who would they be? Her answer was certain and immediate: Oscar Wilde, the notorious British playwright, and Sergei Diaghilev, the famous impresario and founder of the Ballet Russes de Sergei Diaghilev.

We read biographies for a similar reason: to draw closer to persons we otherwise might not have occasion to know. The constraints against meeting notable figures in contemporary history are numerous, insurmountable, and obvious. Socially, few of us have occasion to cross paths with illustrious figures. Geography and the accident of the birth-death continuum intervene to cause further separation. Always, the sentry of reality stands guard, allowing only occasional glimpses into these famous persons' lives.

Who among us has not yearned to be the cat under a certain dinner table, privy to the clever repartee and important banter at a crystal soiree attended by 'the interesting?' Biographies only leave us wanting more. We imagine that we know these subjects on the page, when in reality our literary acquaintances are but fantasy. All we are left with as we close the book are a few discrete facts offered up by historians viewed through the distortions of time, place, and the author's viewpoint.

Reading on, we may learn that some of our subjects crossed each other's paths in real life. One person's biography may provide information not only about our subject, but about others orbiting his sphere as well. Connecting the dots of other times and other places, we live among ghosts of persons who are well worth knowing, yet who are in the end, unknowable. Still, we try. We vicariously attend their parties . . . imagine what they might say to so-and-so, in such-and-such situation . . . placing ourselves at the center of the action.

DINNER AT MR. B'S is one literary stalker's attempt to square the deal. The guests may or may not have known each other. Many of their words are their own however, here their conversations take place without regard to the chimera of 'reality.'

The host of this fantasy party, world-renowned choreographer, George Balanchine, is director of The New York City Ballet Company. He is a complicated man whose view of his own worth is surprisingly humble. Speaking of the many memorable ballets he created, he said, "What I do is assemble ingredients – it is like opening an icebox door and you look inside to see what you have stored away – and then I select, combine, and hope that the results will be appetizing."

In a similar way, guests for **DINNER AT MR. B's** were haphazardly selected, one from over here, another from over there. All are fascinating, accomplished people with larger-than-life stories. All have had numerous biographies, articles and interviews published covering their illustrious lives and careers.

There are ten for dinner this evening. One was kicked out of his country and two others had to emigrate for political reasons. Four began their lives in dismal poverty; the same four are self-made. At least two are Nazi sympathizers, while another becomes a spy in the employ of Israel's Mossad. Four others have changed their birth names other than by marriage and seven are married at the time of the party. Guests' ages range from thirty-two to sixty-four.

So, sit back, have a cocktail, and enjoy the party. We are the cat under the table. Let's join the conversation.

Dramatis Personae:

The Impresario: **George Balanchine**
Director of The New York City Ballet

The Mystery Guest: **David, Duke of Windsor**
The man who gave up the British throne for love.

The Wife: **Wallis, Duchess of Windsor**
The Baltimore woman who stole the King of England

The Gossip: **Truman Capote**
Southern American novelist, author of _"Other Voices, Other Rooms"_
and _"Breakfast at Tiffany's."_

The Coquette: **Pamela Digby Churchill**
Ex-wife of Randolph Churchill, mistress of Elie de Rothschild and
Gianni Agnelli, future wife of Averell Harriman and future Ambassador to
France.

The Fabulist: **Sir Cecil Walter Hardy Beaton**
Photographer and stylist to British royalty, Hollywood and the very
wealthy.

The Chinoise: **Diana Vreeland**
Editor of _Harper's Bazaar_ and _Vogue_ magazines.

The Swan: **Pat Buckley**
Wife of conservative editor of _The National Review_ magazine, William
F. Buckley, Jr.

The Mogul: **Robert Maxwell**
Billionaire Czech newspaper publisher, friend of statesmen, future
Mossad spy

The Star: **Marilyn Monroe**
America's iconic rags-to-riches film star

The Aide: **Rene Deriabin**
George Balanchine's "Man Friday'

The Sommelier: **Andreev Gromov**
Russian Tea Room bartender

The Ballerina: **Tanaquil Le Clercq, "Tanny"**
Ill-fated star of The New York City Ballet and fourth wife of George
Balanchine

George Balanchine's Performing Cat: **"Mourka"**

Curtain Going Up!

The Best People

It was four a.m., Saturday morning, June 21, 1958.

New York's finest and an Interpol officer were on their way; A representative of the British consulate in New York City had been notified; and it was likely that President Dwight D. Eisenhower would be briefed on the incident before the week was out.

The officers, used to being called to parties spinning out of control in the Big Apple, arrived to a uniquely bizarre and troubling scene, even for them. On one side of the room, sobbing, was the Duchess of Windsor. Her nylon was torn and her distraught husband, the Duke of Windsor, one-time future King of England, was on his knees, mopping up a bleeding gash in her leg.

In another corner, an obviously upset Marilyn Monroe, was being comforted by three women. The front of her dress appeared to be torn.

The famous author, Truman Capote, was walking in circles in the middle of the room, repeating, "I'm beside myself! I'm beside myself!" Unlike the others, he seemed oddly happy.

The host of this out-of-control dinner party, George Balanchine, the normally calm director of The New York City Ballet, was speaking intently in Russian to two men. Various white-coated servers scurried around, replacing chairs that were tipped over and righting lamps that had landed on the carpet.

Of more immediate concern was a very large, very drunken man, leaning out over the high balcony, threatening to jump. The man's trousers were missing. Three police officers pulled the man back to safety and restrained him. Inside, the Interpol officer began identifying and interviewing the guests. The officers knew they had to get this one right. When celebrities and police intersect, only one of the two generally escapes unscathed.

The Interpol man was reminded of a similar party scene in an Italian opera. In it, a man is arrested and instructed to report to prison. The man takes great pains to clean himself up and dons a formal tuxedo before reporting. Someone asks him why he is bothering to dress for jail.

His response: "My good man, one meets some of the best people in jail!"

Chapter One
George Balanchine

May, 1958
New York City

"Tanny's in hospital again."

George Balanchine, New York City's preeminent ballet impresario, was talking with his man-servant, Rene. A Manhattan penthouse's magnificent terrace, Balanchine's own '*mise-en-scene,*' glowed in the city's early summer evening just past sunset. The garden's trees and lush shrubbery stood guard as the lights of this spectacular city partnered with Lincoln Center's stage lights to provide Balanchine a gleaming palette for his life and art.

Tanaquil Le Clercq

Beyond the apartment's Russian icons, velvet draperies, and priceless antiques inexplicably mixed with a collection of quirky objects brought in by the impresario to cheer up his ill wife, his terrace this summer evening fairly cried out for cocktails and the sophisticated conversation and village gossip typical of balconies all over the city once candles were lit.

Summer in the City: Women's jewels would sparkle, crystal goblets would drive home the point, and the magical patina of America's favorite city would take over. The delights of an urban evening awaited most participants even as one of its foremost ballerinas was delivered more pain medication in a stark white hospital room nearby.

K a r e n   H a g e s t a d   C a c y

Balanchine's lofty garden was lovingly tended by the patient, his wife, ballerina Tanaquil Le Clercq. The dancer with the impossibly long legs, who on stage seemingly could jump a mile high with the grace of an eland, now two years later, was confined to a wheelchair by the polio that from its cruel onset in Copenhagen while on tour in 1956, now claimed her career, but not yet her life.

---

george balanchine, through the eyes of diana vreeland:
"A dancer's life must be the most exciting thing in the world – and the most excruciating. But, to have performed one arc of the arm, one moment of beauty, one something . . ."

Rene's concern was evident in his serious tone: "Her pain has worsened?"

"They are increasing the morphine. For that, I am told, she must be in hospital. She will be home tomorrow. Then, we shall take her to the cottage. Perhaps the country air will do her more good than this noisy, impersonal city."

For this information, Rene had no good answer. Instead, he lit the candles on the patio, fussed over some dirt that had spilled from a container. He grabbed the vodka from the refrigerator and made his boss a simple drink over ice. Conversation was not necessary. His presence and steady silence was all the famous artist required now.

Rene, like Balanchine, was a Russian émigré. As his employer achieved critical acclaim in America, Rene preferred to observe life from in front of the footlights. He cared for "Mr. B" in every way imaginable. He spoke only in Russian; if anyone addressed him in English, he feigned confusion. He was a Russian through and through. And he was devoted to George Balanchine.

'Tanny' was Tanaquil Le Clercq, Balanchine's fourth wife, one of Balanchine's prized ballerinas. Her long limbs carried the purity and strength of Balanchine's new distinctly American ballet form. At least they had once. Le Clercq and her mentor carried forward the tradition of Petipa, but clarified it to create a fresher version that would lead the way for ballet the world over for years to come.

NY City Ballet Dancers

sergei diaghilev, through the eyes of diana vreeland:
"Diaghilev and his Ballets Russes had an enormous impact on fashion. The first great twentieth-century couturier, Paul Poiret, got many of his ideas from Diaghilev."

If one somehow were to combine Old World elegance with the power and lean strength of the racing horse, then one might begin to understand the Balanchine ballerina. Lithe, long-limbed, and uniquely and athletically American. Yet, with the Russian heritage brought by their impresario, these new dancers showed their pedigrees, with a classical ancestry that stretched all the way back to the Mariinsky Theatre in St. Petersburg. For this pleasing and somewhat surprising combination, they had Balanchine to thank -- the man in velvet smoking jacket who could whip up a plate of Russian piroshkies as easily as he later would choreograph a startling new masterpiece set to Stravinsky's latest work.

Born in Paris, Balanchine's wife, Tanaquil Le Clercq, was the first ballerina wholly trained in his style. At 15, he tapped her to dance with him in choreography he made to be performed at a benefit for a Polio charity. In the ballet, Balanchine was a character named Polio and Tanaquil was his

Karen Hagestad Cacy

victim who became paralyzed and fell to the floor. Children tossed dimes at Le Clercq whereupon she got up and danced again.

Some years later, in 1956, while touring with the company in Copenhagen, in a development too hideous to imagine, Le Clercq contracted the actual disease. Balanchine took a year off from work to tend to his stricken wife. It was two years later and Balanchine was back at the New York City Ballet Company.

Now in May, Balanchine's triumphal 1958 season had just ended, and the city's early summer heat was still a pleasant novelty. New Yorkers were beginning to think about packing for their annual retreats to the mountains to escape the city's summer heat. Balanchine was back to his normal activities as his wife, paralyzed from the waist down and confined to a wheelchair, divided her time between giving company classes and the couple's country home in Connecticut. She would never walk again, let alone dance, lingering evidence of God's folly: a famous ballerina struck down in her prime.

> ### tanaquil le clercq, through the eyes of leon barzin:
> "The best, of course, was Tanaquil Le Clercq. . . . She could dance to anything. She danced to music, not to counts. I remember when she caught polio in Denmark. She had just danced the last movement of *Western Symphony*. I came up and put my scarf around her, she was so wringing wet. The next morning, she couldn't get up. That was the end. It was really a very tragic moment for the New York City Ballet.

As Balanchine accepted the iced vodka from Rene, he said, "Now, more therapy, I expect. Always, more therapy. It never ends, it seems."

Karen Hagestad Cacy

Rene noted Mr. B's distress. Even without an ill wife, he knew that Balanchine would be up nights pacing the floor, listening to the latest musical score, devising in his fertile mind a new ballet season to top the last one. But now he also waited on his dear wife, here, adjusting a lap robe, there, bringing her a favorite cup of Russian tea in a glass with raspberry jam. The furrows on his brow deepened as he told Rene the news.

Rene responded, "Notchka, let me prepare your favorite chakhobili and reheat the eggplant for your supper. A glass of wine. It is not your fault. You must stop worrying so much. Now, about the company, now, about Tanny's health. Never, about yourself. You must take a break."

"A break. To the coast or the mountains, you mean."

"Not at all. Not at all. Look, you have your special guests arriving soon from France. Why not prepare a little party for them? Perhaps they could be your mystery guests. You could plan it all. Forget the stage for once. Let this beautiful Russian apartment be your setting. Stage it, Notchka. Plan it and then step back to observe and enjoy."

Rene kept a close eye on Balanchine's home atmosphere and temperament. He knew when to suggest, when to step back into the shadows. So many celebrities flitted around Balanchine. They all wanted to see him, to touch him, to know him. He knew his boss might warm to his idea of staging a party -- a chance to be in control of others, to manage them, to manipulate them on his own terms. It was not that Balanchine was a superficial, petty man. But he did love a good gossip, the same as anyone. And a trifling diversion now seemed more than appropriate to take his mind off Tanny. And to free up his spirit for the creative juices that would be needed for the coming season.

He knew the idea was being seriously considered when Balanchine answered pensively in Russian, *"Mojet Byeech."*

"Perhaps."

A start to a memorable evening. One like no other. Rene knew Balanchine would arrange his guests at the table as if he were a woman

Karen Hagestad Cacy

preparing a ball. There would be his hand-dried Baccarat glasses for sipping his favorite dry white Burgundy, Chateau de Puligny-Montrachet. And the menu, ah, the menu!

The busy impresario absent-mindedly clinked the melting ice in his glass as he mulled over Rene's suggestion. Invitations would be lovingly engraved. The guest list would be designed to provide an evening of enchanting conversation and perhaps a little drama. He was, after all, Russian. Nothing less could be expected of such a man.

As Rene brought Mr. B. another iced vodka, he noticed him already studying a desk calendar. One day, Friday, June 20, was circled. Above the date floated a small drawing of a champagne glass.

> ### george balanchine, through the eyes of others:
> "His Russian Easter party was always the main festivity of the year. His Russian friends would gather at the apartment to dine right after midnight services. The next day another party would be held for Americans, non-Orthodox, and other friends. For these Easter celebrations he always prepared his most lavish board – roasts, ptarmigans, fish in aspic, specially prepared horseradish and garnishes, Salade Oliviere, and, of course, the traditional pascha and kulitch, which contain all the rich ingredients and exotic tastes one dreams of during Lent: sweet butter by the pound, mounds of sugar, vanilla beans, saffron, cardamom, pressed almonds, raisins."

Good, thought Rene, as he moved into the kitchen to warm the Eggplant a la Russe Mr. B., an avid cook, prepared earlier. Already he could feel the mood lightening. Perhaps things could be put right. Music and laughter would fill the apartment again. To be sure, no summer party would make a difference in Tanny's health. But a memorable evening might provide temporary solace to her husband, the great man of American ballet.

Through the open door, Rene could hear Mr. B. begin to laugh. Rene knew the mystery guest's identity. What he did not yet know were the names of the other guests being selected to amuse that important person.

Obviously, the mere thought of who might attend his Manhattan summer party already was providing the ballet master with much-needed relief.

Rene silently congratulated himself and reached for his own vodka. Mr. B. was fortunate to have such a man in his service, he thought, not for the first time. A fellow Russian, a man of many talents, Rene Deriabin.

---

tanaquil le clercq, through the eyes of ellen moylan:
"Tanny Le Clercq was magnificent as Choleric... Have you ever seen the great blue crane in flight? They are magnificent birds with long necks and long legs... Tanny's movement reminded me of that crane... "

Chapter Two
Marilyn Monroe

Two years in, Mrs. Arthur Miller's marriage was up and down. Today, it was down, and so was she. She was staying alone at her own apartment on East 57th Street, while her author husband was holed up in his Roxbury, Connecticut den, writing.

Marilyn Monroe

Outwardly, the world was at her feet. Film maker, Billy Wilder, said of Mrs. Miller's doppelganger, Marilyn Monroe, "God gave her everything. She does two things beautifully: she walks and she stands still." Photographer of the stars, Eve Arnold, observed, "Her skin was translucent, white, luminous. Up close around the periphery of her face, there was a dusting of faint down. This light fuzz trapped light and caused an aureole to form, giving her a faint glow on film."

Joining a chorus of admirers, Sammy Davis, Jr. added, "She hangs like a bat in men's minds." Yet, on her desk, in a clutter of papers and books (Arthur was after her to read Sandburg's book on Lincoln,) torn scraps of paper revealed the star's present harried state of mind.

Away from the limelight, she was a moody and troubled actress who was a nervous scribbler, an armchair poet. Today's effort was characteristically somber:

K a r e n   H a g e s t a d   C a c y

Life –

I am of both of your directions
Life (crossed out)
Somehow remaining hanging downward
the most
but strong as a cobweb in the
wind – I exist more with the cold glistening frost.
But my beaded rays have the colors I've
seen in a painting – ah life they
have cheated you.

As with other narcissistic actors, Marilyn Monroe, was well aware of the effect she had on others. Agreeing with her many fans, she too admired the creature staring back at her in the mirror. Throughout the years, her mythological star power had snowballed, carrying her to this day in New York. But it all was growing too complicated. Her own coming of age, a past insistent on catching up with her, and the stresses of trying to fit into her husband's world of east coast intellectuals were combining to pull her off center.

In her sparsely decorated, messy apartment, a framed photograph caught her eye. Cecil Beaton had photographed her for a feature in Harper's Bazaar. She cherished this picture. It was slightly grainy, as though it were a color shot that had been transposed to black and white. She noted that in it she looked about sixteen years old. She was holding a rose in one hand.

K a r e n   H a g e s t a d   C a c y

How innocent I look, she thought with regret. In a hand-written note that accompanied the photograph, Cecil Beaton wrote, "You call to mind the bouquet of fireworks display, eliciting from your awed spectators an open-mouthed chorus of wondrous 'Oohs' and 'Ah's.' You are as spectacular as the silvery shower of a Vesuvius fountain; you have rocketed from obscurity to become our post war sex symbol—the pin-up girl of an age. And whatever press agentry or manufactured illusion may have lit the fuse, it is your own weird genius that has sustained your flight."

---

marilyn monroe, through the eyes of billy wilder:
"If she wanted to go to school, she should go to railroad engineering school and learn to run on time."

Arthur read the note. For some reason, it upset him. He made some comment about it being 'from one queen to another.' And that, she knew, was the problem growing in her marriage. Once again, the glare of her stardom was overshadowing people close to her. Even as she strove to fit into his world, to finish James Joyce's *"Ulysses,"* and read Sandburg's book to please Miller, the outside world was driving a wedge between them.

With the world at her feet, all she really wanted was family, stability, and love, three things her younger self, Norma Jean Mortenson, never had. Now, she found herself wanting and needing more. She wanted credit for the real person lurking behind the Hollywood image. But as of 1958, she was still an outcast, especially in the elite village of Manhattan where her intellectual husband was scarcely tolerated for his choice to marry her. When she married Arthur Miller one wise guy even remarked that she'd married her college education.

The phone jarred her from her reverie. It was Arthur. His tone was cold and sarcastic. He'd opened the mail and found an invitation to a dinner party hosted by the ballet master, George Balanchine. He read it to her.

George Balanchine cordially requests

the pleasure of your company

at dinner Friday evening, June 20.

Cocktails will commence at 8 p.m.

Guests are kindly asked to come alone.

A 'Mystery Guest' will be joining us for dinner.

George Balanchine

79th and Broadway, No. 436

R.S.V.P.

Sheldon 6-4431

"Can you believe it?! He's telling his guests to come alone! Can he really be excluding you? I wonder if the ballet master, in his ivory tower, has gotten the news yet that we're married?!"

Marilyn listened to the man she loved, in his indignity, return to her. In a burst of domesticity, her mind wandered to the Spaghetti Carbonara she planned on making for their dinner later in Connecticut. She made a mental note to grab candles, a loaf of French bread, and a special bottle of wine

Karen Hagestad Cacy

before she left the city. As so often happened in their marriage, what she was thinking was different from what she voiced to her husband.

Another thought sprang to mind.

Relief.

So often in Hollywood and New York, she was aware people invited 'Marilyn Monroe, the Star' to their parties as cavalierly as they might engage the services of a performing monkey. Invite the beautiful film star as window dressing. Wittingly or not, one host was saving her from such treatment. Silently, she thanked George Balanchine, a man she'd never met.

She once said, "While it's nice to be included in people's fantasies, you also like to be accepted for your own sake. . . . I'll think I have a few wonderful friends and all of a sudden, oh, here it comes. They do a lot of things. They talk about you in the press, to their friends, tell stories and you know, it's disappointing."

She added, "Of course it does depend on the people, but sometimes I'm invited places to kind of brighten up a dinner table like a musician who'll play the piano after dinner, and I know they're not really invited for yourself. (sic) You're just an ornament."

---

marilyn monroe, through the eyes of actor, sir laurence olivier:
"She has the extraordinarily cunning gift of being able to suggest one minute that she is the naughtiest little thing and the next minute that she is beautifully dumb and innocent."

For now, Marilyn Monroe, nee Norma Jean Mortenson, simply answered her husband. "But you must go. If that's what the invitation requests."

"No, my dear. I have a better idea: We'll play our own little joke on George. What if you invited a novelist and Marilyn Monroe showed up

Karen Hagestad Cacy

instead? He says he has a Mystery Guest. Little does he know! Let's do this. You play the role of his other Mystery Guest. Say yes, darling. It will be fun!"

How could she refuse him? He seemed so pleased with himself. Once again, he seemed to take pride in her. He was including her in the fun. It was enough for now. He wanted her to stop by the bookstore on her way to the country. Would she pick up several books for him? Of, course. That was what a wife should do.

She gathered her things and ran out onto Madison Avenue, noting with happiness the bustle of the city. Everyone seemed to have places to go and things to do. Like herself. She had somewhere to go, someone to go to, something to do. She hailed a taxicab.

Today, she enjoyed once again playing her own little star-game. As so often happened in cabs, her driver swiveled around, looked momentarily puzzled, and commented, "You know, ma'am, if you lost some weight, put on a little makeup, and combed your hair, you would look exactly like Marilyn Monroe."

The cabbie's words were as water to a parched man: affirmation. Good, she thought with satisfaction, I can still be part of the crowd. I am an actress. When I choose, and only when I choose, I shall turn on 'La Monroe,' for your pleasure. But not today. Today, I am just a wife on her way to her husband, who's busy at work.

through the eyes of arthur miller:
"Maybe all one can do is hope to end up with the right regrets."

Her little drama script showed a rampant imagination shared by the very few and the very privileged. Some practiced their craft from inside the ivied walls of sanitariums. Others were still on the outside, walking free. According to Harper's Bazaar editor, Diana Vreeland, a fellow fantasist, "For years, I dreamed I was Bernhardt. Either I was Salome, or I was some Polish tart . . . I was terribly dramatic. I mean, I was never not Bernhardt."

K a r e n   H a g e s t a d   C a c y

marilyn monroe, through the eyes of her photographer, eve arnold: "

"She was already late . . . At eleven in the morning she wore a black velvet gown with straps the width of spaghetti strands . . . When I complimented her on the way she looked, she winked at me in the mirror and said 'Just watch me.' . . . First Marilyn appeared with Olivier, Rattigan and Milton Greene. They were on a balcony and below them were the press. Slowly Marilyn and Olivier came down the stairs and were engulfed by the crowd of friendly professionals. . . . At first Sir Laurence gravely and seriously answered. Then Marilyn settled in, removed her coat, leaned forwards – and broke one of her thinner-than-thin straps. Suddenly the atmosphere changed – she made it fun: laughter was heard, a safety pin was offered and the press conference was hers."

Karen Hagestad Cacy

Chapter Three
Cecil Beaton

"My dear, he's such a snob!"

Balanchine was taken aback by his friend's harsh reaction to the mention of his mystery guest. As someone who dealt with artistic temperaments for a living, he remained silent as his friend continued on the phone.

"The Duke of Windsor has never really liked me, you know. We never got on well. And his face! His face is what happens to a person whose life has no purpose. His face shows his empty life. Tragic, actually: He rather resembles a mad terrier, haunted one moment, then with a flick of the hand he laughs fecklessly."

Sir Cecil Beaton

At Balanchine's silence, Cecil Beaton, famed British photographer, realized he'd gone too far. Lamely, he ended it, "But, I suppose, he is your friend. His wife, the Baltimore divorcee, is rather fun at parties," he sniffed. Then, coming around, Beaton added, "Actually, Wallis has been a good friend to me, I like her. She is a good friend to all her friends. There is no malice in her. There is nothing dislikeable. She is just not of the degree that has reason to be around the Throne."

George Balanchine was invited to elegant parties all the time. As he began to plan his own, he considered mood and tone with the same care he took in composing a new ballet. Balanchine recalled the parties of one of the city's most successful hosts, Leo Lerman, a magazine editor. Lerman held impromptu parties in his Upper East Side townhouse. He served what he called 'nasty wine,' old biscuits and cheddar cheese.

Despite Lerman's meagre offerings, his home always was filled with the most interesting collection of artists and other elites crowding into stairwells and even into his bedroom where he often held court from bed. Once, Balanchine was surprised to come upon Rudolph Nureyev seated on Lerman's floor discussing Kremlin architecture with Lerman and several other guests perched on his bed.

On the other end of the party spectrum were parties thrown by Bennett Cerf, Random House editor for Truman Capote and many other noteworthy authors. *'Chez Cerf,'* every detail was done to formal perfection. His wife, for instance, insisted there be an equal number of men and women. Edna Ferber, a frequent guest, thought the rule ridiculous, observing that guests were getting together to eat, not to mate.

In 1958, change was in the air. Rock and roll co-existed in popular culture with Frank Sinatra and Ella Fitzgerald. The chemise and jet travel were coming on line, white tie, and physical contact with your partner on the dance floor were exiting. General Charles de Gaulle was France's new premier, General Dwight David Eisenhower was President, Elvis Presley entered the U.S. Army.

Also, that spring: the novels, *"Breakfast at Tiffany's,"* by Truman Capote, and *"Exodus,"* by Leon Uris, were best sellers; the Lerner and Loewe play, *"My Fair Lady,"* opened to critical acclaim April 29 in London; the film, *"Gigi,"* premiered in New York City in May; the United States National Air and Space Administration (NASA) opened its doors for the first time; and World Cup soccer competition was set to take place in Sweden.

Balanchine, the Russian transplant, loved everything about America and his adopted city of New York. Just as his ballets freely mixed the traditions of Petipa with the modern classicism of Stravinsky's newest compositions, so too, it was a safe bet, would his party mirror contemporary society. He was a traditionalist who was cognizant of the new age and all it had to offer. No one ever caught Balanchine standing in the past for long.

In the rarified air of New York City's theatrical and cultural community, he was a celebrity, but he was also a common man in many ways. While other successful artists tended to live guarded lives in their own private spheres of narcissism, Balanchine walked the streets of New York, breathing it all in. Some days, he would notice the city's distinctive street smells. Other days, he would look skyward, appreciating the city's unique architecture, gargoyles, and all. Everything and everyone interested him, in no apparent logical order. He was like a clever Russian squirrel, collecting experiences for the winter. Little escaped his keen notice.

By the same token, his many acquaintances fell into every conceivable category. Some, like him, were well known. Others, he ran across in the course of running one of the world's finest, most innovative ballet companies. There was no apparent rhyme or reason to his haphazard collection of friends located around the world.

Rene was not surprised to answer the phone that day to Cecil Beaton, noted British photographer and Hollywood set designer. Beaton had re-decorated Windsor Castle, photographed the privileged, designed memorable sets for Balanchine and the Metropolitan Opera, and travelled the world as an erudite and amusing homosexual house guest to the elite. Beaton, like Balanchine, was a circumspect observer of humanity. It was clear he took pains to nurture his friendship with the ballet master.

The man so critical of the Duke of Windsor at the same time appreciated Balanchine's down-to-earth qualities: The ballet master liked science fiction (he was ecstatic about the creation of a new American space agency,) TV westerns, and American ice cream. He wore bright pearl buttoned shirts, black string ties, a gambler's plaid vest and frontier pants. Today, Beaton's call caught the ballet master at home, ironing his shirts.

Besides the men's professional collaboration, Balanchine always enjoyed the witty commentary this well-travelled insider shared. The men's conversations typically began with stagecraft and set design, but wound up with Beaton's latest artistic rants that invariably included juicy gossip about people whose acquaintances they both shared.

From his kitchen listening post, Rene quietly monitored the call; He waited a discreet amount of time before inquiring. Later, on his second vodka, Balanchine finally opened up. "Cecil was in top form today. Full of stories, as usual. A funny thing about Michael Redgrave: Tony Quayle said Michael Redgrave's problem is he's in love with himself but he's not sure if it's reciprocated."

"Tony Quayle?"

"A British actor."

"Mr. Beaton is always amusing. Did you invite him to your party?"

"Yes. He offered to help. He thinks, and I agree with him, that more elegance is required. This apartment needs his fine hand. If we are to entertain properly, I wish to provide a more appropriate backdrop. I am well aware, Rene, that things around here have grown sadly eclectic with Tanny's situation. Beaton will change all that. He will be our stager. Such a busy man, what with his London opening of *"My Fair Lady,"* and his film, *"Gigi"* opening here this month."

Balanchine continued. "I must say he was less than enthusiastic about my mystery guest."

"I thought Beaton and the Windsor's were friends. Didn't he photograph their wedding?"

"A bit of a love-hate relationship, I imagine. They are fellow Brits, after all. Travel in the same circles. After all, the Duke and Duchess were Beaton's guests only last month in London for the opening of his play."

"My Fair Lady."

"Yes, Beaton designed the costumes and sets for it. And the Windsor's were there. And who knows? Perhaps they also were in Cannes for his film. After all, they live nearby in Paris."

Finishing up, Balanchine carefully wrapped the electrical cord around the iron. "Do not concern yourself, Rene. They will be fine. These cats and dogs will play together."

Balanchine replaced the iron in the linen closet.

As he walked away, Rene heard Mr. B. muttering to himself, "Cats and dogs."

Later, Balanchine picked up where he'd left off. "Cecil and I discussed manners as an art form and we agreed the man with the most exquisite manners of any person we know is the Duke of Windsor."

"You know, Rene," continued Balanchine, warming to his subject, "it is a fact that manners are not the result of good breeding or intelligence for we know many well born and highly intelligent people who are boors. I, myself have known certain day laborers in the village where I grew up who had superb and quite unselfconsciously good manners."

"True good manners are a lot like charm. You either have them or you don't. You cannot teach people these things. While manners may seem to be a question of opening and closing doors and holding chairs and standing up when a lady comes into the room, etcetera, it really has more to do with acting with a sort of indefinably unobtrusive grace. Such as my friend, David."

"David?"

"The Duke."

"Of, course. So, it seems, *'Gospadeen,'* that your mystery guest is the perfect man."

"'Da.' 'Da.' 'Konechno.' I think so."

Several days passed. Rene noticed Balanchine was rarely without an envelope peeking from his pocket. Periodically, he would pause, let out one of his dry giggles, and add another name. Finally, the man whose idea the party was to begin with, got a look at the list. The names were as surprisingly eclectic as their host. Rene could see this would be a party like no other. The Duke and Duchess, it seemed, were only the beginning.

---

george balanchine, through the eyes of felia doubrovska:
"I think no one really knows Mr. Balanchine. He is a mystery. I am comfortable with Balanchine because I never did something wrong to him. He has an elephant's memory if you do something wrong to him."

Chapter Four
The Duke of Windsor

Chez Windsor
4 Route du Champ d'Entrainement
Paris

"David, come here a moment."

The lady of the house called her preoccupied husband from the library of their palatial home near Paris.

"Just a second, darling. I have something on my mind."

"On your what?"

"I know darling, I haven't much of a mind."

Duke and Duchess of Windsor

The Duchess of Windsor, formerly Bessie Wallis Warfield of East Biddle Street, Baltimore, Maryland, was a highly disciplined, critical person. Often, as today, she was irritated by her husband's lax attitude towards appointments and mealtimes. She held an envelope in her well-manicured hand. "

"Who's it from?" asked the Duke.

"Don't be so full of curiosity," said his wife, trying to read without glasses.

Turning her attention to the afternoon tea, the Duchess watched carefully as the man-servant carried in the traditional silver tea service complete with little cucumber sandwiches, deviled eggs, and tiny fresh peach tartlets. Both Windsor's maintained stylishly slim physiques, adorned by hand-tailored clothing, monogrammed items, priceless accessories and one-of-a-kind jewelry pieces. A dieter since his monarchy years, the former Prince cut palace food purchases by two-thirds, and was served salads, fruit, and small cuts of meat. His and Wallis' only indulgence was a delicious Scandinavian dessert called rodgrod, made of crushed raspberries, red currants and rice.

The once future King of England's curiosity got the better of him. Once his wife's back was turned, he began going through the mail himself. Now he approached his wife holding up a letter, newly arrived from across the pond. It was from their friend, George Balanchine. The Duke of Windsor was now in the twenty-second year of a luxurious, albeit irreversible, exile from his homeland in Great Britain. The runaway king and the widely-publicized reason for his departure, the love of his life, the Duchess of Windsor, were about to take their customary high tea in the conservatory of their exquisite Parisian home.

Almost childlike from a distance, the duke's face was puckered and deeply lined from too much exposure to the tropical sun on the couple's many travels. The Windsor's annual rat trail was always the same: Palm Beach, NYC, Paris, Biarritz, Cote d'Azur, Paris and back to NYC.

The duchess, herself a bit dour, was from the start attracted by the duke, her opposite. His even, white teeth frequently displayed an infectious quizzical smile few could resist. A snappy dresser, today he had on a loudly checked tweed suit. His laughing face, always open, innocent, and joyous, in repose was intensely sad as though he were possessed of a secret pain. One habit of the Duke's she could not abide was his smoking. She'd ask him, "Why must you always have something hot in your mouth?"

---

the duchess of windsor, through the eyes of actor, richard burton:
"She had an enormous feather in her hair which got into everything, the soup, the gravy, the ice cream, and at every vivacious turn of her head it smacked Guy sharply in the eyes or the mouth . . ."

K a r e n   H a g e s t a d   C a c y

As she was served, the Duchess noted a tiny stain on the server's white glove. In a small notebook, she habitually kept by her side, she made note of it for mention later. No detail of the household escaped her precise gaze. A dazzling hostess, she supervised minutely her perfect dinner parties, even making sure the lettuce leaves were trimmed to the same size and shape.

At the cocktail hour, the wait staff was dressed impeccably and carried silver trays offering such delicacies as large grapes hollowed out and filled with cream cheese, bacon bits fried in brown sugar, cabbage leaf pieces with shrimps or prawns attached to them by picks, fried mussels, and chipolata sausages. Dinners were served in the couple's blue chinoiserie dining room at two round tables set for eight. There were silver and gold monogrammed cigarette boxes and cut-glass finger bowls. Favored as main courses were roast partridge, Chicken Maryland, grouse, and faux filets, and for dessert, dark chocolate cake called Sacher torte.

Dinner parties at the chateau were small, but formal, and done with great style. Two cloths were put on for evening meals. The first layer was a cloth of gold, the second was fine Brussels lace. The effect was beautiful; The gold shone through under the glistening light of the candelabra. The monogrammed china and silver were of the highest quality. An individual menu was written out in copperplate for each guest and placed on a tiny silver rest in from of him or her. The fowl were brought to the table "dressed" (with their feathers on) so everyone could see and feel them, then they were cooked and served.

Dinner was served promptly at nine, after trays of high-ball's, martinis, sherry, and champagne were offered twice, no more. The Duchess liked to say, "Forty-five minutes of drinking before dinner is quite enough!" When conversations veered off to subjects she disliked, such as the hunt, hounds, and studbooks, the Duchess used a variety of hostess tricks to move the party along.

One such technique was to subtly switch conversational partners with each course, thereby forcing the whole table to switch. "But one mustn't be too obvious about it. It's disconcerting to find a grimacing countenance

Karen Hagestad Cacy

suddenly turning in your direction, its robot-like action saying in effect, 'Here's the fish, and here am I.'"

The story of the infamous couple's life by the fifties was reduced to the irreverent stuff of tabloid fodder. It all began in 1930, when the twice divorced American, Mrs. Wallis Warfield Simpson, first met the future British monarch. The world watched in collective shock as Edward VIII (called David by his close friends,) on December 10, 1936 relinquished the throne for her. The Duke's younger brother, George VI, became the King of England and gave him the title, "Duke of Windsor," as he was heading out of town to marry 'that American woman from Baltimore.'

Their wedding took place June 3, 1937 in the small French village of Monts where locals lined the streets for a glimpse of the famous couple as an American minstrel song summed up the couple's union: *"I got a gal in Baltimo', Streetcars run right by her do.'* The wedding was intentionally small. The British royal family refused to attend. Among the guests who did show up were Hugh Lloyd Thomas, first secretary of the British Embassy in Paris, Lady (Walford) Selby, Walter Monckton, Major Edward Dudley "Fruity" Metcalfe and his wife, Alexandra Metcalfe, the Eugene Rothschild's, George Allen, and Dudley Forwood.

The cavalier manner in which some reporters treated the couple was evident in a couple of reported exchanges at the time. In the first instance, Helena Normanton of The New York Times boldly asked Wallis about her Nazi connections. In an early version of media 'spin,' she denied any close connection to the Fuhrer. In a second instance, guest, Dudley Forwood, was approached by several reporters, one of whom asked, "Do you think the duke has fucked Mrs. Simpson yet?"

Famed set designer and photographer of the royal family, Cecil Beaton, was in attendance before their marriage, taking photographs of Wallis and the Duke. In France at the wedding, friends of the couple entertained Beaton, showing him after-dinner films of Peking, and Wallis's stay at Balmoral. News from the British Isles, however, was swift and cold: Wallis would not be referred to as "Her Royal Highness" following the wedding.

For this insult, and many that followed through the years, the duke grew increasingly bitter and scathing towards his relatives. When Queen Mary died in 1953, and he was snubbed at her funeral by the royals, he wrote to Wallis: "What a smug, stinking lot my relations are and you've never seen such a seedy worn out bunch of old hags most of them have become."

In letters sent to Wallis in later years, the duke became downright hysterical: God's curses be on the heads of those English bitches who dare to insult you!" he wrote.

He would "get back at all those swine in England and make them realize how disgustingly and un-sportingly they have behaved."

Their scars were deep and lasting. Richard Burton reported that at a party "The Duke and I sang the Welsh National Anthem in atrocious harmony. I referred disloyally to the Queen as 'her dumpy majesty' and neither the Duke nor Duchess seemed to mind."

Post-abdication, the Windsor's managed to reclaim some of their former royal grandeur. For both of them, the fiction of continuing royal life and its enviable standards was essential to maintaining their emotional health and perceived social status. At their Paris house the footmen wore the royal colors, and visitors entered under the Duke's personal Garter banner. Care was taken to recreate the sense of a real palace. Full length royal portraits hung in a grand hallway of the home.

Early during their stay in France, they rented The Mill, "Moulin de la Tuilerie," outside the charming but rather gloomy village of Gif-sur-Yvette, a seventeenth century structure, 15 miles southwest of the Paris suburb of Neuilly. Their ever-present pugs, 'Imp,' 'Trooper,' 'Davie Crockett,' and 'Disraeli,' frolicked in the gardens. In each of their various homes, every inch of the duke's rooms, though Spartan, were crowded with pictures of the duchess.

'Royal photographer' and erstwhile friend, Cecil Beaton, thought their homes to be excessive. He disapproved of the use of war medallions, bamboo chairs, and gimmicky poufs. Even so, the Duchess employed a well-known decorator in Paris, Stephane Boudin, chief artistic director at Maison Jansen, a foremost French interior design firm. In her bathrooms, she always hung a portrait of herself in gouache, a form of watercolor, by Beaton.

"In her early years in England," Cecil Beaton later noted in his diary, "Lady Mendl taught Wallis to tone down her personality to suit British requirements. She encouraged her to speak in a softer, more southern drawl instead of in harsh accents and to dress very simply, to accentuate the angular lines of her figure." Wallis's severe, classical clothes became her trademark and emblem.

Throughout the couple's current stay on Champ d'Entrainement, a backdrop of luxury allowed them to maintain a certain *comme il faut* that belied their naysayers, past or present. Their exile, by God, would be a thing of beauty, taste, comfort! Let the British royal family have their silly, drafty palaces. The duke and duchess would live in a splendor not to be equaled in rainy old Scotland.

Now, the duke paused with the letter opener extended in air. "From our Russian friend in America."

"George?"

"Da."

The Duchess carefully picked the fresh peaches from her tartlet leaving the pastry untouched. Her weight was kept in check by an iron will so she could fulfill her own fastidious version of fashion narcissism. No one in the public eye was so perfectly turned out; no one wore the brooches and other priceless specialty jewelry as well as Wallis did.

"George is a Tsarist, you know, not one of those Soviets."

The Duchess was tiring of her husband's well-known hatred of 'the Russians.' He would insist to anyone who might listen that all his predictions had come true: Now, because there had been no WWIII in 1945 and Russia had not been crushed, one had to face the menace of the Soviets. In the presence of the couple's friends, the Rothschild's, or other Jews, he would refrain from repeating his old theme of blaming Roosevelt and the Jews for the confrontation and total surrender policy of WWII.   In the conservatory now, with no one else around except the help, his wife sensed one of his well-known rants on the subject was about to occur.

Nevertheless, she played along. "How so, my darling?"

"He is a man of style. In the ballet world, an artist. But, in daily life: Look at this envelope. The red seal, with his personal insignia. The calligraphy. A man of St. Petersburg. Not the Kremlin."

"Well, open it then. What does our tsarist have to say today?"

The duke continued to hold the unopened letter as he went on: "Like ourselves, he is an exile. Perhaps, when one thinks about it, that is our bond, the source of our friendship. We are alike, in a fundamental way. He left Russia. We left England."

"David, please open it. I am losing patience with you. You always do this, you begin something and then you go on and on, leaving everyone hanging. Really, darling, you must compose yourself. It gets so very tiring. Really, my dear. Really, David."

The former almost King of England hung his head at her scolding. His lady, the duchess, was, as usual, correct. He depended on such moments as these. He noticed a shoelace on one of her Parisian slippers had come undone. Quickly, he knelt down and tenderly re-tied her shoe. The duchess barely glanced at him as she poured herself a cup of tea. His gesture underscored who was the boss of the marriage. She was. First, last, and always.

The duke finally slit open the envelope and removed the hand-written letter. "Shall I read it now?"

The duchess waved her white linen napkin at him in exasperation.

"My dear friends," it starts. He began reading. "You see, what did I say about friendship?"

"Yes, dear." She carefully poured some brandy into her tea cup, took a sip and rang the service bell on the tray. Her man appeared instantly.

"I noticed a stain on your cuff. Please remember our high standards and see to yourself more properly in future."

"Yes, Your Highness, I'll see to it immediately." He left.

The duke continued reading: "At last our season has ended and I have paused to take account of myself. I have been meaning to respond to your planned visit to New York, and to let you know how pleasant it will be to see both of you again. You have inquired after my dear wife's health and I can report that it is stable at present. She seems to do better living in the country, so that is where she is staying at present."

Interrupting, the duchess asked, "Remind me, dear. Is this one French?"

"Yes, another exile, born in France, but now living in America."

"Really my dear, you are like a dog with a bone. One track mind."

"Yes, dear, that's me all right."

He read on. "I applaud you both on your charity work here in the City."

The Duchess interrupted again. "How good of him to notice our effort. Our little clinic has been operating for two years already. Time flies!"

"America is as much our home as Paris now. Remind me, darling. We must schedule a visit to our clinic when we get there."

The Duke continued reading. "I recall that you may be in town on your birthday, June 23. If you would allow me, I would like to throw you a small party the preceding Friday. While honoring your special day, such a gathering would provide a much-needed break from the tedium of my own life currently spent in hospital rooms and doctors' offices. Someone recently suggested to me that I get out of my shell a bit and kick up my heels. So, you see, you both would be doing me a favor by consenting."

The Duke glanced up for a minute. "Kick up his heels? This, they suggest to a ballet dancer?!"

He resumed reading: "I can think of nothing better than to have the pleasure of entertaining two of my favorite people. At any rate, I have several amusing guests in mind who should provide you both with a diverting evening."

> **through the eyes of jane austen:**
> "You have delighted us long enough."

The letter closed, "Please let me know, and plans will commence immediately. I hope this letter finds you both well and that your voyage across the pond is pleasant and without incident. I understand from news reports that very soon, perhaps by this fall, we shall be able to take jet airplanes across the ocean! How wonderful the modern age is! I look forward to hearing from you both soon. A votre service, George."

The Duchess was delighted: "A party! How delicious!"

"I wonder who he has in mind to invite besides ourselves?"

The duchess answered. "I do hope it's not some big rowdy bunch. I much prefer intimate gatherings of the right people."

As an afterthought, she added, "I do hope Mountbatten's not on the list!"

"We entertained 'Tricky Dicky' here just last month, remember? He can be a bit disagreeable. Beginning, with his refusal to be my best man."

"Really, darling. The memory of an elephant."

The Duke added, "Yes, Peaches. Anyway, I know you thought he'd never go. Too boring. Talked of absolutely nothing but himself the whole time. Perhaps George will invite his Russian friend, Stravinsky. Or others from the arts community. At any rate, June's a big month for us. Our anniversary is on the third, and then my birthday. At any rate, we always have a swell time with the Americans! Hooray! Shall we write him back at once?"

The Duchess responded, "Yes, dear. Hooray."

At this, she rose and walked over to a giant bouquet of fresh flowers nearby. Without ceremony, she grabbed the flowers and lifted them out onto the table.

"Am I the only person in this house who knows how to arrange floral bouquets properly? Really!"

The Duke watched adoringly as his wife rearranged the offending flowers. "You are my party girl. What a Queen of England you would have made!"

The duchess stood back to assess her work. Quietly, she answered her

husband: "I like giving parties; I like dressing up."

Karen Hagestad Cacy

Chapter Five
George Balanchine

Balanchine was a changed man. He still tended to his ballerina wife with loving touches in Connecticut, but anyone who knew him could see a familiar gleam in his eyes. It was the same look he had during the season when he was creating a ballet. He had a near-Zen-like countenance as he responded to conversations only absent-mindedly.

Rene watched the party planning take shape from his kitchen post. He was ever-present to carry out small tasks.

George Balanchine and Mourka

Normally, Balanchine was too preoccupied to notice such mundane things as social status or celebrity. In the case of his burgeoning guest list, however, an added level of care seemed to be afoot. The Windsor's, after all, were bona-fide international European royalty, abdication, or no.

On one evening in the mid-1950s, Balanchine attended a dinner party *'Chez Windsor.'* The company included the British Ambassador and Ambassadress to the Quai d'Orsay; Prince and Princess Dmitri Romanoff (the former Lady Milbanke,) and his cousin Prince Yussupoff, who had conspired in the assassination of Rasputin (and was married to Czar Nicholas II's niece, Princess Irina); Cyrus Sulzberger of the New York Times, and his Greek wife, Marina; Count and Countess Czernin, of the Austrian aristocracy; Margaret Biddle, who had been maneuvering for an appointment to the American Embassy; the Philippe de Rothschild's; the Supreme Commander in Europe, Gen. Alfred M. Gruenther, USA, and his wife, Helene, editor and publisher of Elle.

Karen Hagestad Cacy

John F. Kennedy even dined there once before his marriage. The Windsor's never liked his father who consistently disparaged Britain's prospects during the war, but they liked the son. As the Duchess said, "Out of a litter of nine, there's almost bound to be one good pup."

Having dined in the luxury of two of the world's finest party hosts, Balanchine was well aware the bar was set high. His own planning continued apace, but with a hint of frenzy. And Rene continued sneaking looks at the boss's notes. All appeared as before, with Balanchine spending week-ends in Connecticut with Tanny, but Rene watched the party preparations mid-week.

In the country, weekends, Mr. B enjoyed cooking and working around outside as usual. He built a little tool-house and had various projects. He was very informal, always going around with his shirt off, working, getting the sun, digging around in the roses and cutting the grass.

But back in the city, with the date of the party looming closer, any pretensions of calm were cast aside. Beaton showed up to survey the damage. He took notes and disappeared. Gardeners soon appeared and planted tall trees on the penthouse balcony. And all the while, Balanchine was in his kitchen, composing the menu and fussing over the wine list.

In due course, twilight stars in the sky were engaged for the evening. The moon was ordered to shine. An entertainer from the Waldorf Astoria Hotel, who specialized in Cole Porter tunes, was calendared in. A piano tuner showed up. The pain of a wife with polio was dispatched. Joy was on tap as the recent trials and tribulations of 'normal life' were temporarily refused entry.

---

george balanchine, through the eyes of ruthanna boris:
"Everybody is in love with Balanchine in a way, because he teaches and works with love. . . I look at him . . .as an inevitable force – like I would look at lightening, at Niagara Falls, at Mount Vesuvius, at cosmic events."

Chapter Six
Diana Vreeland

Nearby, at 550 Park Avenue, another cultural icon was surrounded by the unique luxury of St. Petersburg, Russia. Diana Vreeland, a New York fashion editor with no discernible familial attachments to anything remotely resembling a Slavic heritage, nevertheless surrounded herself with the luxury of the tsars. On moving in in 1955, she grandly proclaimed, "I want this place to look like a garden, but a garden in Hell." She commissioned the famous interior designer, Billy Baldwin, to translate. Setting off her exquisite collection of antiques, Baldwin painted many of the walls Chinese red, matching Mrs. Vreeland's lacquered nails and bright lipstick.

Her short black hairstyle was slicked back from her forehead revealing a pair of bright dark brown eyes that bespoke a rigorous honesty held by the very few and the very brave. Invariably, there was a vodka martini in one hand and a cigarette holder in the other as she contemplated the world and expressed her opinions in her unique transcontinental accent.

Vreeland's publishing career dated from 1936, when she was tapped by Harper's Bazaar editor, Carmel Snow, to write a regular column in her fashion magazine. Newly arrived with her husband from London, she quickly became known for her quirky commentary. In her regular column *"Why Don't You?"* her suggestions brought a new world of style to American women, many of whom were stuck at home or in stultifying office jobs. Impracticality was the order of the day as her ribald ideas often fired the imagination, to wit: *"Why Don't You* have a yellow satin bed entirely quilted in butterflies?" Or: *"Why Don't You* rinse your blond child's hair in dead champagne to keep its gold, as they do in France?"

> *through the eyes of fashion editor, diana vreeland:*
> "The eye has to travel."

On occasion, Miss Vreeland was Dorothy Parker, sharp in her patois. Other times, she more closely resembled Holly Golightly, traversing her own inimitable terrain: "The bikini is the most important thing since the atom bomb." Your job, as always, was to try and keep up: "These girls . . . If they've got long arms, long legs and a long neck, everything else kind of falls into place."

Or: "Red is the great clarifier – bright, cleansing, and revealing. It makes all colors beautiful. I can't imagine becoming bored with red – it would be like becoming bored with the person you love."

Her trait of unyielding honesty occasionally could land Vreeland 'in the soup' at her job. Her strict standards were presented in a free form stream of consciousness understood only by a limited few anointed fashionistas. With stubborn disregard for publishers' budgets, she assumed everyone understood the 'fashion-as-art' arc of her features.

Safe to say, those blessed with more linear thinking failed to follow breathlessly as she located the perfect sunset in the Sahara, or ordered a thousand white birds to be transported to Russia for a winter's fashion shoot. Not all were fully on board with her earth-crashing necessity for truth, beauty, and precision.

Harper's Bazaar Magazine, in short, was more artists' folio than ladies' magazine, more an induction of fellow dreamers into the esoteric art of the feminine than mere shopping gazette. The damages continued to pile up. One problem was Diana's habit of charging full speed ahead: "Oh, I know how to handle these boys. You just get tougher than they are."

As some of her supporters fell away, she was overheard asking the only male in her department, Baron Nicky de Gunzburg, to explain the situation to her.

"What is the name of that designer who hates me so?"

"Legion," was his response.

As the years passed, Mrs. Vreeland conjured increasingly dangerous fashion stunts. Once, Babs Simpson, John Cowan, Ara Gallant, and two models, were sent by helicopter to the top of a mountain peak in the Andes to photograph evening dresses. Cowan was determined to make it look as if the models were floating in the clouds. At five o'clock, when the pilot told them it was unsafe to stay any longer, Cowan insisted on remaining to get what he wanted. The helicopter took off, abandoning the fashion party on the top of the mountain. The team spent the night on the mountain huddled under Maximilian furs.

"The next morning, they found the Peruvian army waiting, absolutely furious, and pointing to the ground," international super model, Mirabella recalled. "It was covered with mountain lion tracks."

But in the Spring of 1958, Diana Vreeland was in full control of her Chinese red home, her fashion work, and an impressive array of international friends, including socialite C.Z. Guest, composer Cole Porter, and British fashion photographer Cecil Beaton. Her close friends closed ranks around her as she (and her handsome husband, Reed,) hosted memorable parties and sipped her trademark drink, Smirnoff.

Beaton, a recipient of numerous photographic commissions from Vreeland, 'got her.' He shared the Vreeland's elite, pan-European social connections, including but not limited to Parisian couturiers, the Duke and Duchess of Windsor in their French exile, and other well-known members of Europe's royal dynasties.

Today, Vreeland was in a state. She had endured one too many creative differences at work. The 'suits' in accounting were acting up again. It was all becoming simply too much. After holing up alone over a long week-end, in high dudgeon, she invited Beaton to luncheon. Beaton was always a sounding board for the editor. He was pleased to note that she seemed to be in her customary high form, made up of equal parts robust decision and self-creation.

A lingering sensitivity to her recent office contretemps revealed itself as she peppered him with questions about the cost of living in London. Possibly an escape back to the England of her youth was in the offing. She

K a r e n   H a g e s t a d   C a c y

was doing the research. Fall-back plans are always smart. To date, however, not one red cushion, not one ornate gold lamed mirror had yet been touched in her mid-town Shangri-La.

As the two conversed, happily trading industry gossip like a couple of magpies, Beaton could hear Reed in the background, as he moved about the apartment, and he glimpsed a maid carrying perfectly folded, freshly ironed bed linens past an open doorway. In short, if one didn't know the latest back-story, all appeared in order '*Chez Vreeland.*'

As Beaton later told a friend, ". . . I got the full effect of her freshness. Her brain was ticking over with extraordinary quickness and clarity. She was in a rare confidential mood and . . . even has ideas of coming to England to live, and asked me to find out how much it cost me to keep the London house."

After Beaton's departure, merry olde England remained on her mind as she absent-mindedly sorted through the day's usual stack of embossed invitations to art gallery openings, New York soirees, and other social occasions that begged her attendance.

One envelope stood out from the rest. The calligraphy was ornate and in a clear red ink --- just the perfect shade of red, she noted with appreciation. The address was repeated along the bottom of the envelope in ornate Russian script. Charming, she noted with a smile. As she sipped her vodka – how appropriate – Mrs.Vreeland opened George Balanchine's invitation.

Goody, she thought, as she reached for another cigarette from an elegant silver box on the desk. In a flash, memories of Diaghilev, the theatre and Imperial Russia raced through her neat index of a mind. Ah, she thought, the North! Caviar and champagne! Her fantasy carried her onward to St. Petersburg's Hermitage Museum. Riding in a horse-drawn troika, with a fur lap robe on her lap, she could feel the winter snow as it glanced off her reddened cheeks.

Physically, Vreeland resembled a whooping crane, but one with style. Her spine in profile was shaped in a lazy "S," her nose was hawk-like.

Karen Hagestad Cacy

Today, as she contemplated her invitation, her posture momentarily straightened: She soared on stage at the Mariinsky Theatre, all of Russia at her feet. She noted appreciatively the perfect blood-red roses thrown at her feet as she took her final bow, the audience in rapturous applause.

She wasn't totally mad. Mrs. Vreeland knew at some level it was her world-class imagination once again seizing the moment. Fleetingly, she gave a thought for all those not privileged enough to take such flights beyond the footlights. How drab their lives must be, she thought.

Her hand swiftly extended across her desk to an ornate cloisonne cup holding a variety of calligraphic pens. She chose the red ink. Naturally, it was the exact right shade of Red! Red! Red! She lit another cigarette, placing it in its long holder. The woman in her red harem room took a moment to admire her reflection in a mirror. Her sleek, small head was briefly encased in a circle of smoke.

> *diana vreeland, through the eyes of christopher hemphill:*
> ". . . she asked me to find a picture of Maria Callas she remembered clipping from an Italian paparazzi magazine . . . 'If eyes were bullets,' she said, . . . everyone in sight would be dead.'"

She thought, "Looking in the mirror is all right by me. I loathe narcissism, but I approve of vanity." Her response to Balanchine, penned in her usual flowery, theatrical script, was elated: *Darling George, I am sure your kind invitation has elevated my spirits to no end! And a Mystery Guest, to boot! I shall abide by your request that I attend sans escort. Reed will enjoy a peaceful home with me away for an evening. Who knows? Perhaps he'll miss me! Avec plaisir, bien sur, I do accept with pleasure! Of course, I shall attend!" A bientot, Diana.*

Following her friend's example, she carefully melted some red wax for her own personal insignia. There, on the back of her reply was the distinctive "DV." All that was left was to select the most divine cocktail dress for the occasion. The fashion maven began her planning.

One matter, however, required Madam Vreeland's more immediate attention: Unwittingly, Balanchine had put a challenge in play. Mystery Guest, indeed! She'd see about that, or her name wasn't Diana Vreeland!

---

diana vreeland, through the eyes of christopher hemphill:
"Once, during a rare conversational lapse, the (tape) machine turned itself off loudly... 'Poor little thing,' Mrs. Vreeland said sympathetically, 'it has a mind of its own... it got bored. We mustn't let the splash drop! We must be amusing all the time!

Chapter Seven
Robert Maxwell

The phone rang in his back bedroom. Balanchine heard Rene pick up. "Mr. B, it's Lincoln for you."

Lincoln was Lincoln Kirstein, Balanchine's business partner, a man responsible for helping him create and sustain the New York City Ballet company since 1948. As Balanchine passed Rene in the hall, the butler whispered to him in Russian: "I spoke to Fidelma last week." Fidelma was Fidelma Cadmus, Kirstein's long suffering wife. "His latest lover has moved in with them!"

Balanchine's shoulders shot up. "A new one?"

"Da, I've met him. Very attractive. He favors purple vests."

---

diana vreeland, through the eyes of christopher hemphill:
"Once, during a rare conversational lapse, the (tape) machine turned itself off loudly . . . 'Poor little thing,' Mrs. Vreeland said sympathetically, 'it has a mind of its own – it gets bored. We mustn't let the splash drop! We must be amusing all the time!'"

"Do I know about this?"

"Let him tell you himself. Another thing . . . Fidelma likes him too!"

Balanchine took the receiver from Rene. "*Dobri Vecher,* my dear friend. What's new with you?"

"Cecil called and he is delighted with your invitation."

"Have your plans changed? You know, you and Fidelma are welcome."

"No, George. I am still due in Bermuda for our little vacation. I promised her and besides . . ."

Here, Kirstein paused a moment.

". . . besides, I am certain you have learned of my new liaison. Now we are three, and I must take this little trip to smooth the way."

"Have I met him, Lincoln?"

"No, I don't believe so. He's an artist of some talent. That's how we met. But, soon, my friend. Perhaps he will even have something to offer our productions. But, in time. In time. No, I called about your guest list. You know, we mustn't let perfectly good celebrity go to waste."

"Ah, I smell a potential patron is about to be suggested, Lincoln."

"Just so. I have the perfect man in mind. Wealthy beyond anything. International. He owns newspapers. Robert Maxwell. Know him?"

There was a moment of silence.

"George?"

"Who did you say?"

"Robert Maxwell."

"Don't know the man."

Except, he did. Maxwell, another exile from the Caucasus, came to Balanchine's attention several years earlier when he drunkenly disrupted a performance of Sleeping Beauty at Lincoln Center. Guards were called when he shoved his date, a cheap blonde decked out in sequins, mink, and too much perfume.

The Russian billionaire's contretemps at the ballet made the society section of The New York Times the next day. Balanchine asked Rene to learn more about the boor. What he had learned was disturbing. Maxwell, Rene said, traveled with an entourage the size of which many a dictator would envy. There were the young, blonde, long-legged secretaries who traveled with him. His 400 companies.

There was his lifestyle: He ordered pre-checks so that his hotel suites were dust free and the temperature set at 64.5 degrees Fahrenheit. He lived in Headington Hill in Oxford and traveled there by his helicopter. He relaxed onboard his luxury yacht, the *Lady Ghislaine.* People everywhere were at the mogul's beck and call. There even were people who carried his briefcase and provided Maxwell's deodorant and powder for his puff.

Through some shadier Russian contacts, Rene also learned that Maxwell's empire was growing into one of the most powerful crime syndicates in the world, embracing the Russian Mafia, the crime families of Bulgaria, in NY and crime families of Japan and Hong Kong. One could say Maxwell was creating a global criminal network. He was a robber of the first order, setting in motion a chillingly effective structure of global criminals.

Robert Maxwell

In short, the billionaire, Robert Maxwell, was more a man to be feared, than a man to be invited to dine, especially considering the guests Balanchine had in mind. Yet, he also understood Maxwell's low-life criminality created the kind of wealth an impresario could only dream about. Such a man required a veneer of respectability. What better way to achieve an acceptable public face in his operating bases of London and New York than through philanthropy? He wouldn't be the first wealthy man, nor would he be the last, to seek acceptance through his checkbook.

Later, Balanchine sat alone thinking. Rene had left and Tanny was still in Connecticut. The evening had gotten away from him and it was now 2 a.m. The name, Robert Maxwell, served as a dark trigger for him because in Maxwell, Balanchine was looking in the mirror at another man in full retreat from his past.

Invite him for the money, Lincoln had said. He can underwrite a ballet for us next season. Balanchine knew in the end, he would comply. The New York City Ballet was like his child, always coming first in his life. But for now, he needed to revisit the demons from his --and Maxwell's -- past. That painful trip required more wine. Balanchine opened a bottle and resettled in the dark. A small lamp in the corner and his cat, *Mourka,* kept him company.

Closing his eyes, he was back in Russia. The year was 1917 and a civil war was underway. *'Giorgi Mellitonovitch Balachivadze'* moved with his family to Petrograd, while waiting for school to reopen. He lived a hand-to-mouth existence scrounging for food; there was no gas and no electricity, only hunger and cold. To help keep it together, *'Balachivadze'* played piano for silent films, and worked as a messenger boy and saddler's assistant working for scraps of food. He walked miles to find peasants in the country with whom he could trade the salt he had saved for potatoes.

In that time, *'Balachivadze'* even stole from government supplies. Had he been caught, he could have been executed. Cats were regularly caught, strangled and cooked. He recalled that "sometimes we were given horse feed." Horses dropped dead in the streets. Sometimes in the night people with knives took whatever they could. He remembered that at the time he had 30 boils on his body.

While Balanchine could not know the particulars of Maxwell's early years, he could guess. If Maxwell used a frozen ditch in the back of the house to relieve himself in winter, (he did,) and if the floors of Maxwell's boyhood home were dirt, (they were,) Balanchine might have discerned that.

In point of fact, like Balanchine, Maxwell's early years created the man he would become. He was born in 1923 in the village of *Slatinske Doly* in a remote corner of what later became Czechoslovakia. His mother was a wonderful cook of kosher food and – something rare in her village – an intellectual who read books. Maxwell had fond memories of his mother picking up every piece of newspaper in the street to discover what was going on.

Balanchine shuddered in his chair as the past came back. It was a past he was determined to keep at bay. Virulent pneumonia and pleurisy seized him in 1928, and he was put in a sanitarium to recover. The illness affected his health for life and was a large influence in Balanchine's strong sense of fate as a devout Russian Orthodox believer. He once explained to a friend, "You know, I am really a dead man. I was supposed to die and I didn't, and so now everything I do is second chance."

Pouring another glass of wine, Balanchine knew that for him, as for Maxwell, the West always was his dream, even before he left Russia for Paris. He was willing to risk everything for it. Wealthy gangster or not, Maxwell was a self-made man. Balanchine, a man of action and positive thinking, could sympathize with that. And, of course, there was the not insignificant matter of the money. Maxwell could ease the way for The New York City Ballet.

In due course, the desk top was opened, and the red calligraphic pen was removed. Balanchine had no further thoughts as he addressed his last invitation to one Robert Maxwell.

A fellow Slav . . . A man of some success . . . A man not unlike Balanchine himself.

Karen Hagestad Cacy

Chapter Eight
Cecil Beaton

Give Cecil credit. He made it through an entire luncheon with his pal, Diana Vreeland, and never once mentioned Balanchine's party. It was particularly taxing since he spied the tell-tale envelope, unopened and in full view, on her ornate desk. Credit was not entirely due, however. The fact is, Beaton, just off a turbulent trans-Atlantic flight direct from the smash London opening of his musical, *"My Fair Lady,"* had just attended the New York premiere of another of his works, the film, *"Gigi,"* whose costumes and sets he designed.

It all was too exhausting. The timing of his many projects was taking its toll. He wasn't used to the acclaim that didn't let up after he left England. Everywhere, he was trumpeted: The sets! The costumes! All Beaton, all the time! He was the talk of two continents.

And now he'd also opened his mouth and agreed to help Balanchine with the Duke's party. Between press events and premieres, now he also was busily engaging carpenters, selecting Oriental rugs, and having seamstresses measure Mr. B's flat for the luxurious floor to ceiling velvet curtains he ordered for windows and interior doorways. Balanchine possessed a few Russian antiques; Beaton planned to add many more.

His task was to replicate a wealthy town home in tsarist Russia, recreating the luxury of L'Hermitage Museum in miniature for one summer's eve. He went into full set designer mode as he begged, borrowed, and – only when necessary – stole, appropriate furnishings for the host's apartment. When required, he name-dropped and shamelessly traded on his own celebrity to procure what he wanted.

Karen Hagestad Cacy

Finally, he took a night off. No phones. No visitors. No more interviews. No Balanchine party prep. He donned his favorite dressing gown, assembled a shaker of Manhattans, and settled in to watch television. His good friend, Truman Capote, was due to be on "The Jack Paar Show." Beaton always enjoyed the writer's squeaky voice and his wholesale telling of stories, most of them, untrue. When challenged, Truman typically replied, "If it didn't happen that way, then it should have!"

Paar's opening dialogue was one of his usual rants. His audience was along for the ride as he excoriated things and persons he claimed harmed him during the week. America liked Jack Paar because with him, they could get even. Nightly, on The Jack Paar Show, personal laundry was aired, injustices were tackled, and all was accomplished within the witty patter of Paar's hand-selected comedians and guests.

Beaton poured his third drink. He thought he might sleep on the couch tonight. As he began to drift off, he caught the drawn-out syllables of Capote's distinctive voice. Paar was asking him about his famous first novel.

"Truman, how old were you when you wrote *"Other Voices, Other Rooms?"*

"I was only nineteen and I was so brilliant, so brilliant in those days!"

Typical Truman, Beaton thought. His friend was never uncertain about his writing ability. But he sat upright as he heard Truman abruptly change direction.

". . . yes, so imagine a party hosted by a ballet dancer. And I'm invited. It was addressed to me, to 'Troo-man,'" he added in his exaggerated diction. "Well, I mean, it's too strange, my dear. But I'm assured only the best people are being invited. Naturally, that would include myself."

Paar responded, "You go to everything on the Upper West Side, don't you Truman?"

The coy response which, elicited raucous laughter from the audience, "Well-ll, not everything . . ."

What Truman did not say on talk shows was often funnier than what he did say. His high-pitched voice somehow freighted his dialogue with gay innuendo. The southern novelist was a regular talk show guest, a novelty act who enjoyed all the attention and who milked it for all it was worth.

So much for discretion. Now that all of America knew about Balanchine's party, the gig was up. As Beaton fell into a deep sleep, he gave himself credit for one thing: the secret of the mystery guest was still safe. It wasn't his style to kiss and tell, at least not all the time. To be in on such a delicious secret separated him from the others. He, and he alone, would be the chief engineer of the Russian dancer's soiree. Hooray.

Finally, Beaton nodded off.

Sir Cecil Beaton

truman capote, through the eyes of carol matthau:
"Truman would describe everybody – Babe Paley, Slim Keith, Phyllis Cerf, Gloria – everything. He talked about the differences in the various social strata of that special New York City, where and how people were placed, who were the most elite and the richest, where they stood as hostesses, and how New York was really run."

Chapter Nine
Truman Capote

Many who knew Truman attempted to describe him. Friends and enemies alike were fascinated by the short, troll-like man. One friend, ex-patriot author, Paul Bowles, said, "I first met Truman at a cocktail party . . . he was sitting on a love seat with two or three other people, all facing different directions and talking. He was very quick – as I entered he looked up and said to the person sitting beside him, 'Yes, Paul Bowles is a very good writer.' They weren't talking about me at all, but he said it in such a way that I could hear. He was a consummate actor. He wrote all his roles and acted them out."

The English language has its drawbacks. Capote might be described more accurately in the French, because he was truly *'un type.'* Make no mistake. Truman Capote, Southern Gothic author, and New York man-about-town, bore little resemblance to young Truman Streckfus Persons, of Monroeville, Alabama. At 24, he met Jack Dunphy, the writer, who became his life partner. The two men traveled to Europe, met Cecil Beaton, and spent time with him in London and Tangier, where Beaton maintained a house. Beaton became an artistic role model for Capote, observing the young man's career was *"like a carefully planned military campaign."*

Now, Capote was riding high. He'd just published his novel, *"Breakfast at Tiffany's,"* and he was the darling of the talk show circuit. The book follows the turbulent adventures of Holly Golightly, a beautiful *'ex-patriot'* from America's South who takes Manhattan by storm. Drawing on his own childhood experiences in Louisiana Capote said, "Always write about what you know about. Don't write a book about how to care for your poodle. You don't have a poodle."

> **truman capote, through the eyes of diana vreeland:**
> "We became friends immediately . . . His particular charm was an endless, non-explanation of anything."

Capote's apartment, located at the UN, was a mix of the southern child, the accomplished author and the society pal he had become since moving to the City. He had a curious collection of animals including a bronze giraffe, carved lions, porcelain cats, dogs, rabbits, and owls. There was an ornate Victorian sofa, and antique paperweights, a collection started by Colette when Truman was in Paris, covered every surface. Someone commented that "Truman's eclectic treasures somehow remind you of the contents of a very astute little boy's pockets." On the wall was a portrait of Truman painted by James Fosburgh, Minnie Cushing Astor Fosburgh's husband.

Capote befriended the rich and powerful. As he collected his porcelain pet menagerie, so too Truman collected people, first beguiling them, then later using them, according to his needs. No one who knew him failed to have an opinion about the diminutive author.

John Richardson, the actor, saw him as a "manipulative court jester. With his wit, shit-stirring and conniving ways, he could twist rich people around his finger. It was very important to him to feel that people preferred him to their husbands, wives, or children. And quite often they did. They'd choose Truman because he was so beguiling and then they'd become addicted to him."

Truman Capote

Film director, John Huston, said: "I immediately fell for him – it didn't take me five minutes to be won over completely as he did with everyone I ever saw him encounter. He had a charm that was ineffable. He exerted this charm freely."

He would call someone on the phone: "Beauty? Gorgeous? Adorable One? This is 'Troo-man.' Do you want to have lunch?" He always came rehearsed. Someone who knew him said he would never just have lunch with you, he'd lined up things to tell you. He came loaded for bear. Always. Always had stories about who had had the latest shots at that clinic in Switzerland, or some scandalous gossip about some cardinal of the Catholic Church.

Capote's friendships with several hand-selected society ladies helped launch a new term in the lexicon of the mega-wealthy: *'the walker.'* Most often doyennes' wealthy and powerful husbands were too busy to socialize, much less 'do lunch.' They had little interest in art openings or the symphony. Wasn't it enough that they gave freely to the arts?

More to the point, men of such stature felt no compunctions about taking their due from wherever it was offered, especially when it included an attractive mistress here or there. Truman's own mother had endured such treatment when he was a child. Possibly from those experiences, he could empathize with betrayed wives.

He even coined a name for his society women: He called them his 'swans.' Truman was inspired to use the word by a passage he'd read in a nineteenth-century journal by Patrick Conway, who wrote that he had seen *"a gathering of swans, an aloof armada . . . their feathers floating away over the water like the trailing hems of snowy ball-gowns,"* and was reminded of beautiful women.

As he listened to their sad marital stories, his counsel was always pragmatic: "My dear, women always have problems. Just tough it out. Consider yourself a very expensive personal secretary. Executive secretary. Just hang in there and take all the perks, go to all the parties, buy all the clothes, enjoy your life." The road to a brilliant marriage and those "waters of liquefied lucre," as Truman lyrically described the big bank account required to support swan-dom, was often long and arduous.

Capote especially gravitated to the women's wealth, their beautiful homes, and their international travel. He grabbed hold of their coat tails tightly and never let go. He adopted their ways, repeated their sayings, and lived his life as closely as he could to their lives. From them, he learned the ways of the wealthy.

Nothing escaped his careful eye. For instance, the baby vegetable. He noted that his swans viewed the dinner party as a showcase for their talents. Serving the tiniest, most expensive vegetables at a time when they were rare was a way they established their hostess credentials, competing on the field of the dinner party

Truman decided that the size of a vegetable was indeed an indication of class. "The real difference between rich and regular people is that the rich serve such marvelous vegetables. Little fresh born things, scarcely out of the earth. Little baby corn, little baby peas."

Today, he was meeting his publisher. First, he retrieved his mail. In it was Balanchine's fancy invitation. Opening it, he reacted with his usual flamboyance: "I'm beside myself! Beside myself! Beside myself!" As usual, his delight was accompanied by a series of agile handstands. He propped up the dancer's fancy invitation on the mantel where he could gaze at it with anticipation. Then he left for his appointment. There was a skip in his step as he considered what to wear to the party. If the summer weather cooperated, he thought, he might wear his black velvet suit, the hat with the maroon feather, and perhaps a long scarf to waft around the room. His friend, John Huston, once told him he was the only male he'd ever seen attired in a velvet suit.

But, enough about friends and parties. Today, Capote had serious business to contract. There was a film producer who was expressing interest in making his book into a movie. The clever troll already had an actress in mind. It was a woman both clever and child-like. Both breathtakingly beautiful and manipulative of men. A woman not unlike his own mother, who left him for her many liaisons, and on whom his book was based.

The actress he had in mind to play Holly Golightly was there from the start. As he wrote, he pictured her standing there alone on the sidewalk in front of Tiffany's, dreaming of jewels and success. His actress bore a striking resemblance to his southern naif: He knew the woman he had in mind would be playing herself.

Marilyn Monroe, like Truman Capote, came from a troubled background. They both knew poverty. They both knew how it felt to be nobodies. Yet, both of them rose from the ashes. Each was a self-invention. Marilyn playing his Tiffany's heroine would in many ways be Truman's twin. Because Marilyn was Holly Golightly. And Truman was Marilyn. No one else could know what these three knew.

No one could know what these three had endured.

Truman imagined: *"Breakfast at Tiffany's,"* with . . . Marilyn Monroe, as the star . . . Truman Capote, as the author . . . and Holly Golightly, as the glamour puss.

Star-crossed lovers, all.

Karen Hagestad Cacy

Chapter Ten
Pat Buckley

"The mind boggles!"

"I simply don't understand why the President just doesn't pass the bloody bill himself."

"Well, if you ask me, it's all too ridiculous for words."

"That woman is so stupid she ought to be caged."

"It is of an imbecility not to be credited."

In 1958, the world belonged to Pat Buckley; everyone else just lived in it. She was a modern-day version of Nora Charles, of *"The Thin Man"* detective series. Her husband was her straight man, an adoring presence orbiting her star. Theirs was one of the great love stories. She was, in the view of her son, an old-fashioned wife. She was Bill's cheering section, making certain her columnist husband was surrounded by all the comforts of a well-kept home.

Pat Buckley and William F. Buckley, Jr.

All, was served up with a ready wit and her own unique air of maddening insouciance. She also was one of Truman's "swans." Here, too, she failed to fit the mold. Unlike his other swans, she had a good marriage, was not emotionally needy. She was a "Lady Who Lunched," appearing at New York's finest restaurants with her well-heeled society girlfriends, including the witty gossip, Truman Capote.

Her author son, Christopher Buckley, lovingly described his mother's entrances to gatherings as being "in full prevarication." Like some of the others invited to Balanchine's dinner party, Pat Buckley could, and did, lie. Her version of the truth never was used for the usual reasons – self-promotion, advantage, larceny. Rather, her lies, which some might characterize as 'white lies,' were used solely for their entertainment value; the unvarnished truth so often fell short of the mark.

Patricia Buckley was the wife of conservative columnist and well-known author, William F. Buckley, Jr. Early on, when Bill Buckley traveled to her hometown of Vancouver, British Columbia to ask for her hand in marriage, Pat instructed him to wait downstairs in the foyer. Pat scrambled up the stairs and excitedly informed her mother of the purpose of their visit. Buckley overheard the entire conversation, at the conclusion of which could be heard the sounds of extended hysterical laughter. It seems the young Canadian socialite regularly brought young men home with the same story.

Fortunately for Buckley, she chose him. Their dinner table conversations must have been something. The couple was always lively and slightly combative, but in an old-fashioned, sophisticated way. Cleverness was the rule of the day. For instance, her husband had a passion for sailing. His was a serious avocation as he made numerous trans-oceanic crossings. At the news of yet another voyage, fraught in her mind with danger, Pat told a friend, "If he comes through this thing alive, I'll kill him!"

Years later, her writer son reported on one of his mother's more outrageous whoppers, to wit that "the king and queen always stayed with us when they were in Vancouver."

"When Mum was in full prevarication, Pup would assume an expression somewhere between a Jack Benny stare and the stoic grimace of a 13th-century saint being burned at the stake. He knew very well that King George VI and Queen Elizabeth did not routinely decamp at Shannon . . . Her fluent mendacity, combined with adamantine confidence, made her really indomitable . . . She was really, really good at it.

She would have made a fantastic spy. . . She was beautiful, theatrical, bright as a diamond, the wittiest woman I have ever known . . ."

The shining lie meant to entertain, it turns out, is the exclusive province of the truly charming, fun guest. Within Pat Buckley's rarified Le Cirque luncheon clique was Diana Vreeland, another accomplished liar. She freely copped to it: "Now social lies are something else again. I don't mind if you say 'I can't dine tonight because I have a business dinner.' That's almost conventional, isn't it?"

"I once had a marvelous Irish temporary maid whom I was absolutely impossible to. I made her tell lies – social lies – on the telephone by the hour. 'Madame has not returned from lunch . . .' 'Madam is taking a nap and cannot be disturbed . . .' And if I really didn't want to talk to someone, 'Madam is out of town.' After six months, she finally left me. And as she was walking out the door, she said, 'Goodbye, madam. And now I'm going straight.'"

Vreeland, known as an amusing raconteur in her circle, told many stories on herself. Another one dealt with her own unique definition of honesty: "The best raspberries, too, are the black ones, and they should be tiny – the tinier and the blacker, the better! Strawberries should be very big and should have very long stems attached so that you can pull them out easily. Yvonne, my maid, used to choose them individually for me at Fraser-Morris. Very splendid. God knows what they cost nowadays. Once I asked how much they were apiece. Yvonne was shocked. 'Ask, Madame?' she said. 'Listen, Yvonne!' I said. Everybody asks. 'But madam . . .' So, you mean to tell me, Yvonne, I said, that you'd walk into Harry Winston's to buy a tiara, and not ask? One asks! Truth is a hell of a big point with me!"

But among this class of liars, Truman Capote was the gold standard. According to one acquaintance, "He was very amusing. If you had him for dinner, an evening of talk, he had these glasses he'd bring along: a clear pair, a slightly shaded pair, and a really dark pair. It was quite apparent that he couldn't lie properly unless his eyes were covered. So, he would change glasses. When they were really dark, you knew a huge exaggeration, a lie was coming. We called them the 'shades of truth.'"

"The Dupont's have a house over there on Fishers Island, and when they gave a lunch, they sent over this massive boat for Truman. He was very pleased with himself. When he came back he said that 'there were one hundred for an outdoor lunch.' *(Medium-shaded glasses.)* 'There had been a young girl there, in her teens. Hundreds of gulls – it was the mating season – were circling around the dock. As lunch went on, this girl was dying to go down to the dock and look at the gulls. Everyone said, No, don't. They're very vicious at this time of year.' *(Darker glasses.)* 'Finally, she went with an umbrella to watch them. On the docks, the umbrella collapsed in the wind and the gulls tried to peck her eyes out.' *(Darkest, darkest shades.)*"

The Buckley's received their mail from a variety of sources: They kept a maisonette on East 73rd Street in Mid-Town, a large home in Stamford, Connecticut, and Bill Buckley's "National Review" magazine offices on Lexington Avenue. Today, Balanchine's letter was messengered to the East 73rd home from National Review, where it mistakenly had landed.

"And Bill said to me, 'Ducky, you look absolutely gorgeous. Where's the rest of the dress?' It was up to the kazoo!" Pat Buckley was up late and talking on the phone, doing a post-mortem on the night before – she and her husband attended a fund-raiser for her charity, the Memorial Sloan-Kettering Cancer Center. Seated in her shiny green chintz bedroom in one of her trademark caftans, she was holding an un-opened invitation in her well-manicured hand. She'd decorated her bedroom with the help of her friend, English decorator Keith Irvine, who observed "She had very bad taste, but she was adorable."

through the eyes of anthony trollope:
"I think the greatest rogues are they who talk most of their honesty."

Another decorator, Todd Romano, took a more charitable view: "These ladies, Pat Buckley, Nan Kempner, and CZ Guest, were really comfortable in their own skin and that extended to their décor." He described Mrs. Buckley's style as "high camp boudoir."

She hung up and finally opened Balanchine's invite. A mystery guest, she thought. How delightful. But she had a similar reaction to that of her good friend, Diana Vreeland. She took it as a challenge to her social perspicacity. Immediately, she began reviewing her sources, her social circuit spies. She would get to the bottom of this mystery!

And select a frock.

pat buckley, through the eyes of christopher buckley:
"Even when Pup was despairing of her behavior ---as he did only occasionally – and sought refuge on the lecture circuit, or wherever, he would call her every night, trying reconciliation with, 'Hi, Duck.' 'Duck' was the formal, *vous* version of 'Ducky,' their term of affection for each other."

Karen Hagestad Cacy

Karen Hagestad Cacy

Chapter Eleven
"Piggy Bird"

There was the old version: "You must present foot to floor."

And there was the new version: "You get your heel forward so you could hold a martini on it."

"Do not step on bent knee, step on straight knee."

Tanaquil Le Clercq, Balanchine's fourth wife, sat in her Connecticut garden reminiscing about the many hours she'd spent in her husband's company classes over the years. One day she'd shown up with a bandage across her small nose.

Tanaquil Le Clercq

"What happened?" he asked.
Another dancer answered for her. "She kicked herself."

Balanchine laughed, knowing better than anyone the range of the coltish dancer's leg extensions: Her legs were so long they went all the way to . . . there! Combined with her athleticism and quickness, Tanny was a very special Balanchine dancer. She was noticed whenever she stepped on stage; her mere presence raised the level of electricity in the theatre.

And now, look at her.

Crippled, she soldiered on, keeping herself engaged. She wrote a children's book about their family cat, *"Mourka: The Autobiography of a Cat."* She cooked and collected dancers' recipes. A crossword aficionado, she even created puzzles for The New York Times. In a cruel irony, she wheeled herself into the ballet studio and used her upper body and

K a r e n   H a g e s t a d   C a c y

expressive arms to direct classes. It was not uncommon for Balanchine's former wives to be lined up at the barre – Tamara Geva, Vera Zorina, and Maria Tallchief.

---

through the eyes of anthony trollope
"Life is so unlike theory."

Melissa Hayden was a ballerina who danced contemporaneously with Tanaquil. Like other members of the company, Tanny's illness struck her personally. Every dancer must rely on his body as the instrument of his profession. Lose that, and you lose everything.

"Tanaquil loved to dance, and I would dream that she was on stage and that I was excited about her dancing and was congratulating her. She had been so special. It was a tremendous loss to the company, to the shape of the company. I had been struck by her from the very beginning . . . We shared a dressing room, and I thought she was so intelligent, so sensitive, and talented. She had a real feeling of drama about her body, and ballets she felt comfortable in made her glow"

Tanny's illness already had taken the master away from his craft for a year to tend to her. Not only did she bear the guilt of a husband so inconvenienced, but of the New York City Ballet's loss as well. Of that dark time, Hayden said, "We pulled together very strongly when she got sick and Balanchine left to take care of her. I think most of us felt as if a parent had gone away for a long time. But we knew he would come home."

Tanny did her best with the cards Mother Nature had dealt her. She continued to be a loving wife, trying to lessen her husband's burden as much as she could. Today, as always, she had on an expensive French perfume. She was never without it. Years before their marriage, Balanchine had taken her aside after class and gifted the young teen with a bottle of rare and expensive perfume. "For you, my dear. Your name tag." He gave all of his ballerinas their own perfumes, not out of any sense of romance, but so he knew where they were in the building.

Karen Hagestad Cacy

With her illness, Tanaquil was often alone. Even when she was in the company of others, she was still alone. Her marriage had become tenuous. She thought it was only a matter of time before she and George might call it quits. In 1958, however, neither partner acknowledged her illness was turning their love into duty, embarrassment, and guilt. The daily-ness of caring for a deteriorating body, while noble, was nevertheless destroying any thoughts of romanticism, with "Polio" an unwelcome third party.

The day before she was stricken, in Copenhagen, Tanny was on her way to company class at the theater. She briefly paused on the cobblestone street to look at something. Many years later, she couldn't recall what caused her to stop. Standing there, she noticed a bird perched on a wire high across the busy street.

With traffic zooming past, the bird suddenly took flight, aiming itself directly at her feet. He landed, and in every way impersonating a messenger on a serious mission, he looked directly at the ballerina and squawked insistently. At the time, she thought nothing of it. Just one of those things that happen in the gaps between one's life.

The next morning, drenched in perspiration, unable to move, she recalled the bird. Was he trying to warn her of the impending illness that would forever alter her life?

Now, outside her Connecticut home, there was another bird. She began their dialogue by lining up almonds along the fence. Seated in her wheelchair, she watched as the cautious bird gradually trusted her enough to approach, take the nuts in his beak, and fly off to his nest. Eventually, Tanny placed the almonds in her hand. The greedy little bird hopped on and gave her his curious bird-look, head cocked. This made her laugh out loud. Then he jammed up to nine almonds at a time into his beak. Tanny knew how many. She kept count.

Before flying off, he paused to say, "Do not leave. I'll be back for the rest."

And Tanny always answered him, "I'm here. I'm not going anywhere."

Karen Hagestad Cacy

From then on, he woke her each morning. "Squawk! Get up now! I want my almonds!"

She named him "Piggy-Bird."

When one sees a bird in flight, no bird will ever again fill that space in quite the same way. And when one watches a prima ballerina take flight, that experience also is irreplaceable. Her soaring leaps that defy gravity as though she's floating on air remain recorded solely in memory.

Someone observed, " . . . think of the grains of sand against the wavy silken sea of *Figure in the Carpet,* or the cavalier with white glove raised to protect his eyes from too much beauty of his Liebesliederwalzer-fraeulein, or the prodigal son crawling off after the orgy with the worst hangover in the world ever, or the delicious forbidden entanglements of three girls and a man in *Serenade,* all moments that will never happen quite the same again and you're glad you were there when they did."

As Tanny fought the illness, her mind was heavy with conflicting emotions. She knew Balanchine. He was surrounded by beauty. Friends commented on his dance 'family,' how attractive they all were. He loved women. They were his inspiration as he choreographed his memorable ballets. Never angry in class or rehearsal, his soft voice would repeat what he wanted them to do. Sometimes he would need to repeat himself several times before a dancer got it. It was common for dancers to say it was because of Balanchine's quiet determination that they had the courage to attempt the near impossible.

Tanny accepted him as he came to her. Both simple and complicated. Tempted and loyal. A shy flirt. Demanding and sweet. These years, good and bad, belonged to her alone. She would make the best of things.

In the meantime, Balanchine returned to work. For a man, so complex, his explanation of his work was surprisingly simple: "I make some steps for my friends. They are nice. Sometimes it's all right. But I will tell you what you have to do." (to be a good choreographer.) "You have to be a very good dancer yourself. I didn't say famous, I said, good. You have to know how dancers feel. You will never know unless you have done it. Then you

Karen Hagestad Cacy

have to know music very well. Then you have to look everywhere, everything, all the time. Look at the grass in the concrete when it's broken, children and little dogs, and the ceiling and the roof. Your eye is camera and your brain is a file cabinet."

It was June now, and Balanchine was spending much of the time in the city preparing for his dinner party. Tanny knew that he was following the directions of set designer, Cecil Beaton, to redecorate their apartment for the event. Walls even were being removed, Rene reported. She felt guilty as her illness dragged on, bringing them both down. She agreed with Rene that a fancy party was just what the doctor ordered for her restless husband, particularly now that the ballet season was over and he had so much time on his hands.

Balanchine, always a quiet man, lately had been dwelling in the past too much, on the old days in Russia, on religion, and other bits of nostalgia. He described to her the Mariinski Theater in old St. Petersburg and ballets by Petipa. There was real water with cascading fountains and huge shipwrecks, he told her. The American theater's Cecil B. De Mille-type special effects were every day for ballet productions under the tsars.

"At the Imperial Theater, everything grand was possible because of the Imperial Treasury and the Tsar's commitment to the theater. Soldiers labored below stage to create stage miracles, and cheap labor was readily available, as was a vast children's corps de ballet."

Out of the blue, one Saturday, he looked at her and announced, "I go to church but nobody knows."

Another time, he mused, "You know, those men in Tibet up in the Mountains. They sit nude in the cave and they drink only water through straw and they think very pure thoughts."

"Yes," she answered, "you mean the Tibetan monks. The lamas."

"Yes. You know, that is what I should become. I would be with them. But, unfortunately, I like butterflies."

George Balanchine

An accomplished pianist, he would sit at the piano, playing entire Tchaikovsky concertos straight through. Increasingly since the onset of her illness, he seemed to be living in his own world. Tanny knew many people didn't realize his sensitivity. He was a solitary person, set apart from others. When he would play the piano, he would not even know who existed. She called him to dinner but he didn't hear. As he finished the piece, finally he looked up, noticing her in the room with him for the first time. "Ah, hello."

One by one, dancers visited Tanny offering her food, sympathy, and news of the company. One visitor was Tamara Toumanova. She told her how much Balanchine meant to her. "When my father died, we were sitting having coffee. And it was a bright, sunny day. Balanchine said 'You see, Tamartchka, Papa is not gone. The sun shines. He is here with you.'"

More and more, late at night, Tanny could hear her husband up pacing through the house. He could be heard softly repeating to himself, "Must believe. Must believe."

---

george balanchine, through the eyes of mary ellen moylan:
"I could never tell you how Balanchine creates; it would be like trying to hold running water. . . . He had a sense of humor, and there was a feeling of camaraderie at rehearsals . . . In Balanchine's work the individuality of a dancer always comes into play."

Karen Hagestad Cacy

Chapter Twelve
Pamela Churchill

"Hide the men, Pamela's in town!"

Pat Buckley was in full caftan mode, manning her boudoir telephone for an important call-to-arms. Her task today was to alert the troops. Secure enough in her own marriage, she feared for her friends' relationships. Notorious European courtesan, Pamela Digby Churchill, finally had played out all the eligible men after several decades spent in England and France, and was now setting her sights on America, land of milk, honey, and other women's husbands. The wealthier, the better!

Pamela Digby Churchill

"Everyone always talks about the rich men I have slept with, no one ever talks about the poor men I have slept with," Pamela Churchill once told a Parisian friend.

So, she said.

Pamela Beryl Digby began life as an English rose in provenance and complexion. She was born in Hampshire, England and raised in the countryside with her own pony, was sent to a Munich boarding school, where she met Adolph Hitler, and 'finished' at the Sorbonne. Thus, Pamela's expectations of life's gifts were high indeed. Her upper class start set the menu for a future of social carpet bombing never seen before or since in polite society.

After a six-year 'starter' marriage to Randolph Churchill, she moved on to Paris and a liaison with Gianni Agnelli, among others. The romantic

Karen Hagestad Cacy

chameleon adopted his ways including an Italian accent, answering the phone during their affair, "Pronto, Pam."

Next, she was on to Baron Elie de Rothschild, acting as his "European Geisha," with only slight alterations from the Agnelli assignment. With Elie, she now answered the phone, "Ici, Pam." There were a number of other suitors along the way, but Pamela, now age 38, could see the handwriting on the wall. Approaching forty and unmarried was no place for a courtesan to be, no matter how charming and accommodating.

"I simply cannot bear the woman," Pat was saying to her longtime friend, Nan Kempner.

With that, the word was dispatched all over town. The "Ladies Who Lunch" were girding themselves for Pamela's arrival, an unwelcome intruder in their midst. It would not be an overstatement to say the wagons were being circled and the muskets were being loaded.

Pat Buckley's phone was ringing off the hook. One call came in from her friend, Diana Vreeland. Naturally, the two discussed the "Pamela matter."

"Darling," said Diana, "I suppose I could feature her in the magazine, send her somewhere offshore."

"But that's only temporary."

"Quite right. Anyway, I must report she's already arrived. I ran into her several days ago, at the Plaza's Oak Room. She was alone. I greeted her, carefully, of course."

Pat Buckley responded, "Watch it, Diana. Reed's very pleasant looking."

"Oh, I'm not worried. We have no big money. Pamela's into big money. Or celebrity."

"Or both," answered Buckley.

K a r e n   H a g e s t a d   C a c y

"Quite right. Or both. Now listen to me. I hear she is coming to Balanchine's little soiree," added Vreeland.

"And it begins! I suppose we shall just have to deal with the situation. Bill knows Elie, you know. I could tell you things . . ."

Vreeland loved her women friends. "Let's do lunch soon. This could be fun for us, if we approach the matter thoughtfully."

In their conversation, and in many others like it all over the island of Manhattan, Pamela's arrival was noted. To have the United States forces aligned against you in the European theater was one thing. To have the "Ladies Who Lunch" sign a unification pact against you, quite another.

Of course, all of this was part of Balanchine's careful staging. The Russian was amusing himself not only through menu *Winston Churchill, Pamela's former father-in-law* selection, set decoration and the wine list. Oh, no. The impresario was having his fun, mixing and matching. The guests, after all, were the performers in his little play. And improvisation was the order of the day.

Let the fun Begin!

Karen Hagestad Cacy

george balanchine, through the eyes of mary ellen moylan:
"You know when I was a student, Balanchine gave me some advice, He said, 'Don't ever get fat and don't ever get married'. . . . He would rather have his girls on stage than in the kitchen or nursery."

Chapter Thirteen
The Duchess of Windsor

Thursday, June 19, 1958
Waldorf Towers

Ensconced in their usual suite of rooms at New York's Waldorf Towers, the Windsor's were in full anticipation of Balanchine's party. It was the day before the impresario's party and the couple, as was their custom, was reviewing the guest list in preparation. A constant stream of hairdressers, masseuses, manicurists, and chiropodists were making their way through their rooms. The duchess's hair was shampooed and set. She tried on her sets of jewelry several times. Gift baskets were delivered. The phone never seemed to stop ringing.

The coming party was a bit of a departure for the Windsor's. Usually the pair was hosted by known quantities – members of America's social elite, Anglophiles, and others sympathetic with their "romance-of-the-century" story and its unfortunate consequences.

Frankly, they were not close friends with the impresario, but hosted him whenever his company performed in Europe. As a guest, George Balanchine was a quiet presence. He added a certain *Je ne sais quoi* to their parties – call it culture, call it elegance. The man's posture was perfect, his demeanor courtly. In a room, full of narcissists, Johnny-come-lately's, and the idle rich, Balanchine's mere presence provided a certain gravitas.

The Windsor's soirees were memorable for many reasons. Along with the impeccable presentation of food, drink and atmosphere, there often was a soupcon of scandal. The couple's one-time friend, Jimmy Donahue, heir to the Woolworth fortune, used to embarrass the footmen by making loud remarks about their genitals.

Actors Richard Burton and Elizabeth Taylor were friends of the Windsor's, but even they had their limits where the couple's Parisian guests

Karen Hagestad Cacy

were concerned. Wrote Burton, " . . . we'll never be invited again to the Duke and Duchess of Windsor's soirees. And Thank God, he said fervently. Rarely have I been so stupendously bored." A decade later, the British Ambassador went so far as to term the couple *'declasse.'* Added Cecil Beaton, "Cafe society in Paris is downright trashy, a weird collection of social derelicts."

No one meeting the Duke and Duchess for the first time lacked a reaction. Richard Burton observed that "It is extraordinary how small the Duke and Duchess are. Two tiny figures like Toto and Nanette that you keep on the mantelpiece. Chipped around the edges. Something you keep in the front room for Sundays only. Marred Royalty."

Someone else described the Duchess: "Her mouth was too big, her nose was too long, and her clenched teeth grin was almost grotesque. But her eyes and her hair were nice; so was her voice also. Her figure was trim though too thin to be exciting. She shone at parties – always full of vitality. She could dance up a storm and match drinks with anybody. She would hold forth to a group of people."

Wallis, Duchess of Windsor

The hostess also was a raconteur, with a seemingly inexhaustible supply of risqué stories: "What is the difference between a night on the beach at Coney Island and a night on the beach in Hollywood? Answer: At Coney, the girls lie on the beach and look at the stars. In Hollywood, the stars lie on the girls and look at the beach."

Still another reported, "She played poker hard: One poker night we had a big pot going and Wallis suddenly jumped up and knocked the table over, and all the cards and chips fell on the floor. She said a cat had startled her by rubbing against her leg, but I think she saw she was going to lose the pot. As somebody said, 'She saw the kitty, but not the cat.'"

And: "She was an awful little flirt."

About the Duke, Diana Vreeland observed, "There's never been a blue like the blue of the Duke of Windsor's eyes. When I'd walk into the house in Neuilly, he'd be standing at the end of the hall. He always received you himself, which was terribly attractive, and he always had something funny and friendly to say to you while you disposed of your coat. But I'd see him standing there, and even in the light of the hall, which was quite dim, I could see that blue. It comes from being at sea. Sailors have it. I suppose it's in the family --- Queen Mary had it too. But he had an aura of blue around him. I mean what I say –it was an azure aura surrounding the face. Even in a black and white picture you can feel it."

Now seated across the room, the Duke was precariously balancing an ice pack on a chronically sore hip. At the same time, he was attempting to write in a journal as his wife addressed him.

"At least we won't be enduring your girlfriend tomorrow."

No reaction.

"Coco Chanel."

Silence. The Duke was absorbed in his work.

"David! Who'll want to read about a boyhood as dull as yours? It's a waste of time!"

"I'm sorry, darling. But you may enjoy what I have written."

"I rather doubt it."

"It's about '*the French.'*"

"Didn't you mean the *filthy French?*"

The Duke's glasses slipped halfway down his nose as he leafed through the diary pages, reading parts in no apparent order:

"The Eiffel Tower is huge and hideous; the French are gluttons; a certain French painting of a British naval review is frightful; the curator of a museum in the Marais is a senile idiot; Gerard Marais came to dinner and proved to be a bounder; a celebrated photographer talks nonsense; the Jardin d'Acclimation is a wretched sort of zoo."

"You will get no arguments from me," was the Duchess's reaction.

"Did you just mention Coco Chanel?"

Exasperated, "Never mind. I was simply seeking your attention. We need to go over George's guest list. Put that journal away."

As her husband took his seat, she readjusted the ice-bag on his hip and placed a woolen shawl over his shoulder. "Now, then. Comfy? All warmy? Let us begin."

"First off, Cecil tells me our secret is safe. No one knows we're the mystery guests! Won't this be fun?"

"Hooray. Shall we arrive in costume?"

"Don't be silly. Now, then. Cecil says there will be ten, including ourselves."

"Good. Intimate."

"No crowd, thank God. And Cecil's practically the co-host. Apparently, he's gone to great lengths to remake the apartment. Matters have gone downhill lately *'chez Balanchine.'* Of course, Cecil is just in from his opening in London." Be sure to compliment him."

"On the décor or the play?"

"Both, of course! And his film, *'Gigi,'* is opening here this week as well."

"Remind me, dear. The play's *'Pygmalion'?"*

"Yes, dear. Redone as a musical, *"My Fair Lady."* That brings me to Truman Capote. His new novel is just published . . . *'Breakfast something or other.'* We shall be surrounded by artists tomorrow!"

"Are he and Cecil . . . you know?"

"You mean 'a couple?' Who knows? They are in Tangier together rather regularly. All I know is Mr. Capote has been something of a pest lately. Following poor Cecil all 'round the world. Adopting his mannerisms. It's both complimentary and rather strange."

"What shall I say to them? No doubt, something literary. There, I'm in trouble, I think."

"You certainly are! When did you last read anything? Never mind. Don't answer that. Just do what you always do. Change the subject!"

The Duchess paused to pour them both a cup of tea before she continued her party tutorial.

"The thing Cecil says to remember about Mr. Capote is that he lies."

"My, word. Doesn't everyone?"

"Yes, but apparently, his are rather world class. He tells the most outrageous stories, according to Cecil."

"Like the 'Monster of Glamis.'"

"No dear, nothing at all like the Queen Mother. Our Mr. Capote, I'm told, is a frequent talk show guest. Cecil predicts we'll take a shine to him off the bat. He says he has a funny take on things, just hilarious. Apparently with his fertile imagination he can just go off at a moment's notice. He told Cecil he had plans to start a 'Just Ducky' restaurant and serve duck-burgers, duck soup and duck dessert. Said he'd be the 'Go-Go Girl' in the Tar-Baby bar there."

Karen Hagestad Cacy

"How very odd."

"Our lovely friend, Diana Vreeland."

The Duke took a moment to adjust his ice pack. "Didn't we just see her and Reed at El Morocco?"

"Yes dear."

The Duke started laughing.

"Now what have you come to?"

"Speaking of ducks . . ."

"Really, Edward. I have no idea what you're thinking sometimes."

"Diana is quite the story teller herself. Remember her story about the Marquess of Bath?"

The Duchess joined in: "He owned Longleat . . ."

"Yes. He went through the whole war with a duck on a lead, praying for bombs to fall so that his duck would have a pond to swim in. He always had that duck, looking to the sky, both of them, and if they heard the crunch of a nearby bomb, the two would set off on the dead run to see if the bomb crater would fill up with water so the duck could swim."

"Yes, Diana will be fun, *'comme d'ordinaire.'*"

"Hooray, again."

"Yes. Hooray, again. Next, we have Arthur Miller, the novelist."

"More literature. My word!"

"Remember, he's married to Marilyn Monroe, the film star."

"I'd quite rather she'd attend."

"You would, Edward, that's for sure. However, as we said, when talking with Miller, you can just keep changing the subject. You're good at that."

The Duke beamed at his wife's compliment. "I am rather."

"He's very political, I'm afraid. I have learned that a member of the House Un-American Activities Committee asked him to name names before they would issue him a passport. He stood firm. No names. The committee member offered him a deal: if he, the member, might be photographed with Marilyn Monroe, no more questions would be asked. But Miller was adamant: no pictures."

The Duke concluded, "Excellent. A man of principles, like ourselves, my dear. 'Fight the Almighty State,' I like to say!"

"Yes, dear. Our next name is Pat Buckley."

"Who is it?"

"She's the wife of William Buckley, Jr., a prominent political conservative in America. Owns his own magazine."

"Remind me, darling, what are we over here?"

"I probably would be a democrat. As for you, with your politics, conservative, I'm afraid."

"Why afraid?"

"David. Do not start with me."

"No dear."

"We have two more guests to cover. First, 'that woman.'"

"Pamela?"

"The same. Seems she's over here for a new man."

"Pamela Churchill. The queen of dinner parties and marrying well."

The Duchess said, "That's her, all right. She's apparently already befriended our Mr. Capote. He has a list of ladies for his lunch dates. Besides our Pamela . . ."

Interrupting, the Duke said, "Randolph Churchill's former wife . . ."

Sighing, the Duchess said, "England must claim her, whether it wants to or not. As I was saying, besides 'her,' Mr. Capote's ladies include Mrs. Buckley, Babe Paley . . ."

"Television . . ."

"Yes, very good. Her husband's the president of CBS. Also, Marella Agnelli . . ."

"Who shared her husband with Pamela some years back. See dear, I do keep up."

"Indeed, you do . . . And, Gloria Vanderbilt, Gloria Guinness, C.Z. Guest, Lee Radziwell, and Slim Keith."

"Those ladies."

The Duchess concluded, "Yes, all those ladies."

"Counting us, you have only mentioned nine names so far."

"Hooray. My husband, the counter."

"I'm rather good at counting actually."

"Robert Maxwell."

"Who'd you say?"

"He's a Jew."

"Oh, Gawd! Pray how did that one slip through?"

The Duchess continued. "We are in America. Land of the free, home
of the brave. Robert Maxwell is a Czech-born British media
proprietor. He's very, very, very, very . . . wealthy. Has his own yacht, his
own helicopter, a home in Headington Hill in Oxford. Publishing
companies. He even offered to service Bulgaria's foreign debt with a bank
he created."

"I suppose we might have heard of him before now."

The Duchess answered. "I am advised that in Bulgaria, he is the
undisputed ruler, offered anything he likes there – cars, a mansion, even a
palace. They say he may be the first authentic tycoon of the Eastern Bloc."

"A tycoon?"

"Yes dear, a tycoon."

"But he's a Jew, you say?"

"Yes dear."

"I suppose one must get by that somehow."

"Yes dear."

"I suppose great wealth can make an excellent sort of thing."

"Yes dear. Quite."

george balanchine, through the eyes of richard buckle:
"George Balanchine is the man above all others in the world who can make those impressions and images visible. Like a diver, he plunges into the dark depths of music and comes back quietly with a pearl."

Chapter Fourteen
Arrivals

Friday, June 20, 1958

Celebrities would soon be arriving. Each had an important life. With travel plans. Steady schedules of soirees. Gowns to fit. Jewels in their safes. Books to sign. Film premieres to attend. Queen Elizabeth to greet at London play openings. Airplanes. Limousines. Private railcars. And taxicabs.

Inside Balanchine's apartment, candlelight shone on polished mahogany and newly-placed period mirrors graced the walls, reflecting newly placed paintings, priceless Russian tapestries, and fine silver. Cecil Beaton, a fabulist for all times, had worked his magic. Old St. Petersburg did indeed await Balanchine's guests.

Diana Vreeland was first at the door. She swept in with an unlit cigarette in its long holder at the ready. "Did you know I'm always having the most extraordinary conversations with taxicab drivers? They have views, I can tell you, on everything!"

Balanchine was in the kitchen giving final instructions to his serving staff. Rene met Diana at the door. He greeted her, lit her outstretched cigarette, and took her wrap. The fashion maven was dressed elegantly in a red silk kimono. The black chrysanthemums etched in the fabric complimented her sleek black hair to perfection. Her Chinese red nails and lipstick finished the job.

"My God, Rene, taxis are expensive! I should take a bus like the rest of the world. You can't picture it? Neither can my grandchildren. They tell a story about me:

Karen Hagestad Cacy

Nonnina – that's what they call me; it's Italian for 'little grandmother' – Nonnina took a bus with Grandpa once, and you know what she said to him? 'Oh, look! There are people here!'"

Rene showed Madam into the living room. The several steps they took down the apartment's hallway may as well have been a sixteen-hour plane flight to pre-revolutionary Russia. As she entered the scene, Vreeland noted with appreciation a lit candelabra atop the ebony grand piano. A newly added stained glass window set off French doors to the outside garden Tanny lovingly created before her illness.

Rene apologized for his boss's delay in greeting Mrs. Vreeland, and escorted her to the main room by the penthouse garden. Beaton's fine hand was everywhere in evidence. Plush velvet curtains reached from high ceiling to floor. Russian antiques glowed in the apartment. With dusk coming on, tiny lights sparkled on the balcony, a precursor of the costly jewels certain to adorn Balanchine's guests.

Rene, *'ca ne fait rien.'* I am always early, I'm afraid. It's terribly poor manners, the product of too many years having to meet magazine deadlines. I'm like a horse, saddled up and ready to go! Still, you have to begin somewhere. It's like when I was thrown by the taxi . . ."

The First Lady of Fashion was on a roll. Rene gave her his undivided attention as she continued.

"I had one foot in the door of a cab, the cab started to go and I was thrown back on my head and dragged along the ground . . . And then the driver saw me, stopped the cab, and looked at me on the ground."

"'Oh, my God, what have I done?' he said.

'You started to move and I wasn't in the car. Why did you move?'
'I have no idea.'

'Now listen, there is a mirror, but never mind. No bones are broken. No one's hurt. Let's get on with it.'

So, I got in the cab and the driver said to me, 'Lady I've got to tell you something, this is my first night out in the cab and you are the first person I've driven.'

'You've got to begin somewhere. Never look back, boy! Never look back. But still, you've got to look in the mirror to see if the person's in the car!'"

Rene decided to have his fun. As he mixed her a martini, he inquired, "Would Madam like to know the identity of our mystery guest?"

"I'm quite certain I already know! It's Cecil Beaton, of course. He's just opened *My Fair Lady* in London. And his film, *Gigi's* just opened here. Who else could it be? He's the toast of the town, darling! I have sources."

Rene slowly shook his head.

"Truman Capote, then! His marvelous book, *Breakfast at Tiffany's*, is all the buzz."

Rene leaned in and whispered the Duke's name.

"My word! Why was I not informed? We three go way back. There is no better hostess on the planet than the Duchess! One might as well consider us part of "the British invasion." The Yankees may have left England, but I can tell you, they never fully rid themselves of the Monarchy. They still gaze across the pond with a certain amount of envy, I can tell you."

Rene answered, "Of course, I am only an assistant. I've never had the pleasure of meeting the Duke. How do you find him? Are the stories we hear true?"

Rene took a break from his customary silent service. This was his chance to rub shoulders and get information. Knowing other people's business was very Russian, after all.

"What stories? Oh, you must mean about the abdication. The year must have been 1930, because I remember Reed was here in New York on business that year and I was home alone in London. One night a friend was going to take me to dinner and to a movie at a divine movie house on Curzon Street where you called up to reserve tickets and where everybody knew everybody – it was rather chic to go, but it was important to be on time. My friend was to pick me up at precisely eight o'clock."

She continued. "Eight o'clock arrived. Then, eight-fifteen. I was standing in front of the fire downstairs, wondering. I couldn't believe it, because my friend was always extremely prompt, as all Englishmen were in those days."

Madam Vreeland paused to take a sip of her drink and take a satisfying look around at her surroundings. "My goodness, how exquisite things are! I feel as though I am at L'Hermitage all over again. I suppose you know all the wonderful dancers! Oh! I can tell I have misspoken! You must have been a dancer! I can tell by your excellent posture. How delightful! How I envy you all!"

Rene waited patiently. Finally, Madame continued her story. "Anyway, as I was saying, at ten minutes to nine, in walked a man who hadn't shaved since morning, whose tie was askew, whose collar was rumpled. You simply didn't see men like that at ten to nine in the evening in London. . . . He'd be clean as a whistle – and *on time.*"

Rene glanced nervously at his watch. The others were late.

She noticed Rene's nervousness. "Never mind the time. This is an important story I'm about to tell you. Nearly no one knows it!"

She continued her story. "'Diana,' he said, 'I have just lived through the most terrible day of my life. At nine o'clock this morning, I was called to Buckingham Palace to meet the King and the Prince of Wales. I sat in the room with them, lunch was served, a bottle of wine was passed . . . we made conversation – stiffly. Then, . . . '"

Rene heard ominous sounds coming from the kitchen. Oh, hurry, Madam, pray do, he thought.

"The man who was telling me. . . Fruity Metcalfe was the Prince of Wales's aide-de-camp, don't you know. You see he was invited to lunch with King George and the Prince as a sort of buffer. And Fruity told me that the Prince looked his father, the King, 'straight in the eye and told him that never, under any circumstances, would he succeed him.'"

Diana Vreeland

"Because of Wallis Simpson, now the Duchess."

"No, no, no, Rene! Listen to me. Mrs. Simpson was not yet on the scene!"

Rene could scarcely contain his glee. What a piece of news! What an evening this was going to be, if the start was any indication.

Meanwhile, busy backstage, George Balanchine was preternaturally calm as he put the finishing touches on a meal to end all meals. It was, after all, more than a *dinner*; it was a *production*. No cost or effort was spared. His hand was warding off fate. Tonight, he would put life on hold. The finest Russian vodka rested on ice. Silver caviar spoons were at the ready.

Karen Hagestad Cacy

The baton was poised over the orchestra, awaiting the down-stroke that would signal the show was beginning.

But the audience was not entirely seated yet. There always were stragglers.

Just as he began each dance performance back stage peering out at the audience from behind the velvet curtain, so too tonight, Mr. B collected himself behind a door in his own kitchen. With a last-minute adjustment of his characteristic bolo cowboy tie, he emerged to receive his guests. On cue, his pianist began playing a medley of Cole Porter and George Gershwin tunes.

He overheard Rene and Diana talking in the living room as he greeted his next two guests. Pat Buckley and Pamela Harriman, Capote's 'swans,' arrived at the same time. Instinctively, Balanchine correctly read their false gaiety and their high voices. Their society poses were a poor mask; Even

George Balanchine (center)

the ladies' traditional badges of honor of competing perfumes and costly diamonds, could not cover the quantum distance dividing the two. Good, thought Balanchine. Some tension always adds interest. His productions were staging grounds for the unpredictable. No two performances were ever the same, tonight, no less than in the theater.

> *diana vreeland, through the eyes of christopher hemphill:*
> "Allure: Now I think it's something around you,' she said, 'like a perfume or like a scent. It's like memory . . . it pervades.'"

Chapter Fifteen
Upstairs/Downstairs

Meanwhile, upstairs, his two mystery guests also were preparing for the party. According to Beaton's instructions, a bedroom was prepared to serve as a comfortable holding area so his guests of honor might already be comfortably 'in residence,' and able to choose the time and manner of their arrival downstairs. Grand arrivals for the royal pair were customary.

Duke and Duchess of Windsor

"There's nothing wrong with your tie! For heaven's sake, leave it alone."

As with any married couple of some years, the Duke and Duchess still got on each other's nerves. The Duke was fussy about trifles like the pudding knot of his tie and the set of the flower in his buttonhole. He tugged at the knot again, and again. Tonight, he wore a Scottish plaid of the Black Watch – black and green kilt and a sort of white shirt – very smart.

Although the couple's good friend, Cecil Beaton, was informally co-hosting the party, his photographer's eye nevertheless could be ruthless in its observations. As he reminded Balanchine, ". . . the Duke's face is rather wizened, his teeth, yellow and crooked, and his gold hair is becoming rather parched." Not content to leave it at that, Beaton added, "His face now begins to show the emptiness of life. It is too impertinent to be tragic . . . He looks like a mad terrier, haunted one moment, then with a flick of the hand is laughing fecklessly."

Karen Hagestad Cacy

Nevertheless, as all who met him agreed, the Duke's charm remained unmatched in the social world, and his American wife's regal taste and unforgettable parties kept them both 'in the swim,' as they would be again tonight in New York.

The Duchess had her own pre-party jitters: She teased her back hair, repeatedly pursed her lips, pressed her cheeks upward between her palms, and fondled a small gilded unicorn that she liked to carry. Tonight, as always, the Duchess was elegantly turned out.

Adorning her long designer gown in a midnight blue silk blend, she had such jewels! There were two huge leaves or feathers on the left side of her dress, one in diamonds and the other in rubies, and she'd added a pair of diamond and ruby earrings, diamond and ruby bracelets, and a ruby ring.

The Duke, as always, admired his wife: "Will you look at me, married to such a lady. You are so far removed from my putrid relatives."

She answered, "You mean *'that fat Scotch cook'?* "

"Yes, the royal ' Loch Ness monster.'

"Thank you, dear, for your compliment, even if you do compare me with the *'fourteen carat beauty.'*"

"No, no, no, Peaches! No comparison! Did the Queen Mother have such a party thrown for her when she was over here? She had the official recognition, of course . . ."

The Duchess was growing exasperated. "Might we stop talking about your relatives for a full two minutes? Really! Such an odd lot, they all are. You're free now. Please do not remind me of those people!"

"Yes dear, as always you are quite right. When shall we descend?"

"George will call us down once everyone has arrived."

Karen Hagestad Cacy

"So kind of him to provide the pre-prandials. Tell me, Peaches, is it eight yet?"

"Yes, dear. I know your standard. It is indeed time for tiddly's. We'll be a step ahead of everyone."

"My lady is always a step ahead, with or without the benefit of a cocktail."

As her husband poured her first martini of the evening from a silver shaker, the Duchess again peered in the mirror at her own reflection. She decided to add a last-minute ruby pin to her hair. So good, having jewels of one's own, she thought. So much better than being a little wifey from Baltimore. Her royal posture stiffened. The Queen was about to meet her subjects. Peaches' jewels caught the lamp's light.

Perfect, she thought.

How very perfect.

Karen Hagestad Cacy

Chapter Sixteen
The Procrastinators : Robert Maxwell

At least two of the evening's guests equated the act of showing up on time with being ordinary and uninteresting. One was Robert Maxwell: Power was a key part of his make-up. His studied lateness was tactical. Unlike Madam Vreeland, so spontaneous and open, arriving early and loaded for bear, this member of the late set was more careful, closeted, and secretive by nature. If he'd ever consent to spending any time on a psychiatrist's couch, he also might read as being somewhat unsteady.

The billionaire, according to his personal code of behavior, rarely arrived on time. He needed to make a noticeable entrance, to underscore his presence by *finally* showing up: *make 'em wait.* Maxwell, as Balanchine came to learn, was a dark presence operating on the fringes of international law. But there was far more to know about this overweight, cigar-smoking mogul. His braggadocio, as it turned out, was a studied cover for certain other activities, not to be mentioned in polite circles. Or, in fact, in any circles.

Maxwell, while courting persons of power in Washington, D.C., held an abiding hatred for America. His wealth, access to those in control, and political views no doubt played a role in his eventual recruitment for service to the State of Israel: Alongside his important 'business' activities, Maxwell would sign on as a spy for the Mossad. The world's most secretive agency would find in Maxwell a fellow traveler: a Jew who could walk the halls of power, dine with kings and heads of state, and keep secrets.

His recent trips to America were about business, not pleasure. There was a certain defense system for sale to the right government for the right price. Maxwell was in the country to broker a deal. Unbeknownst to his potential American buyers, however,

Israel had already 'pre-programmed' the product to meet their particular needs. When operational, information obtained automatically would show up in Israel's security offices through a cleverly installed programmatic 'trap door.' The great governments of the world are all about tactics. Rather than arriving late to parties, Israel's policy was to get there before the others, eat up all the hors d'oeuvres, and leave before anyone was the wiser.

In fact, as the guest planned his own timing to Balanchine's party, he had just arrived from the nation's capital, where he was party to the cuckoldry of America. But tonight, tonight he would be all smiles, charm oozing from every pore. Always, his poor mother's parting words were with him as his guiding light: If you are ambitious, there is nothing that is impossible. She taught him success came to the English gentleman.

Maxwell's powerful will to survive helped him break free from his grimy young life in the former Czechoslovakia, to enroll in the 'London School of Propriety,' and enter the drawing room, expensively clothed and well-spoken. A well-developed upper class British accent provided Maxwell with a veneer of respectability. But if truth is the first casualty of war, then Robert Maxwell became one of its victims.

Eventually, the refugee's past caught up with him as niceties took a back seat to expediency. There was his obsessive need for self-aggrandizement and the easy way he played fast and loose with the truth. And there were other traits: an overarching personal vanity, a blustering manner, and his relentless bullying followed by fearful rages.

Karen Hagestad Cacy

Early on, Maxwell's dark good looks and erect military posture combined to cut a dashing figure. Twenty years later, Maxwell's body weight was nearly double.

By 1958, he was gorging himself on huge portions of lobster, salmon, caviar, choice meats, all washed down with copious amounts of vintage wines and champagnes. He was known to eat two full dinners in one sitting, wolfing down the food at ravenous speed. Afterwards, he smoked one of the Cuban cigars he claimed were ordered for him at the order of Fidel Castro.

He carried everywhere a powder puff. He would use it to dab his nose and forehead quickly before going into an important meeting. He had an abiding belief that any hint of perspiration on his face could leave him at a disadvantage in the deal he was going to make. To cope with his body odor, a secretary always carried a stick of antiperspirant – he would do this up to a dozen times a day.

From intelligence agents, he met along the way, Maxwell learned truth is an acquired taste. A Mossad agent later told him 'our job is to create history and then hide it. On the whole, we are honorable, respect constitutional government, free speech, and human rights. But in the end, we also understand that nothing must stand in the way of what we do.'

As he traveled the world, Maxwell enjoyed being seen in the company of kings and queens and Hollywood stars. He was not averse to hiding behind certain respectable figures, including the Rothschild's, the Lehman Brothers, and that epitome of respectability, the governor of the Bank of

Karen Hagestad Cacy

England, Robin Leigh-Pemberton, even as he fronted for some of the world's most powerful godfathers.

Maxwell was invited by Lincoln Kirstein to Balanchine's party for his money, nothing more. But every transaction has two sides. What Maxwell would extract in return for his invitation was yet unclear. Respectability? That ship had sailed. The Czech never walked away empty-handed. Balanchine's party would be no different.

Chapter Seventeen
The Procrastinators : Marilyn Monroe

Marilyn Monroe, a woman who could stop traffic, who thrilled movie-goers the world over, who seemingly had life by the tail, off-screen was shy and insecure. Now married to playwright Arthur Miller, her desire to be perfect, to fit in with his New York intellectual set, was beginning to weigh heavily on her.

Sam Shaw was one of her regulars. The photographer met her on a Billy Wilder movie set some years back, and became a shoulder for the star to cry on through two marriages. She trusted him, their friendship was tested and durable. Said he, "I just wanted to show this fascinating woman with her guard down, at work, at ease off stage, during joyous moments in her life and as she often was – alone."

The day of Balanchine's party, he had shot her at the Pulitzer Fountain outside the Plaza Hotel in an assignment for Vogue Magazine. She looked fresh and breezy in her white linen summer sheath, matching open toed sandal heels, and short white spotless wrist gloves. Her hair was less tamed – a cascade of wind-blown curls circled her elfin face.

"Oh, Sam. Let's start early."

The photography session was over, it was already 6 o'clock, and the star needed to talk. They went inside to the famous, cozy Oak Room. The Plaza, she thought provided real comfort. It was a massive building, with marble steps, well-polished oak walls, chandeliers, and glittering, happy people moving through from around the world.

> *marilyn monroe, through the eyes of diana vreeland:*
> "Marilyn Monroe! She was a geisha. She was born to give pleasure, spent her whole life giving it – and knew no other way."

In short, when she was feeling the least bit apprehensive or blue, the Plaza Hotel's Oak Room bar often could do the trick, if only temporarily. Tonight, she had a command performance at the impresario's dinner. For many reasons, she craved Sam's company, along with several stiff drinks. Her attendance would be a surprise, as she performed a 'mitzvah' for her husband, replacing him as his own personal mystery guest, a joke to be played on the host.

After many years, Marilyn could handle Hollywood parties. They were all formulaic: the lecherous old men with fantasies of casting couches spinning in their balding heads; the film agents pushing their latest star brand; the anxious hostesses trying unsuccessfully to mask their jealous guarding of their husbands from Marilyn's so-called wiles. The star had long since learned to handle these circumstances.

But a New York City dinner party was quite another matter.

With a ballet impresario as host.

And a Manhattan grouping of writers and other East Coast denizens.

Marilyn was about to enter the rarified air of America's true elites: "In the event of an unexpected landing, oxygen masks will appear . . ."

The problem was, they were expecting the trumpeted, erudite author, Arthur Miller. Instead, they were getting his wife in a practical joke of a star turn. Simply by showing up, she'd disappoint. Instead of the darling of New York's literati, they were getting 'Norma Jean' in white sheath and wrist gloves.

> **marilyn monroe, through the eyes of margot fonteyn:**
> "She was astoundingly beautiful, without the trace of a line or wrinkle on her beguiling face. What fascinated me most was her evident inability to remain motionless. Whereas people normally move their arms and head in conversation, these gestures in Marilyn Monroe were reflected throughout her body, producing a delicately undulating effect like the movement of an almost calm sea. It seemed clear to me that it was something of which she was not conscious; it was as natural as breathing, and in no way an affected 'wriggle,' as some writers have suggested."

Once more, she was being used. Not for herself, for the image of herself. Sam followed the tell-tale swiveling female hips to a booth in the back of the bar. Heads turned, but here at the Plaza, no one wanted to be seen watching. Soon, the two were seated, their drinks ordered from a fawning waiter, and the bar's normal conversational hum returned. The subtle message was, "It's New York City and the Plaza. Celebrities come and go. We are not impressed."

Nevertheless, Marilyn and Sam, seated in their dark booth, were 'out.' This meant that even in private conversation, Marilyn was fully inhabiting the 'star persona' --the half-open mouth, the whisper baby voice, the thrust of two perfect breasts just far enough above the table to suggest more to follow. Stars, unlike others, are expert in fully using their physical assets. Marilyn, as usual, was a performance in search of a script.

The young actress studied her predecessors carefully. Her journey to fantasyland began during a rejection-filled childhood. In reality, she was a lonely foster child, but in her own mind, she always was a star. She was Garbo. Marilyn wasn't the only one living on the dream-celebrity grid. Magazine editors like Mrs. Vreeland were there too: "If you knew Garbo, if you'd ever been to a Garbo dinner, meaning you're three or five at the most . . . but don't let me go grand on you. I'm only talking about the way she holds her mouth when she's talking to you. I can't say what it is she does. If I could say it, I could do it myself."

Today, as always, Sam read the star's mood. He'd seen it all before. She was once again recreating herself. Today, she was the New York intellectual who was, only incidentally, an international film star. In this script, Marilyn read the right books, hung out with important people who had big thoughts, and even married one of the east coast's leading playwrights.

Mission Accomplished.

Almost.

But a crack was beginning to appear in the nymph/egg-head marriage: jealousy. There was also the matter of a disconnect between the civilian population and Hollywood. Arthur Miller already appeared to be wondering what part of his marriage was real, what part was publicity tour, and what part was yet another fantasy by a troubled beauty.

"Okay, beautiful. Talk to Sam. Tell me what's troubling you. Your photos, by the way, will be fabulous! I think we nailed it."

She began her second drink. There was a long, sad sigh. She took Sam's hand under the table and gave it a squeeze. Then she let go.

Sam waited. He'd been here before. Sometimes, all she needed was a sympathetic ear. God knows, he had no answers. Not really. He hovered on the periphery of the glamour scene. He was wise enough not to get too close. He struggled to keep his photography on a professional level. Marilyn was a glaring exception. He couldn't resist the waif. Again, he waited.

Marilyn appreciated his silence. So few people knew how to do that. Everyone wanted to talk. Everyone always had an opinion. About everything, especially her. Or at least, about her marriage. The one they read about in the newspapers.

Karen Hagestad Cacy

Now, though, even her Arthur was being infected by the chatter. Why couldn't he just back off? Why did he need the approval of all his snobby artist friends? Why had Beaton's kind note to her been such a threat to him? The British photographer was a sweet professional friend. There was nothing else to say.

Finally, she spoke. "I feel better now."

"The alcohol helping?"

"Yes. No. Yes. And you. Your quiet presence. I should write you a poem sometime. About what you mean to me. You, with the lens in front of your face."

Their low-key friendship continued. He was the balm. She was the wound.

Sam happened to glance toward the bar. He saw a large man enter, notice Marilyn, and seat himself to have a clear view of them. The man was gobbling raw oysters, washing them down with martinis. He kept watching them. Who was he? A fan? Another man with a hard on? There was something crude about him; He made Sam nervous. Fortunately, Marilyn didn't seem to notice him. That, or her well-developed disinterest was in effect. Wherever she went, there they all were. How else could a girl react?

A waiter approached apologetically with a chilled bottle of champagne.

Sam reacted, "We never ordered this."

"The gentleman at the bar has sent this over with his compliments. He is an admirer of Miss Monroe."

Marilyn roused herself briefly to correct the waiter, "Mrs. Miller. Mrs. Arthur Miller."

"Yes, ma'am. I meant, Mrs. Miller."

The waiter left. Sam noticed the man glancing at them expectantly. He acknowledged him with a half-hearted nod. Done and over. It happened a lot.

Marilyn tried the champagne, and Sam followed suit. It was very expensive. Why, the hell not, was their reasoning. The star needed to leave in a few minutes for her performance at George Balanchine's dinner party. A little more fortification, for the road.

> *marilyn monroe, through the eyes of others:*
> "She was very directed, a self- improver. Lots of lists and to do's. She wanted to play Shakespeare – Juliet and Lady Macbeth. Wanted to create a new production company with Marlon Brando."

"Look, honey-bun. You are one smart lady. You read. You think. You light up my lens. Go to that party and make your husband proud. There's no one in this entire town who can hold a candle to you!"

Marilyn reached over. Her friend's collar was crooked. She straightened it. Then she gave him a sisterly kiss on the cheek.

"I love you, Sam. You do a girl good."

Fade out.

> *marilyn monroe, through the eyes of john huston:*
> "After dinner, we went into the bar to shoot craps. When (John) Huston gave Marilyn the dice, she asked: 'What should I shoot for John?' His answer: 'Don't think, honey, just throw. That's the story of your life. Don't think – do it.'"

Chapter Eighteen
Pamela Churchill

Pamela Churchill was well aware of the effect she was having on New York's entrenched "Ladies Who Lunch." On one level, she really couldn't blame them for closing ranks. After all, she was a predator in their midst. She had conquered the men of Europe. Her track record for bagging prey remained unchallenged in the society world.

Beware an English Rose on the prowl.

In fact, Pamela was adrift. The powerful men she'd bedded over the years were becoming too numerous to mention. After an early marriage to Randolph Churchill, son of Sir Winston Churchill, her lovers included: Averell Harriman, chairman of the board of Union Pacific Railroad, and presidential emissary during the war; Frederick L. Anderson, in charge of the America's Eighth Air Force Bomber Command; William Paley, President of CBS; Jock Whitney, prince of New York's early cafe society; Edward R. Murrow, World War II reporter of note; Aly Khan, the fabulously wealthy son of Aga Kahn, Imam of the world's Shia Imami Ismaili Moslems; and Gianni Agnelli, head of the Agnelli fortune and Fiat.

She was still reeling, however, from the demise of her latest love affair to a married man, Elie de Rothschild. The romance began in 1952 when she met this scion of one of Europe's wealthiest and most influential families. His wife was in an extended period of mourning and off with her sister when Pam moved in. A friend close to the Rothschild family at the time observed that Pamela always seemed to move in on people when wives were off duty.

> *pamela churchill, through the eyes of others:*
> "Prince Aly Khan, was the son of Aga Khan III and the second of his four wives, Theresa Magliano, an Italian ballerina. Aly had a well-known affair with Pamela Harriman, then married Rita Hayworth in 1949."

The abandoned husband was ripe for the picking. As de Rothschild bragged to a friend, "She brings me my drink and keeps quiet."

Pamela's romantic conquests were the result of extensive care and study on her part. Along the way, she was growing into a great lady, a hostess extraordinaire. Marian Shaw, an actress, observed Pamela's transformation: "One dinner at our house . . . she kind of held the floor. But later she seemed to change her style and listen a great deal more."

Shaw continued, "At her own apartment, Pamela introduced guests individually by taking them by the arm, escorting them quickly around the room, whispering the name of each guest in their ear. She was an extremely deft and gracious hostess. She was very discreet and very considerate of the men she was with."

Now, alone again in New York, Pamela was licking her wounds. Wasn't it enough that she was the perfect English lady with the skills and outlook of a courtesan? That she was a gracious hostess? That she kept her men's homes and environments to a level of sophistication and ease few could imagine? After all, it was she, and she alone, who could spend their vast fortunes to keep them in a style they never knew they wanted.

Still, not one of the men, following Churchill, saw fit to marry her. In the end, none of them saw fit to buy the cow when they could get the milk for free. Now she was 38 years old. Enough was enough. Tiny lines were making their way to the edges of her beautiful blue eyes foretelling a future of diminishing returns.

> *pamela churchill, through the eyes of others:*
> "There was nothing covert about Agnelli's long-standing relationship with Pamela. She lived openly in one of his houses, served as hostess at his parties, and was the happy recipient of extravagant gifts of jewelry, designed clothing, and money. But Agnelli could not be faithful to one woman, even to his mistress."

The lady was fading. With her characteristic strength, she knew it was time to dust off, reinvent herself, and tuck into the peace a good marriage

Karen Hagestad Cacy

could afford. Time to return to respectability. On the agenda now was locating a husband for herself, a man with homes, connections, and status. Pamela Digby Churchill would continue to dine off the finest china, with silver cutlery, elegant chandeliers, and penthouse views. And repair to the country home festooned with bouquets of field flowers refreshed daily by an attentive staff. To her horses in well-tended stables, state dinners, and the company of the 'Best People.'

Clearly, if it were mere luxury Pamela wanted, she would long since have achieved her goal. But this Englishwoman sought power as well as privilege. Her man needed to have a certain *Je ne sais quoi,* a star power to propel her into the finest dinner table conversations, to place her inside the action. She was not, nor would she ever be, 'the little woman.' She would never be a member of the 'Ladies Who Lunch' set. These women were too self-satisfied for her taste.

She wanted more, always more.

And Balanchine's dinner party was an opening. The arts, she knew, would provide her with another entry to the right people. She could keep her ear to the ground and learn the gossip around town: What marriages were on the rocks? Which couples were living separately? What wife was on extended vacation?

The hunter had placed herself in the center of New York City, America's financial mecca.

She may as well have hung out a sign:

"English Rose for Sale!"

---

pamela churchill, through the eyes of leonora hornblow:
"When Pamela met a man she adored, she just unconsciously assumed his identity, as if she were putting on a glove."

　　　　Karen Hagestad Cacy

Pamela could guess what the others would be wearing this evening – exquisite gowns, priceless jewels. The 'gown' she selected for the dinner was not a gown at all, but a quietly sexy silk business suit. The blue of the jacket and matching pencil skirt perfectly matched her sky-blue eyes. The cut was Dior; the designer's creation showed her still-slender figure to advantage. Pamela's custom-designed French underwire bra would guarantee that no one would miss a perfect decolletage. Her only overt play would be in her choice of jewelry: The triple strand of pearls at her throat was held together by a diamond clasp the size of the Bronx, an earlier gift from Gianni.

It was nearly seven; her driver would be downstairs soon. Pamela took a last look at her reflection – she saw red curls framing a still slender face. Not bad, she thought to herself. I still have it. Yes, I do. She took a final sip of her first martini of the evening, for courage.

A little-known fact about Pamela was that going out alone, sans partner, for her, always took courage. Tonight, as on other occasions, she knew she would face the usual phalanx of females, intent on slowing her down. She recalled a mere three years ago, when concerned about their brother's self-destructive lifestyle, the Agnelli sisters successfully conspired to depose her. Their work done, a new Mrs. Gianni Agnelli put Pamela out in the cold in short order.

But that was then, and this was now. Once again, it was show-time. The car had arrived. Attention, New York: She's back!

---

pamela churchill, through the eyes of babe paley:
"Entertaining Pamela was expected when she crossed the Atlantic. After all, no one was a more hospitable host than she when American friends visited Paris. But Babe Paley did not like Pamela, whom she called 'that bitch,' and was not enthusiastic about this visit. Barbara Cushing Paley was Betsey Cushing Whitney's sister. Both Cushing girls were wary of a Pamela Churchill on the prowl, given her history with their husbands, Bill Paley and Jock Whitney, and their fears that she was coming around for another try. . . . That did not mean that they avoided each other; simply that everyone was careful."

Chapter Nineteen
Cocktails, at Eight. Dinner, at Nine.

Balanchine's dinner party may have been Rene's idea initially. But the ballet master was a master chef at heart. He was a kitchen elf who, each year put his domestic skills on display. Constantly missing his homeland, Balanchine recreated its definitive tastes once a year.

His Russian Easter party was always the main festivity of the year. His Russian friends would gather at the apartment to dine right after midnight services. The next day another party would be held for Americans, non-Orthodox, and other friends. For these Easter celebrations, he always prepared his most lavish board – roasts, ptarmigans, fish in aspic, specially prepared horseradish, and garnishes, Salade Oliviere, and, of course, the traditional pascha and kulitch, which contain all the rich ingredients and exotic tastes one dreams of during Lent: sweet butter by the pound, mounds of sugar, vanilla beans, saffron, cardamom, pressed almonds, raisins.

Walls were removed. Artisans painted frescoes. Crown molding appeared. Cecil Beaton's fine artistic hand was evident throughout Balanchine's apartment. The stager created his ideal of a St. Petersburg townhouse in tsarist times. In the rear, away from workmen and out of sight, the other master was bringing in his own party crew.

Rene's close friend, Andreev Gromov, was sommelier at The Russian Tea Room. It was his pleasure to step in to help. Andreev Gromov and Rene Deriabin had been friends for many years. The two were known throughout New York's Russian ex-pat community as 'Mutt and Jeff.' Their running commentary was often xenophobic, but always amusing as they took digs at the inconsistencies and flaws in New York's passing scene.

At parties, on the street, wherever two or more Russians gathered in the City, Rene and Andreev kept people laughing. Many of the jokes were ones only emigres from the Russian experience might understand. That made the two all the more in demand. The two party boys were perfect adjuncts to Balanchine's plans.

Balanchine adjusted his usual Easter menu to suit his guests. Gone were the Russian pastries. In their place were memorable, and costly, wines and spirits. Under Andreev's expert guidance, only the most perfect and exquisite wines were now sitting on the bar awaiting corkage. Knowing the meager financial straits of the ballet world, Beaton stepped forward early, flush with recent winnings from his two hit shows, and offered to foot the liquor bill. The often financially-strapped Balanchine was pleased to oblige.

A week before the party, the three Russians convened to test the food and its pairings with the wines.

"Gospodeen Balanchine. I greet you today, not as Rene's friend, but as your personal oenologist."

"Andreev, if I wanted a doctor at my party, I might have invited one."

"No, No. That is only my official title at The Russian Tea Room – an oenologist is a wine connoisseur. It is in that spirit that I introduce you to your first wine of the evening. It will pair well with your Blini Hors d"Oeuvres served with sour cream, Caspian Sea smoked salmon and dill.:

A Recipe from Mr. B's Kitchen

Blini Hors d''Oeuvres

Served with Sour Cream,

Caspian Sea Smoked Salmon and Dill

2 cups milk

one package granulated yeast

2 cups un-sifted flour

1 tablespoon melted butter

2 eggs, separated

½ teaspoon salt

2 teaspoons sugar

¼ cup heavy whipping cream

melted butter

Directions:

Scald milk; cool to lukewarm. Place 1 cup of milk in a small bowl and sprinkle in yeast; set aside. Place the other 1 cup milk in a large bowl with 1 cup flour; stir to combine. Stir yeast-milk mixture and add to milk-flour mixture, beating well. Beat in remaining flour and 1 tablespoon melted butter. When well-blended, cover bowl with a damp cloth and let rise in a warm place for 5 hours. Beat 2 egg yolks, add salt and sugar, and add to batter, stirring 1 minute. Beat whites into stiff peaks. Add to the whipped cream and fold mixture into blini batter. Brush a 6- inch skillet with melted butter and use a gravy ladle to spoon mixture into skillet, tilting pan quickly to spread.

When blini is golden on one side, turn and cook other side. Stack cooked

blini on a dish and keep warm in a very low oven.

Yield: 24 - 6-inch blini

Allow me to present your first wine of the evening: Veuve Ambal Cremant de Bourgogne. The grape varieties of this sparkling wine are the Burgundy grape Pinot Noir with a hint of Gamay. Renee opened the bottle and filled three champagne flutes for the tasting. Balanchine had the blini on a plate before them.

Rene asked, "The wine is in a white bottle, Andy? Why is that?"

"Presentation in a white bottle highlights the beauty of this Burgundy Cremont rose. It is dominated by red fruits --raspberry and red currant. The fine bubbles and pale rose color will delight the most delicate of taste buds."

Balanchine took a sip and smiled. "Andy, you sound like a wine commercial."

"Then, let me continue. The Maison Veuve Ambal was founded in the heart of the Burgundy wine-growing region. The estates are located in four different wine-growing regions and this diversity gives the rich and complex aromas that can be found in the Maison's wines. In fact, Veuve Ambal's Cremont de Bourgogne uses the special features of each Burgundy wine-growing region like a painter uses a large palette of colors to enhance the qualities of his work."

The men helped themselves to Chef Balanchine's sample blini, and sipped the sparkling wine.

Balanchine complimented his sommelier, "You do not disappoint, Andy. I think my international guests will savor this wine."

The men continued their menu tastings through the week, comparing Andreev's selections against Balanchine's menu. Once they were in agreement, their information was sent to a New York City Ballet Company calligrapher. Elegant menu cards were placed at each guest's seat at table.

Karen Hagestad Cacy

When Balanchine was safely out of earshot, Rene beckoned to Andy.

"How you like Cecil's Coromandel screen, Andy?"

"'What is this 'Coromandel?'"

Rene waved his hand.

"Is antique from China. But, listen to me, Andy. After Cecil leave, I move it here. You see now?"

"Nyet."

"For us. Now we stand behind it on our way to the kitchen."

"Ne poneemayoo, Rene." (I don't understand.)

"To listen, Andreev. To listen."

Finally, Andy joined in.

"Ah. *Slooshatch.* (To listen.) *Tepyer, ya poneemayoo.* (Now, I understand.)

Da. Poneemayete. (Yes. You understand.)

Slooshatch! (To listen!)

Da. Slooshatch. (To listen.)

THE BALLET COOK BOOK
DINNER SERIES: PART V

SATURDAY, FEBRUARY 2, 2013 | 8:30 PM

THE RECIPES OF

TANAQUIL LE CLERCQ

GUACAMOLE

SWORDFISH TARRAGON

CELERY ROOT SOUFFLÉ

"JUST YAMMY"

TARTE À L'ORANGE

GREAT-GREAT-GRANDMOTHER BLACKWELL'S
EGG NOG

Karen Hagestad Cacy

Chapter Twenty
Ten for Dinner

The Duke was growing restive.

"Peaches, it's 8:15 already. What's keeping them?"

"You worry too much. There are cracker crumbs on your chin."

"Yes, dear. Good save, as usual. I do hate people who lack punctuality."

"I know, darling, and in this I suppose you would exclude yourself."

"I am rather on royal time, aren't I?"

The Duke used a cloth napkin from a tray to brush the crumbs from his chin.

"There, all clear now. How do I look, Peaches?"

His wife's back was turned as she re-filled their glasses. She didn't hear him, and didn't respond. There was a quiet knock on the door. It was their host.

"My dears. How wonderful you both look. I am so happy you are here this evening. Just an up-date on our guests. We are missing two so far – Arthur Miller, the playwright, and Robert Maxwell, the, er, 'comment vous dites en francais?' Le Baron."

The Duchess smiled. "Well said, George. Le Baron, indeed. Acting, no doubt, as he believes a Baron should behave, showing up late."

"My question is, if it would be your pleasure to delay the party for these late-niks." The Duchess spoke for them both.

"George. Listen here. Give us ten minutes and then you may announce us."

"That's fine, then."

The Duchess took Balanchine's arm in a firm grasp. "Now see here, Maestro. Tell us about your lovely wife, Tanaquil. Will she be joining us this evening?"

Balanchine, for a moment, stared out of the window, as if he were alone. Slowly, he came around. "You see . . . it has been difficult. I don't want to speak."

The Duke interrupted. "My dear George, we are friends. There's such a thing as too much forbearance, my good man."

"Tanny is tonight at our country home in Connecticut. Her pain has recently intensified. She has adequate medication, I believe. There are friends staying with her. Tomorrow, of course, I shall join them. Perhaps she will sit in the garden and take the sun. I feed her fresh vegetables. Always the best food I can find. Always the best. Sunshine. Health. We are hopeful . . ."

His voice trailed off. More than his words, his body conveyed his sorrow. The Windsor's both squared their shoulders and made a tacit decision. Enough of sorrow for one evening. We are all here together. It will be our duty to provide this great man with a respite from his worries. We cannot help Tanaquil. But we can be good guests. We will 'sing for our supper.' We may be royalty. But we are also human. And we recognize agony when we see it.

Perhaps the Windsor's own life experience kicked in. Only when one has lost everything can one fully appreciate the pain of another. In their humanity, at this moment, the Duke and Duchess of Windsor displayed their true colors. They could be the most loyal of friends. Their own sorrows and disappointments served a purpose: on rare occasions, the couple was able to empathize with others who were losing their bearings. It was a fleeting moment. But it was enough that it was there at all.

Balanchine felt it. His party truly began at this moment. As he had asked God, he got his answer: sorrow would stay away this evening. Joy, humor, and interesting guests would provide him a diversion on this summer's eve in the City.

The mood in the room suddenly lightened. George Balanchine, the impresario, returned to his host duties. "By the way, I hope you both will enjoy blini with smoked salmon, a canape I prepare special for you."

The Duke clapped his hands together. "Yes indeed, hooray."

Duke and Duchess of Windsor

A more subdued Duchess echoed her husband, "Yes, George, Hooray."

As an after- thought, she asked, "By the by, how is our Pamela?"

"Who, you say?"

"You know. Pamela Churchill. We know that Elie has abandoned her. She's in New York alone. How does she seem to you?"

"Oh, my dear lady, I will save that for you to know. I am but your humble host."

The Duchess laughed. "George, you are about as humble as I don't know what! Not for nothing do you direct an entire company full of prima donnas! We are suspicious of what you are about tonight. After all, you have assembled a rather curious list this evening. Sparks may fly!"

The Duke spoke up, "Yes, Sparks. Hooray."

The Russian shrugged, "We'll see. We'll see."

Karen Hagestad Cacy

Outside in the hall Balanchine's face broke into an impish grin as he descended the stairs to greet his guests.

"Cats and dogs," he thought again.

George Balanchine & Mourka

---

the duke of windsor, through the eyes of others:
"By 1947, the duke was drinking heavily. The duke drank only gin; the duchess took only a Dubonnet or one of those nasty weak Vermouth tasting things."

Karen Hagestad Cacy

Chapter Twenty-One
Blinis

As Balanchine arrived downstairs, he heard Truman's voice from the entry hall, true to form, already dishing the latest tribal news.

"So, Jimmy said to his chauffeur, 'Where are we?' And the chauffeur responded, 'Lexington Avenue, Mr. James.' And Jimmy ordered him, 'Take me over to Fifth where I belong!'" The story was followed by laughter, as his guests arrived at the door in a bunch.

Pat Buckley, Pamela Churchill, Cecil Beaton, and Truman Capote were talking at once as they crowded into the doorway. One by one, they tossed their wraps at Rene on their way inside. Balanchine attempted to greet them, but, they were distracted by Truman's stories.

Apparently the four already guessed the identity of Balanchine's mystery guest. In the elevator, they posited the Windsor's were in New York. They rather hoped it might be them. In anticipation of that possibility, Capote was getting the party rolling by dishing about a former friend of the Windsor's, heir to the American Woolworth fortune, Jimmy Donahue.

They all knew Donahue, who lived with his wealthy mother on Fifth Avenue and was a bon vivant on three continents. He was a close friend particularly of the Duchess for several years until the three had a storied falling out in Switzerland. Just warming up, Capote decided to follow up with his most lascivious Donahue story.

> *truman capote, through the eyes of others:*
> "As a gossiper, he had the fascination of a candied tarantula."

"Now listen, this all took place nearly ten years ago. You simply must hear this. It may be my best story. Donahue walked into Cerutti's, that homosexual bar on Madison Avenue. You know the one, Cecil. You and I

Karen Hagestad Cacy

have been there. Anyway, the bar was full of men in uniform. Jimmy was with the jewelry designer Fulco di Verdura."

Beaton chimed in, "I know Fulco. I photographed some of his creations for a feature in Harper's recently."

Besides the four, Capote's audience by now had grown to include Diana Vreeland and Balanchine. Andy and Rene also were listening from their post behind the screen. This was why they'd signed on to work the party: Inside stories. What fun!

Vreeland interrupted. "Oh, I know the story. Truman, you may not want to begin the party with this one. Be warned, everyone. Close your ears."

"Don't be silly, Diana. This is just the ticket. As a writer, you know I'm fascinated by the back story. It's not what's on the printed page that's important. It's what they don't want you to know. All literature is gossip.

Pat Buckley joined in. "Please, Truman. Don't just begin a story and then walk away."

Capote replied, "No worry, Pat. Life is nothing more than a moderately good play with a badly written third act. But, this story takes the cake!"

It was clear to Balanchine he'd already lost control of his own dinner party. For a moment, he was overlooked. His guests were happily chattering on. Knowing the Windsor's were just upstairs, Balanchine preferred a more measured start to the evening. Cats and dogs!

But Capote was on a roll. There was no stopping him.

"The year was 1946. Donahue took a number of sailors, soldiers, and marines to a party at his mother's apartment over here on Fifth Avenue. They stripped one of the GI's, and began shaving off his body hair. They were using an old-fashioned open razor. I wasn't there. So, don't blame me."

Cecil didn't like where the story was going. "Truman, why don't you save the rest until we've had the benefit of a cocktail?"

They all could see the excitement building in Truman's face as he came to his finish. He ended his little entry hall performance with a grand sweep of his velvet cape.

"Then Jimmy castrated the soldier!"

Vreeland reacted. "This, he tells us without so much as a martini!"

Ignoring her characteristically trenchant comment, Truman continued his story: "Naturally, everyone became hysterical, and the man was thrown into Jimmy's car, driven to the 59th Street Bridge, and tossed onto the sidewalk. Donahue was arrested but released when Mrs. Donahue paid the poor man, I hear, a quarter million dollars to drop the charges."

There was a stunned silence as the story sank in. Even for people used to Capote's theatrics, the story was a bit too much to take.

Pat Buckley was the first to recover as Rene appeared with a tray of drinks.

"Jesus, God. Rene, what are those, martini's? Be a doll and hand me one. At once!"

The group moved like a flock of geese into the main room. The French doors were thrown open to the balcony beyond. A chandelier hung over the grand piano, where a pianist was softly playing Cole Porter tunes. Rene ran around lighting the rest of the candles as Andy manned his fully stocked bar off to the side.

The guests were used to opulent surroundings. But Balanchine's place tonight was a visual feast. It was no longer a New York apartment, as much as a lavish set from a Cecil Beaton production. The apartment's newly created St. Petersburg theme was a product of the designer's uncanny ability to invent scenes nothing short of ethereal.

Karen Hagestad Cacy

Carte
Blini Hors d''Oeuvres
With Sour Cream, Caspian Sea Smoked Salmon
and Dill
VEUVE AMBAL's Cremont de Bourgogne
(a Burgandy Cremont rose)

Slow Beef Borschok
With Rye Toast Points
1957 Domaine de la romanee-Conti La Tache Grand Cru
Monopole from Cote de Nuits, France
(a pinot noir)

Sole Bonne Femme
1950 Domaine Huet Vouvray Moelleux Le Haut-Lieu
(a Chenin blanc also known as Pineau de la Loire)

Poulet Braise au Champagne
Buckwheat Kasha
1953 St. Julien Bordeaux

Cheese Selection
Selection of German Rieslings
Kabinett (dry,)
Spatlese (medium-dry)
Auslese (sweet)
Beeren & Trockenbeerenauslese & Eiswein (very sweet)

Tonight's theme might as easily have been 'Nicholas and Alexandra in 1915,' as a 1958 New York dinner party of 'The Best People.' Velvet curtains swept the floors. Satin tapestries and burnished Russian antiques offset newly gold filigreed walls and ornate sconces.

Karen Hagestad Cacy

Outside on the penthouse balcony, a large round table was set with white linens, two candelabras, gleaming silverware, and large bouquets of white roses, set low for easy conversation. The number of wine glasses at each place foretold an elegant and complex meal to come.

Drinks in hand, the group finally remembered their manners and turned to their host, greeting him in turn.

There was a twinkle in his eye as Balanchine addressed them:

"Welcome, my friends. Welcome to a humble ballet master's small apartment."

Diana spoke first: "Hardly so humble, my dear George. This is a fantasy of bygone 'Roo-sha!'" The fashion editor rolled her 'r' as though she, herself were a member of Russia's royal family.

"Cecil, you have quite outdone yourself!"

Balanchine replied, "Da. Da. All of this is Cecil's handiwork. I cannot tell you how many artisans and workmen he's had here. You see . . . with Tanny's illness, I've been busy tending to her needs lately. So, Cecil come with magic wand. The commotion! Oh, the commotion! Like our stage sets over at theater. Friends, we do this for you. I am glad you have agreed to join me and also, I hope you will enjoy a few delicacies I have prepared specially for you. You know how much I am American now. But just for tonight, we shall impersonate tsars. Na Zdorvyeh, friends!" (To Your Health!)

Beaton responded, "George, you are our impresario tonight. And we are yours to command."

Truman spoke up. "Speak for yourself, Beaton. I'm at nobody's command."

Pat said, "Obviously."

pat buckley, through the eyes of leo lerman:
"The Buckley's gave a celebration of Estee Lauder at Mortimer's, and all the *gratin* was in gushing attendance."

George could tell it was going to be an interesting evening. Ignoring Truman, he held up his drink glass. "My dears, let us enjoy the evening. My darling wife, Tanaquil sends along her regrets as she is in the country this evening. Please, does everyone have their drink?"

Everyone nodded.

"And now . . ."

George raised his glass in the direction of the staircase. The others followed suit. They knew what was coming. White orchids were wound along the railing. The pianist, who'd been playing softly in the background during the host's remarks, now began playing Britain's national anthem.

"Ladies and Gentlemen. My I present our special guest of the evening, our Mystery Guest, the Duke of Windsor accompanied by Her Royal Majesty, the Duchess of Windsor."

So, they were right. The guests turned to each other silently acknowledging their social acumen. Good show. They'd figured it out!

The party's mystery guest and his wife suddenly appeared at the head of the staircase, and paused before making their way carefully down the stairs. Their entrance, while lacking the mounted palace guard and buglers dressed in red velvet capes of the Duke's former home in England, was nevertheless, as gracious as many still taking place at "Buck House." The Duchess's fabulous jewels caught the light as she approached. And the Duke's quiet posture communicated class and 'lege majeste.' The two near-royals knew how to make a grand entrance. The guests below welcomed them with smiles and an impromptu round of applause.

Balanchine's respectful introduction and the playing of their national anthem clearly touched the pair. Here in America, even a Russian host knew enough to present them with the formality due them. The warm welcome was yet another reason the couple adopted America as their second country. France, where they lived near Paris, was never in the running.

"The couple made no attempt to understand the French. Indeed, they didn't like them. An American woman arriving in a storm at their Paris home complained 'What a storm. This country of yours . . .' 'This is not my country!' the Duke snapped."

The Duke and Duchess of Windsor rose to the occasion. They might as well have been receiving guests at their elegant home in Clarence House. All of England might as well still have held them in royal esteem, hanging on their every word, noting their clothing and accoutrements. Discussing their comings and goings in the London papers.

Rene returned to the kitchen to grab the tray of blini's as Andy began opening the Veuve Ambal. He returned and moved a small table near the Duke for his hors d'oeuvres and drink glass. The Duke turned down the sparkling wine, preferring gin. The Duchess requested her customary Dubonnet.

Truman and Cecil stood in the corner discussing the Duke. Rene leaned in to catch their conversation.

Beaton was saying, "I just dined with them in Paris last month. We were at the Berkeley."

Capote said, "Over at the Avenue Franklin D. Roosevelt and the Rue de Ponthieu?"

"Yes, that's right. So, the Duke says, 'Perhaps some of you would prefer smoked salmon. Two hands. Good. Waiter, two caviar, two smoked salmon. I recommend a melon next.' Those delicious little Charentais melons were in season. Then he moved to the entree: 'I recommend a double mutton chop, with soufflé potatoes and fresh asparagus.'"

Tasting a blini, Capote smiled approvingly. "You know, swell food is one of the main joys of the upper class. Oh, we had wonderful, fresh vegetables in the South, growing up. But since I have developed certain friends . . ."

Diana Vreeland chimed in: "Lettuce is divine, although I'm not sure it's really food. The consommé at Maxim's! That, to me, was food. It had every bone from every animal, every vegetable . . . it's the best nourishment in the world . . . Toast should be brown and black. Asparagus should be sexy and almost fluid . . . alligator pears can never be ripe enough – they should be black. What you throw in the garbage can, I eat!"

Cecil said, "You know, I used succulent foods as visuals in 'Gigi.' Food can be very decorative."

Truman added, "And sexy. There's been many a seduction over the perfect bowl of fresh strawberries!"

Vreeland agreed. Here was a subject close to her heart.

"I quite agree. And raspberries! The best raspberries . . .are the black ones, and they should be tiny – the tinier and the blacker, the better! Strawberries should be very big and should have very long stems attached so that you can pull them out easily. Yvonne, my maid, used to choose them individually for me at Fraser-Morris. Very splendid. God knows what they cost nowadays. Once I asked how much they were, apiece. Yvonne was shocked. 'Ask, Madame?' she said. 'Listen, Yvonne!' I said. 'Everybody asks.' 'But Madame . . .' 'So, you mean to tell me, Yvonne,' I said, 'that you'd walk into Harry Winston's to buy a tiara, and not ask? One asks!' 'Truth is a hell of a big point with me.'"

Capote, as usual, had the last word: "You do know this dinner has a theme: Two of the men, and one of the women have slept with the Duchess."

---

cecil beaton, through the eyes of others:

"Cecil was a man of great elegance. Through vanity, he always ordered his clothes a size smaller than he required because it looked better. . . He had been an outsider when young, and he thus developed the facility to observe, first with nose pressed up against the glass, and then from within."

Karen Hagestad Cacy

Chapter Twenty-Two
"Norma Jean"

Rene greeted Balanchine's second to last guest as the others circled the Mystery Guest and his wife in the main room. At the door was a vision, a mirage. It was Marilyn Monroe, the film icon, blonde, shining, lips slightly parted in hesitation. Ready for your close-up, Miss Monroe.'

Norma Jean

"Good evening. I do hope I am not intruding. My husband, Arthur, asked me to stand in his place this evening."

Rene couldn't answer. His reaction was similar to everyone's the world over. He was staring at a legend. But the woman before him seemed shy and polite to a fault.

Stammering, Monroe filled the silence. "You see, 'I am invariably late for appointments – sometimes as much as two hours. I've tried to change my ways but the things that make me late are too strong and too pleasing.'"

Rene's heart was melting. He couldn't help himself. He, too, was stuttering: "Miss Monroe . . ."

Marilyn corrected him. "It's Mrs. Miller, actually . . ."

"Sorry. Mrs. Miller. Of course, I am certain Mr. B. will be more than pleased you're here. You really are beautiful, Mrs. Miller."

Marilyn knew the effect she had on men. She overlooked Rene's reaction as one might trip over a piece of broken glass on the sidewalk.

Karen Hagestad Cacy

Balanchine joined them. He too was surprised to see the film star standing in his entry.

Rene quickly filled him in: "Her husband couldn't make it, so Miss Monroe, er . . . Mrs. Miller, is here in his place."

Marilyn still had on the demure sleeveless white linen sheath of her earlier photo shoot at The Plaza. She was happiest in white. It was rare for her to wear colors. Also, it was her one act of defiance to forego slinking in wearing some gold lame number. She was assigned a certain role by her husband. Instead, she chose a co-starring part. Tonight, she would not be the sex symbol. Tonight, she would be the dressed-up Norma Jean. That would just have to do. She thought, "A sex symbol becomes a thing; I just hate to be a thing."

George recovered quickly. "Zdravstvweecha, Miss Monroe."

"Please, call me Marilyn."

"Marilyn. Actually, you will be pleased to know there is one other guest still behind you. We are just enjoying our first drinks. Come, please join us."

Marilyn operated on an animalistic level, trusting her instincts in dealing with others. She immediately picked up on Balanchine's vulnerability. People in pain can appear distant and closed off to others. Marilyn immediately identified something lurking behind this particular Russian soul, despite his pleasant demeanor.

With the discovery, she began to relax. Her host clearly was a fellow traveler. "You know, George, I've been on a calendar, but I've never been on time," she told him.

The humor endeared her to Balanchine. They would be friends, he felt. He was not some slathering male, sniffing at her heels. They would talk. He wanted to know her better. It was an auspicious start to their evening. Finding someone who gets you is a gift to be treasured. Arm in arm, the two new friends entered the party together.

Balanchine was pleased. Three mystery guests already! No telling where this was all heading!

Every encounter for Marilyn was a performance. She did that thing she did, whenever she entered a room full of strangers. She turned on a switch. It had something to do with the relationship between her spine and hips. Whatever it was, it always worked like gangbusters. There was an audible gasp as they entered into Beaton's tsarist setting.

Truman was the first to speak. "Work it, baby!"

Pat Buckley, not understanding their close friendship, took umbrage at Truman's crude greeting.

"Really, Truman, a simple 'Hello, and Welcome' might have done the trick. "

Approaching the star, Buckley swept her into a hug with her caftan sleeve. "Hello, and Welcome. What a pleasant surprise indeed."

> *marilyn monroe, through the eyes of elton john:*
> "Goodbye, Norma Jean, Though I never knew you at all . . . it seems to me you lived your life like a candle in the wind, Never knowing who to cling to when the rain set in . . ."

Turning to Truman, "See how easy?"

Marilyn, a good friend of Truman's explained. "Thank you so much . . ." She struggled to know her benefactor's name.

"Pat Buckley. Wife of the often misquoted and much hated conservative columnist, William F. Buckley, Jr. who, I can assure you, is a living doll. Although, come to think of it, he does overdo it a bit with the sailing. I mean, the man could get killed out there on the open ocean one of these times!"

Marilyn said, "Actually, Truman and I know each other quite well. What he said . . . well, it's one of our little communications. Sort of like, 'How's it going? Long time-no see."

Truman asked, "So, where's the great playwright this evening? Up in Connecticut, I suppose."

"Yes. He had to work. So, he thought I might be a replacement. I do hope no one minds that I came along instead."

The shy girl used her actress charms on the group. It worked. Her wide-eyed sincerity caught them all off guard, as they momentarily abandoned their usual world-weariness. Rene stepped forward with her drink and blini canapé.

> **marilyn monroe, through the eyes of henri cartier-bresson:**
> "I saw her bodily – Marilyn – for the first time and I was struck as by an apparition in a fairy tale. Well, she's beautiful – anybody can notice this, and she represents a certain myth of what we call in France 'la femme eternelle.' On the other hand, there's something extremely alert and vivid in her, an intelligence. It's her personality, it's a glance, it's something very tenuous, very vivid, that disappears quickly, that appears again. You see, it's all these elements of her beauty and also her intelligence . . . last night I had the pleasure of having dinner next to her and I saw that these things came fluidly all the time . . . all these amusing remarks, precise, pungent, direct. It was flowing all the time. It was almost a quality of naivety . . . and it was completely natural . . . she's very good that way; one has to be local to be universal."

Already a little tipsy from her drinks at The Plaza, she whispered to Pat, "If I'd observed all the rules, I'd never have got anywhere."

Pat warmed to the star with that remark.

"Me either, doll-face. Me either."

> **marilyn monroe, through the eyes of eve arnold:**
> "Her imitators tried to recreate her walk, but they never even came close to that swivel of the hips that was her trademark. Like Chaplin, she built her film character around her walk. . . .as with everything else (the smile, the voice, the glow) she could turn on the undulating hips at will. . . . No wonder she often spoke of herself in the third person. "

Karen Hagestad Cacy

Chapter Twenty-Three
The Man from the Bar

Marilyn's good humor was short-lived, unexpectedly replaced by a curious sense of unease. Balanchine's final guest arrived just as she was gaining her sea legs. His arrival momentarily overrode Pat's friendliness, and Truman's quirkiness.

As soon as the man entered the room, her mind flashed to the hard, nubby, cheap fabric of the casting couch. A girl never forgets some things. She recognized Robert Maxwell right off as the man from The Plaza Hotel bar. It was his expensive champagne that she and Sam enjoyed earlier in the evening. Now, in a twist of fate, here he was again.

He was expensively, if not well, dressed and packing more than a few extra pounds. There was an air of crude entitlement about him. She could feel herself physically recoil. Pat Buckley, her self-designated protector, immediately and correctly read her negative reaction.

Pamela and Diana joined Pat and Marilyn in short order, forming a coven of feminine sensory perception. All seemed knocked off balance by Maxwell. Something was wrong. He didn't belong here. He was not from the theater. He was not even a New Yorker. It became apparent once he spoke that he was British; at the same time, it was reasonably clear to everyone he was no English gentleman.

One thing about the assembled:

To a person, they practiced an age-old practice. They kept their boundaries secure whenever anyone *'Not of Our Class, Darling,'* attempted to scale the walls of societal propriety. There was nothing the poor man could do about it.

Karen Hagestad Cacy

Maxwell was tonight, and would be forever, *'NOOC, Darling.'*

In America, no less than in Europe, one doesn't choose one's social class.

It chooses you.

At the same time, the man was interesting. He had an air about him, as though he were keeping a secret others wanted to know. Oddly, he averted his eyes from Marilyn. Instead, he paid his respects one-by-one to the other guests. He approached the Duke as though he were still the King of England. Maxwell was mannerly, obsequious, accommodating. He even performed the royal bow to the couple.

So far, so good.

But then, the Czech intruder uttered the unthinkable, "I understand your friends call you David. May I, Sir?"

The Duke was so taken aback by Maxwell's effrontery that he turned to his martini, taking a large gulp. Maxwell was left to sort things out on his own and move on. He tried to recover by kissing the Duchess's hand. Everyone but him could see it was going to be a *'no go.'*

Diana chose to ignore the newcomer entirely and instead, engaged her host about the world of dance.

"George, between yourself and Cecil . . . I feel as though I've been dropped down a well into the world of Diaghilev tonight! You know, there was the flavor, the extravagance, the *allure,* the excitement, the passion, the smash, the clash, the crash . . . this man smashed the atom!' You were in Paris at the time: You, of all people know, his influence . . .was complete."

"Diaghilev's Russia and the Maryiinski Theater are never far from my thoughts as I create ballets for the company . . ."

Clapping her hands together, Diana interjected, dramatically, *'The Prodigal Son!'*

"Yes, 'The Prodigal Son,' for one.

Diana wanted to spend the evening peppering Balanchine with questions about the ballet. The majesty and aura of the art never failed to fascinate her. She was a *ballet groupie,* or in politer terms, a *patron of the arts.*

"You know, George, my parents were racy, pleasure-loving, gala, good-looking Parisians who were part of the whole transition between the Edwardian era and the modern world . . . Money didn't seem to be of any importance to them . . . because of the life they led with fascinating people and events. All kinds of marvelous people came to the house – Diaghilev was very impressive. He had a streak of white hair and a streak of black hair and he put on his hat in the most marvelous way. I remember him very clearly."

---

through the eyes of marilyn monroe:
"Sometimes I've been to a party where no one spoke to me a whole evening. The men, frightened by their wives or sweeties, would give me a wide berth. And the ladies would gang up in a corner to discuss my dangerous character.

Their conversation was interrupted by a loud cry. A leering Maxwell finally had reached Marilyn, and was attempting to kiss her hand. But she withdrew it. The soft, breathy voice that was the Monroe trademark, momentarily disappeared, replaced by Norma Jean's distinctly less pleasant one as she recoiled from his touch. George Cukor, her director for *"Something's Got To Give,"* observed, "I once heard her talk in her

145 |

Karen Hagestad Cacy

ordinary voice, which was quite unattractive. So, she invented this appealing baby voice . . ."

"No! I'm sorry. Please, no."

He was no Hollywood producer. Rather, just another rich guy on the make. And here, of all places. This was her Maginot Line. Her defenses were full on and would remain so for the rest of the evening.

Pamela quickly intervened, escorting Maxwell away.

"Mr. Maxwell, you are British, I understand. I also am English. How long will you be staying here in America?"

At least there was one welcoming person in the crowd. Why was he here anyway? With these people, he did not know. The answer was obvious. His money, as always, led the way. Everyone wanted to be near him for what he could do for them. Of course, payment for the evening would be the underwriting of one of Balanchine's ballets in the fall. Lincoln Kirstein had made that fact abundantly clear.

But, make no mistake: Maxwell didn't consent from kindness or any sudden love of the arts. His sponsorships were nothing more than carefully calculated shields of respectability. For a man to build a world-wide crime syndicate, the more hide-outs he had, the better.

And so, as Pamela led him away, he played along. He knew who she was. At least, she could appreciate big money. Maxwell's wealth, by now, well exceeded that of her former European boyfriend, de Rothschild. He knew all the details. As they spoke quietly, he could not help noticing the slight rise of her bosom under the expensive Dior suit.

Like many men before him, Maxwell found the English Rose hard to resist.

Karen Hagestad Cacy

stas radziwell, through the eyes of others:

"Stas Radziwill (Prince Stanislas Radziwill (1914-76), Polish nobleman, sits silent throughout dinner party in South of France. Mrs. Kellock, rich American, turns to Stas and says, 'Do you realize you have not addressed one word to me the whole evening?' Stas replies, 'When I sit next to women like you, my best friend is potato.'"

Karen Hagestad Cacy

Chapter Twenty-Four
Politics Start at the Water's Edge

Robert Maxwell charged full steam ahead, oblivious to the affect he was having on others. Fueled by alcohol, he misread Cecil Beaton, a fellow Englishman, as a new friend. The photographer was explaining minor adaptations between the English and American versions of *"My Fair Lady."* His descriptions were nothing more than polite parlor talk.

But Maxwell reacted, "Americans! I do not like them. I do not like their principles; I do not like their manners, I do not like their opinions."

Given Maxwell's extreme wealth, his next comment was more puzzling:

"Here in New York, every man worships the dollar, and is down before his shrine from morning to night."

Beaton had nothing more to say. Hoping for more up-lifting conversation, he moved to the piano where Truman was mid-story to Pat and Diana:

"Mind you, this took place in 1948. Miss Barney's circle was not limited to lesbians . . . though certainly all the more presentable dykes in town were on hand. Sometimes she had rather curious or unexpected people . . . but it was always very proper . . . talk about this concert or that concert, or so-and-so's paintings, or 'Alice has a fabulous new recipe for eggs.'"

Truman paused briefly and changed his glasses to a darker pair before he continued. "The only shocking thing I ever remember was when Carl Van Vechten came for tea and peed on the sofa by mistake. Everybody said, 'Oh-oh, wait a minute,' and then they turned, and down the line Esther Murphy, with the same problem, was peeing on her sofa."

Karen Hagestad Cacy

Beaton lifted his glass to Rene. "Rene, pour. This cautions to be a rather long night."

Balanchine approached.

"Cecil, listen to me: Lincoln asked me to invite Maxwell. Is business, you understand."

"Isn't everything these days?"

"Was mistake. Best we keep him away from our special guests. I must check on the kitchen. Dinner's nearly ready. Will you keep an eye on them for me?"

Beaton answered, "George, you must know the Windsor's are anti-Semitic. They've never made a secret of that."

Overhearing them, Truman approached, adding his two cents: "Darlings, the Czech's a Jew. And none other than Adolph Hitler, himself, sent the Windsor's a wedding gift! Did you both not know that little piece of history? Oil and water, darlings!"

The little shit-stirrer was getting warmed up.

"No. No politics!" George complained.

George's worried brow may have fooled Beaton, but not Capote. Truman was delighted to discover that 'ballet man' was a fellow traveler, and he didn't mean a Communist. In a flash of intuition, Truman saw that his host, like himself, was adept in the 'fine art of human interaction.'

Karen Hagestad Cacy

It takes one to know one!

Capote and Balanchine. One, a social butterfly, the other a near recluse. One, an emotional wreck from a mother's repeated abandonments, the other, home sick from lifelong exile from 'Mother Russia.'

Edward, Duke of Windsor

In separate acts of self-preservation, over the years, both men kept introspection at bay by using human nature against their fellow humans. But, only when necessary. Their skills were best used in moderation. Truman performed a quick calculation: Balanchine's wife was down with polio, a summer of inactivity yawned before the impresario, and no doubt an undiagnosed depression lurked behind the Russian's pleasant party face. In an instant, the perceptive author arrived at a fresh understanding of the reasons behind the party, the guests, and the puppet master who'd brought them all together.

. In his best Bette Davis impression, he said, 'Fasten your seat belts, boys; It's going to be a bumpy ride tonight!'"

Truman already was having a good time, and the party barely had left the ground.

George walked away shaking his head.

Beaton grabbed Truman by the shoulders and planted European kisses on each cheek. "Now, Truman, we are here to cheer up dear George. Don't let's start anything tonight."

K a r e n   H a g e s t a d   C a c y

Unnoticed by the two, the Duchess stood nearby, listening. Truman and Cecil were both friends. She wanted to know what they were about.

Truman answered Cecil.

"Moi? You give me too much credit. Listen, did I ever tell you this one? It was when the Loel Guinnesses' visited me and Jack in Verbier in Switzerland for dinner: I made the perfect dinner for them at our house and we had the perfect wine and the house was beautiful. Everything was perfection. Suddenly, Jack looked at Loel and said 'What the fuck are you doing here, you big fat Nazi?' After that there's nothing you can do. You can't excuse yourself. You can't excuse him. You just have to sit there and die. Can you believe he would do that?"

Finishing, Capote said, "However, I agree. We must keep the parties separated this evening."

From the corner of his eye, Truman saw Maxwell zeroing in on Marilyn again. Oh, no you don't, buster! The evening was turning into a series of police actions! Oh well, thought the elfish writer, at least it's interesting!

Truman grabbed Marilyn's elbow and steered her onto the terrace. In the night sky, a thin strip of brilliant pink and orange was the final vestige of another hot summer day in the City. Beaton's twinkle lights created a most congenial fairy-like setting in the penthouse trees surrounding the table. Renee was busily lighting the two massive candelabras, signaling the sit-down meal would soon begin.

"We like it out here. It's a nice safe place to talk."

"Oh, Truman. You are such a friend. Thank you. What a disagreeable man."

"You are my own Holly Golightly. My inspiration! Will you do the movie? Say yes, do!"

Karen Hagestad Cacy

"You know I'd love to. But I have so many new projects. I've been asked to a film festival. They're showing one of my production company's films, *"The Prince and the Showgirl."* You know, the one with Sir Laurence Olivier. Do you know him, Truman?"

---

through the eyes of cecil beaton:
"It was more cafe society than gratin, mixed in with 'newspaper celebrities.'"

Truman sniffed. "Another phony. I know how he treated you when you were filming. The man has a very high opinion of himself. Insufferable. But, I'm sure you handled him okay."

"Sometimes people can get to me, you know?"

"Oh, me too! Listen, toots. I could tell you stories of my childhood. Every once in a while, you're going along. Everything seems fine. And you run across someone, or something someone says, and 'Boom!' It all explodes! My mother was such a beautiful woman. She had all these men friends. She would park me in this hotel room and go off. To this day, some hotel rooms can give me the creeps. Particularly the ones painted all in white. I think I may have a phobia about white rooms!"

Truman and Marilyn fell back into their familiar pattern: two adults looking in a rear-view mirror in near disbelief at how far they'd come. Their friendship always included some 'one-ups-man ship,' a bit of 'My childhood was worse than your childhood.'

Marilyn answered him.

"White. That's interesting. I'm the opposite. White for me is a safe color. Without emotion. There's no decision with white.

It's clean.

Pure.

K a r e n   H a g e s t a d   C a c y

Uncomplicated."

Truman thought she was finished speaking, when she softly repeated herself.

"White."

The Duke and Duchess approached the pair. The Duchess addressed them first.

"How lovely it is out here. Inside it was getting a bit . . ."

Her husband finished her sentence,

". . . stuffy, darling."

"Yes, that's right. Stuffy. Now then, Truman. Between you and Marilyn, you are the two most interesting persons at our party. Do tell us all about your new novel."

"It's called '*Breakfast at Tiffany's.*' It's about a small-town Southern girl who makes her way to the big city."

The Duchess responded, "Much like myself. I am from the South, you know– Baltimore. Then, off I went to London! The rest, as they like to say, was history!"

Truman laughed. "No, Duchess. Holly Golightly is nothing like you, I'm afraid. The novel, truth be told . . ."

He paused to trade his glasses for a darker pair before finishing.
". . . is autobiographical."

"With you as the small-town girl?" the Duchess asked with a giggle.

Karen Hagestad Cacy

"That's it. Now you're getting the picture, Your Highness."

Laughing, the Duchess turned to Marilyn to include her in their conversation. "Whatever can we say about that, dear?"

She leaned in close to inspect Marilyn's face.

"My word, it's true what they say. Your face really does glow!"

Recovering, she continued speaking.

"Anyway, the Duke and I were just down in Florida. We stay with the Guinnesses' every season. They wear summer attire year-round down there. And David insisted on wearing this powder blue pullover to luncheon one day. His slacks were a sort of yellow and navy blue plaid."

The Duke interrupted her, "Actually, the blue was more on the aquamarine side, Peaches."

"Yes, well, whatever. My husband is a stickler for some things. Then for others . . . well, no comment. As I was saying before I was interrupted, the combination, to my way of thinking was something just short of hideous. And, of course, I said so."

The Duke interrupted again. "Here comes the punch-line. Wait for it."

"Whose picture do you think was on the cover of *'The Tatler'* the very next week, and furthermore, when do you think the men in Palm Beach began wearing bright pastel colors?!"

"I do know a thing or two about colors. Not much else, I'm afraid," added the Duke.

With those remarks, Marilyn knew she'd just made another new friend. Lost puppies, authors with lousy childhoods, abused trees.

And now: now, a Duke, with a shyness that appeared to rival her own.

Karen Hagestad Cacy

hollywood, through the eyes of marilyn monroe:

" . . . in Hollywood important people can't stand to be invited someplace that isn't full of other important people. They don't mind a few un-famous people being present because they make good listeners. But if a star or a studio chief or any other great movie personages find themselves sitting among a lot of nobodies, they get frightened as if somebody was trying to demote them."

K a r e n H a g e s t a d C a c y

Chapter Twenty-Five
Places, Everyone!

Trays of food began arriving at the outdoor table. Hand-dried Baccarat glasses were lined up on a silver tray. Andreev busily relocated his operation to a small wine bar positioned nearby on the balcony. With the strains of Cole Porter playing in the background, the party of ten made their way to their seats. With this crowd, naturally, no one sat as directed. Not one of the guests was known for taking orders well.

Diana and Truman ran around the table, checking the place cards. When the seating arrangements weren't to their choosing, the self-designated 'social team' changed the cards. Thanks to their handiwork, poor Maxwell was now seated at the end of the table, in, as Truman directed, 'Outer Hebrides'!

As everyone finally took their seats, Andy poured the wine, an Alsatian Riesling. Their sommelier offered: "This wine, dryer than German, will pair well with our Pear and Bleu Cheese Salad. Southern Pecans finish the dish and the wine holds lots of pear notes, perfume, mineral, a racy mixture, with spice and a soft, but balanced acidity."

The Duke was the first to comment. "Excellent wine, Andreev. Jolly good choice!"

Diana agreed. "Yes, Andy, simply divine. Everything, George. Really, how delightful this all is! To see old friends, and meet new ones."

At the last statement, she and Pat exchanged meaningful looks, as did Truman and Marilyn.

Diana continued holding court.

"The only real elegance is in the mind; if you've got that, the rest really comes from it. What I'm talking about is general conversation. Country-

Karen Hagestad Cacy

house stuff. I adore someone who has the attention of the whole table. Too much these days there's this ritual at dinner of talking to the person on your right and then turning to your left. And people are much too keen on even-steven numbers at dinner."

Pamela instinctively turned to Maxwell. She knew they both were at the end for a reason. The two were allowed in only temporarily. Maxwell, for his money. And Pamela, well, she had yet to figure that one out. Perhaps for her European connections.

"I am always fascinated by successful people. Tell me, Mr. Maxwell, however did you accomplish so much in your short life?"

At the other end of the table, Vreeland droned on.

". . . Of course, it helps if there's some preposterousness in the air . . . something outrageous or memorable. Greta Garbo always brought a spark that ignited everyone around the table. A great gusher of language. Garbo never called anyone by their first name. 'Mrs. Vreeeelanddd.' Everyone called her 'Miss G.' . . . I learned everything in England. I learned English!"

Marilyn said, "Oh, I just adore Garbo!"

Maxwell ignoring the others, directed his attention to the rather spectacular pair of breasts to his right.

"Is it the truth you are after, Miss Churchill, or a clever dinner table response?"

"The truth, always the truth. You may know, I have been close to my share of wealthy and powerful men. The subject interests me, that's all."

"Then here is your answer: 'Boorishness.' With a soupcon of the English gentleman."

"I beg your pardon, but did I hear you say 'boorishness'? How very odd."

"That's right. You see, coming from very limited circumstances . . ."

"You were very poor once . . ."

"The word 'poor' does not cover it, I can assure you. Anyway, as I was saying, once one has been to the depths, so to speak, nothing is at risk. Do you understand what I am saying?"

"I think so."

"Business is a form of tyranny. The winner is always the one least worried about methods or risks. Winners have no thoughts of propriety. Only, of winning. Now do you understand, my dear?"

"You are speaking of the law, are you not, Mr. Maxwell?"

"Miss Churchill, given our discussion, I suggest you call me 'Bobby.' And, I shall call you 'Pamela.'

The raw honesty was at the same time pleasing and frightening. She would have to keep this one at an arm's length, despite his money, she thought. She lowered her eyes in a silent response, and dug into her salad.

---

leo lerman, through the eyes of diana vreeland:
"Leo Lerman was saying, 'Anxiety like a distant ship, very far off. What is it? It rises like a miasma from my deep feeling that I am not working enough to earn my pay. All those years of unceasing work, and now – shreds.' Diana Vreeland responded, 'Listen, buster, you must get used to leisure!'"

Karen Hagestad Cacy

Chapter Twenty-Six
Slow Borschok / Fast Company

The Duchess was in her element. Parties were her forte. She gave the most amusing dinners in Paris; nothing escaped her attention as she achieved the title of "Hostess with the Most-est." She responded to Pat Buckley who asked her to share a few of her entertaining tips.

"Chefs are curiously color blind," replied the Duchess. "Leave them to their own devices, and you may end up with an all-rose dinner – Crème Portugaise, Saumon Poche with Sauce Cardinal, Jambon with Sauce Hongroise, and Bombe Marie-Louise. . . . Whatever else might appear on the menu, it should not be soup. One of my firmest rules is, 'Don't start a dinner with soup. It's an uninteresting liquid that gets you nowhere.'"

As she spoke, a server removed her salad plate and empty wine glass. As the wife of the guest of honor, she was first to be served. Here came a low, wide bowl set on an elegant serviere, filled with . . . soup.

It was George's well-known Russian Slow Beef Borschok, accompanied by sour cream and rye toast points. The soup was a curiously heavy choice for a warm summer's evening, but its aroma was earthy, meaty, delicious.

Pat reacted first. "Well, at least we didn't begin the meal with it!"

Diana Vreeland recovered quickly for her. "Oh George! Borschok! Authentically Russian! How divine!"

---

the duchess of windsor, through the eyes of others:

""It was she (Mrs. Simpson) who gave the chef and butler their orders; and as she directed the flow of conversation, the King visibly rejoiced; he was like a soloist waiting confidently for the conductor's nod. An observer described the scene to the writer Geoffrey Bocca: the King 'watched her happily as she

---

Karen Hagestad Cacy

A Recipe from Mr. B's Kitchen

Slow Beef Borschok

Served with Sour Cream and Rye Toast points

8 large or 12 small beets

Salad oil

6 cups homemade meat stock

6 peppercorns

1 bay leaf

1-1/2 teaspoons wine vinegar

1-1/2 teaspoons sugar

1 lemon sliced

Sour cream

Directions:

Wash beets, remove tops. Brush with salad oil and bake on a piece of aluminum foil at 350 degrees for 1 hour, or until tender. Cool, remove peel, and grate. Place stock, peppercorns and bay leaf in a saucepan and bring to a boil. Add beets, vinegar, and sugar. Stir, taste, and correct seasoning. Strain to remove bay leaf, peppercorns, and beets. Serve in cups with sour cream and lemon slices separately. Float small rye toast points on top before serving.

Yield: Serves 6

Karen Hagestad Cacy

The Duchess avoided making eye contact with her host. However, as she took her first sip of the wine Andreev paired with the Borschok, she realized they were in competent hands. She recognized the exquisite notes of a pinot noir, but not any run-of-the-mill pinot noir. A simple Russian soup was one thing. But the wine! Ah, the wine! Andy's selection would elevate a lowly baked potato!

Cecil also was impressed. Andreev was taking full liberties with the wine budget he provided. He knew this second wine was excruciatingly expensive! Befitting its high quality, Andy proudly announced his selection with a flourish.

"Next, I am offering an exquisite 1957 Domaine de la Romanee-Conti La Tache Grand Cru Monopole, from Cote de Nuits, France. The Borschok is meaty enough to stand up to the earthy notes of this pinot noir. I hope you enjoy my selection."

Balanchine addressed the table. "You see, we take care of you. Never fear, my friends. There is more in store. 'Na Zdorovyeh!'" *(To your health.)*

The impresario raised his glass in a toast.

The Duke interrupted. "George, dear friend. Let me add to your toast of Good Health. We all wish your dear wife the best of health and that she will soon improve. So: To Tanaquil, everyone."

The Duchess looked at her husband, a little surprised. "David, that's why everyone loves you. You really should be leading England, my darling."

Quietly, to Wallis, the Duke said, "If I were King, we'd rather be having my favorite, Chateau de Puligny-Montrachet."

The Duchess admonished him: "Shush, David. No need to express your every last thought."

Diana said, "David, I quite agree with your lovely wife. You would make a marvelous King!"

Karen Hagestad Cacy

She continued, now to the others at the table.

"The English are quite the most amazing people. I recall during the war . . .do you know my friend Ray Goetz? The most amusing man who ever lived. He was married to Irene Bordoni. He was big in the theatre. He brought over that divine Spanish singer, Raquel Meuller, who sang '*Who Will Buy Me Violets?*' Anyway, once during the war, I said to him, 'Oh Ray!' Isn't it awful about the war?' He turned. He looked at me for just a minute – just a split second – and asked, 'What war?' And with that, he walked right past me like a shadow."

The Duchess answered. "Thank you for that, Diana. But of course, we both consider you as British."

"I quite adore monarchy!"

> *george balanchine, through the eyes of tamara geva:*
> "He was very religious, his faith so deep that normal troubles of existence never touched him. He was absolutely sure that God was on his side. Politically, he was of the almost extinct species –a monarchist. He loved pomp and crowns and never forgot that as a young boy he was presented to the Tsar after one of the performances of the Maryinsky Theater. . . His hatred of the Soviet Union was maniacal."

George chimed in. "Me also, Diana. There is a pageantry, an order that reminds me of the rigor of ballet. Nothing wrong with rigor. Too bad the Soviets lost sight of that with their so-called 'new Russia.' Sterile. No humanity. No spontaneity. Colorless."

The Duchess answered him.

"I quite see your point, George, particularly with regard to Russia. However, as David and I can attest, the monarchy can be carried a bit far from time to time. They punish my husband like a small boy who gets a spanking every day of his life for a single transgression. There is the matter of the monarchy's lack of dignity toward my husband. It has occurred to me over the years how ridiculous it is to go on behind a family-designed, government-manufactured curtain of asbestos that protects the British Commonwealth from dangerous us . . . This man, with his unparalleled knowledge, trained in the affairs of State . . . was first given an insignificant military post during the war. Eventually, he was quote, 'put out of harm's way,' unquote, with an appointment of little consequence – the 'Governorship of the Bahamas.'"

Cecil raised his wine glass.

"To His Royal Highness, the Duke of Windsor."

Truman interrupted. "Listen, darling, if we are going to toast a man, let's do it properly. He stood up and raised his own glass toward the Duke.

"To His Royal Highness, the King of England!"

The party was in high spirits. All raised their glasses in the odd toast to the former monarch.

Andreev was glad he ordered extra bottles of the pinot. It was all he could do to stay even with the revelers.

On the other side of the table, Maxwell and Pamela quietly ate their soup and enjoyed the wine. Pat Buckley sat nearby. Truman was holding forth to her in a disjointed and rambling commentary on the passing scene.

About one of Pat's friends, society walker to The Ladies Who Lunch, Jerry Zipkin, he commented, "He's as queer as a two-dollar bill. His face is the shape of a bidet!"

Without waiting for an answer, he added, "Sinatra was an artist; the Stones are just entertainers."

Trying to change the subject, Pat asked, "Have you been to Venice lately, Truman? I was just there. By chance, I found myself sharing a gondola ride with . . ."

Karen Hagestad Cacy

"Venice! I adore Venice! Venice is like eating an entire box of chocolate liqueurs in one go. As for your friend in the boat . . . that one's about as sexy as a pissing toad."

"Truman, I really am trying to have a polite conversation with you. Lord, no wonder Bill didn't care to come with me! And speaking of my wonderful husband, tell me, how are you and Bill's favorite person getting on these days?"

Pat decided to bring in the shock troops. She knew Truman and her husband shared one view – they both feuded with, and despised, Gore Vidal.

At her question, Truman rose from his seat. He did a curious turn about the terrace, flapping his arms limply in a sort of charade. Then he re-took his seat and turned to face Pat.

"Oh, you mean '*La Gore.*' Another has-been. Put it this way, doll, he carries a whip for self-flagellation. Trouble is, he forgets, and uses it on others."

At this point, it was clear Truman was well on his way. Like several of the others, he'd enjoyed a few drinks before he arrived at the party. Pat turned her concentration to Pamela and Maxwell to her other side. Thank God dinner partners came on two sides, she thought.

In a bid to make conversation, Pamela tried a bit of European gossip. Maxwell already was enjoying Truman's throwaway remarks. Now he joined in as Pamela and Pat began talking. They spoke softly so the others couldn't overhear them. Naturally, that meant the whole table was paying attention.

Pamela leaned across Maxwell and asked Pat, "Do you by any chance know Jimmy Donahue?"

"I've met him. As you must know, Pamela, Manhattan is very like a small village. One runs into this person and that person. Sooner or later, we all meet each other. Why do you ask?"

Karen Hagestad Cacy

"Some disturbing stories have reached Europe about Donahue. Someone I know calls him a Manhattan Caligula."

The mogul hit pay dirt. Continental gossip was precisely his cup of tea. The Czech-turned-Englishman dined out on such stories wherever he went. World leaders he met depended on Maxwell for fresh stories of the 'rich and famous.' Now, as a full moon rose over the terrace wall, Maxwell was ready to hear more. He feigned boredom and concentrated on his soup. He wanted the women to talk as freely as possible, given the circumstances.

Pat knew plenty about Jimmy Donahue, one of Manhattan's more outrageous denizens. Good Lord, who on earth didn't?! She quickly scanned what she'd heard. There was the several years long friendship between Donahue and the Windsor's. But their friendship had crashed, following a terrible row in Switzerland. Stories about the three, however, remained legendary, and persisted.

Hostesses often received instructions when they issued invitations to the Duke and Duchess to include the couple's good friend, Jimmy, as well: "Can my naughty boy come too?" the Duchess playfully wrote, more than once.

Pat remembered one of Capote's stories from around 1951. Noel Coward met Capote in Portofino and had a frank discussion with him on the Windsor-Donahue-Windsor triangle:

"I like Jimmy," Coward told Truman. "He's an insane camp, but fun. And I like the Duchess; she's the fag-hag to end all – but that's what makes her likeable. The Duke, however, well, he pretends not to hate me. He does, though. Because I'm queer and he's queer but, unlike him, I don't pretend not to be. Anyway, the fag-hag must be enjoying it. Here she's got a royal queen to sleep with and a rich one to hump."

Rather than share her risqué story with Pamela and a rapt Maxwell, she chose to offer up a consolation prize instead: "He's a rather amusing fellow, I gather. At one of his parties, I heard he set Princess Ghislaine de Polignac

Karen Hagestad Cacy

up with a handsome other guest. She complained to Jimmy and he said to her 'Oh chou-chou, I'm sorry. I told him you were a transvestite.'"

Maxwell joined the conversation. "So, he's a bit of a trouble maker . . ."

Pat continued. "Well, he is the heir to the Woolworth fortune. They say he has a certain comical arrogance about him. Here's something else I heard from a friend: Once he was bored by leisurely service in Mexico, so he bellowed at the proprietor: 'Just tell me the name of your country and I'll instruct the State Department to stop your foreign aid.'"

Maxwell said, "I might have said something like that myself!"

Pamela threw him a bone.

To Pat, she said, "Apparently, our dinner partner lives in the stratosphere, financially."

But Pat wasn't having it.

"Obviously," was her terse reply.

Pat might have been more forthcoming with Truman or Cecil. She knew a lot. The Ladies Who Lunch knew a lot. But one of their best traits was the ability to know when to tell and when not to. Clearly to Pat, this was a case of the latter.

Truth be told, she knew some whoppers with regard to Jimmy.

She knew what he'd said about the Duchess after their falling out: "She married a king but she screwed a queen." That particular line was repeated up and down Fifth Avenue for months.

And other truly wicked things. She'd heard, for instance, that Jimmy, for Wallis, was a last throw of the dice. Count Jean de Baglion, gay, plump, wickedly funny, and exceptionally clever, was reported to have provided the Duchess and Jimmy with his apartment. Jimmy's apparent homosexuality shielded the couple from revelations in the press. The Duchess rationalized their 'friendship' by saying she could relate very easily to him because they both were Southerners, even though there was a generation gap. He played the piano, he could tell jokes, he was so witty.

But Pamela was not entirely lacking in Jimmy stories herself. She knew the Duchess lunched with Jimmy at the Mediterranee and dinners at the Relais des Porquerolles. When asked about her lunches with Donahue, the Duchess reportedly said, "I married David for better or for worse, but not for lunch."

---

george balanchine, through the eyes of lucia davidova:
"When Stravinsky came to live in America, George had an apartment on East Fifty-Seventh Street. . . .He had been quite strapped financially, but he was going to give a dinner for Stravinsky. . . .Besides having cooked all day and bought the most expensive things, he found two bottles of wine he couldn't possibly afford. When Stravinsky appeared, George said, 'Now we have lovely wine.' 'What for?' Stravinsky replied. 'I always bring my own, because nobody at the moment can offer me what I drink.' George was crestfallen; he had spent practically a month's salary on those two bottles."

Truman turned to Marilyn seated beside him and teasingly said, "Ah, if it isn't the 'late Miss Monroe!'

"Sweetie, really, I can't help being late. I know what people say about me."

"I'm not 'people,' I'm Troo-man. Talk to me, doll."

"It's not important."

"Let me be the judge of that. Now, spill it. Uncle Truman is listening. The doctor is in."

"Well, when I have to be somewhere for dinner at eight o'clock, I will lie in the bathtub for an hour or longer. Eight o'clock will come and go and

Karen Hagestad Cacy

I still remain in the tub. I keep pouring perfumes into the water and letting the water run out and refilling the tub with fresh water. . . . Sometimes I know the truth of what I'm doing. It isn't Marilyn Monroe in the tub but Norma Jean. I'm giving Norma Jean a treat. She used to bathe in water used by six or eight other people. Now she can bathe in water as clean and transparent as a pane of glass. . . . . People are waiting for me. People are eager to see me. I'm wanted. And I remember the years I was unwanted. All the hundreds of times nobody wanted to see the little servant girl, Norma Jean – not even her mother. I feel a queer satisfaction in punishing the people who are wanting me now. But it's not them I'm really punishing. It's the long-ago people who didn't want Norma Jean."

"That's the mean reds talking! I should know. They talk to me all the time."

He repeated himself.

"All the time."

Truman continued.

"Listen, darling, we both need to get over our pasts. I mean, just look at us! Me, a famous novelist. You, an international film star. Here, have some more wine. If you want, later, I have some white powder in my pocket. We can have our own little party, just you and me. I find that always helps matters."

Then, like a little boy playing with a friend in his tree-house, he added, "I'll let you try on my new cape later."

No one talked to the star that way. But few people possessed the wherewithal to understand her childhood monsters. She told someone that ". . . I went out and looked in the hall. My mother was on her feet. She was screaming and laughing. They took her away to Norwalk Mental Hospital. . . . It was where my mother's father and grandmother had been taken when they started screaming and laughing."

Karen Hagestad Cacy

Such were her fears that "the thought of having a baby stood her hair on end. She could see it only as herself: another Norma Jean in an orphanage."

Capote had his own monsters just below the surface. His magic white powder . . . wine . . . living the good life . . . even writing – all helped him 'deal' with them. He moved through literary circles, the international set, and other circles associated with celebrity and wealth. An amusing guest, who only occasionally got out of hand, the professional 'bad boy,' was on everyone's 'A List' of invitees.

> *truman capote, through the eyes of john malcolm brinnin:*
> "Small as a child, he looked like no other male adult I'd ever seen. His head was big and handsome, and his butterscotch hair was cut in bangs. Willowy and delicate above the waist, he was, below, as strong and chunky as a Shetland pony."

When challenged, the diminutive writer could respond like a bull-dog. One illustrative story took place in 1948 in Paris, recounted by Karl Bissinger:

"Truman's in the middle of a story and hears: 'For Christ's sake! Wherever I go I hear that American faggot-y pansy voice! Can't I ever get away from you guys?' Truman bristled and got up: 'Just you shut up! Wherever you go you cause fights and trouble . . . fights and trouble . . . Just you shut up! Don't wreck people's lives. Stop calling people faggots.' Then Truman resumes the story calmly."

His life experience gave him the ability to see himself more clearly than others did. At the same time, the short writer with tri-colored eyeglasses could 'read' others as clearly as if he were reading the dictionary. He had a surprising working knowledge of psychoses, traumas, and unfair childhoods, matched up with a lengthy list of other people's dirty laundry.

Everyone opened up to him. The man with flamboyant satin-lined cape, always knew what to say.

Marilyn reached under the table and took his hand.

Karen Hagestad Cacy

"You are such a friend. I wish Arthur would be a friend like you."

Truman asked, "Am I? He isn't?"

"Yes."

"And, no."

Truman squeezed her hand. "Men! They never get us!"

---

marilyn monroe, through her own eyes:

"But there was something wouldn't let me go back to the world of Norma Jean. It wasn't ambition or a wish to be rich and famous. . . . There was a thing in me like a craziness that wouldn't let up. It kept speaking to me, not in words but in colors – scarlet and gold and shining white, greens and blues. They were the colors I used to dream about in my childhood when I had tried to hide from the dull, unloving world in which the orphanage slave, Norma Jean, existed."

Karen Hagestad Cacy

Chapter Twenty-Seven
Sole Bonne Femme

Balanchine's dinner party progressed to a light fish course after the criticized soup. Andy, who'd been sampling his own wine behind the bar, directed servers to remove the spent wine glasses, in preparation for the next course.

George announced to his guests: "Tovarischee, next with Sole Bonne Femme, Andreev has once again outdone himself. Cecil, the wine budget you provided continues to be stretched with this next selection."

Truman spoke. "Good thing you have all these 'Gigi' royalties rolling in, darling!"

George directed Andreev, "Andy, tell us about this one."

Andreev walked around the table, pouring the new libation.

"Now for you is 1950 Domaine Huet Vouvray Moelleux Le Haut-Lieu. This Chenin blanc is also known as Pineau de la Loire. It is of a white wine grape variety from France's Loire Valley. I will direct you to the wine's brass color. In the nose, there is candied lemon and smoky notes. If I may boast for a moment, this is a rather restrained, but very elegant wine. I hope you will enjoy it."

In the lull, the Duchess could be heard scolding her husband.

"David. You are no longer on the throne. Please wait for others to be served."

The Duke answered her, "One of my leftover royal habits, I'm afraid, darling."

George addressed the Duchess.

"Tonight, in our minds, your husband still is the King of England. And we are honoring you both. Please, my good friends, proceed. A votre sante!"

The Duke offered, "Going first at the table is not exactly the very worst thing . . ."

"No, David . . .," answered the Duchess.

"The very worst thing was that time, remember, darling, what one of our guests did with his wine glass?"

"I don't recall."

"Yes, you do. It was an Englishwoman, the peeress, who told us."

"Now I remember. Not exactly the topic of polite dinner table conversation I might choose, but, knowing you . . ."

Truman chanted, "Go there! Go there!"

The Duke needed little encouragement.

"This was at our house in Neuilly, "Chez Windsor," as the French like to say."

The Duchess interrupted, "And we all know how you love the French!"

"Anyway, this woman's neighbor at the table, a South American, emptied his largest wineglass and concealed it in his lap, under the tablecloth. She was mystified until a moment later he put it back beside his other glasses, full."

Cecil commented, "I say!"

Truman, teasing, "Everyone, check Cecil's wine glass. Does it look a bit pale, to you?"

Karen Hagestad Cacy

Beaton replied, "Oh, stop and eat your sole. Or should I say, 'Have a soul?'"

Truman and Cecil, old friends, could go back and forth for hours. Truman wasn't finished with Cecil: "Sweetie, I remember Michael Pitt-Rivers when he asked you, 'Cecil, why is it that you are so loathsome in London and yet so delightful in the country?'"

No sooner than the two engaged, each turned to their other dinner partners. Truman's comments ran the gamut: ". . . but I'm reading the most divine scandal . . . I'm going to send you this wonderful African pornography . . . Fame is only good for one thing – they will cash your check in a small town . . . I don't care what anybody says about me as long as it isn't true."

The Duke could be heard telling George, "I went up to Queen Mary and kissed her on both hands and then on both cheeks. She was as cold as ice. When I approached my brother, now King George VI, he completely broke down. So, I said to him, 'Buck up, Bertie. God save the King!'"

The Duchess, known for her risqué cocktail stories as usual rose above her rather ordinary looks. The combination of jewels, impeccable dress, and a sparkling personality did the trick. While she was an excellent hostess, it could be said that she was an even better guest. In her words, "I sing for my supper."

Now she was entertaining George with two of her jokes.

"Then there was the man who offered the girl a scotch and soda, and she reclined." Or, the one about the wife, who welcomed her husband home:

"'Oh, darling, I've missed you,'" she cried, and fired the gun again."

George was pleased at the mix of company. Everyone seemed to be enjoying themselves. Rene was on point. Andy's wines, thanks to Cecil's generous budget, were winners. He shared the cooking duties with a chef from The Russian Tea Room, Andreev's restaurant. The feast seemed to be impressing his well-travelled guests.

Rene could see his libations were having their desired effect. The sound level on the open patio was escalating. Waves of laughter ran around the table. Truman, when he wasn't busy lying or telling outrageous stories, was up, dancing around, flashing his linen napkin, playing matador. The mood was spontaneous, joyful, and disrespectful of cold, white hospital rooms. Suffering was on holiday, as Rene had hoped it would be.

With those observations, Rene gave himself a small pat on the back. But while he had called the evening correctly, he still didn't really understand his boss. There were so many facets to the man: There was Balanchine, a creator and gifted choreographer; Mr. B., a personnel manager, shaping the fortunes and vicissitudes of competing dancers; Counselor Balanchine, dealing with the psychology of clashing egos and insecure artists; George, a domesticated nurturing husband; and Balanchine, a businessman, constantly on the look-out for ways to bolster the company's fortunes.

Tonight, Rene could add one more facet to the man: Tonight there was Balanchine, the social butterfly, who flitted from guest to guest, checking wine glasses, asking the Duchess if she felt a chill, introducing his performing cat, Mourka, to perform somersaults.

Someone else, besides Rene, had their eyes on Balanchine. Marilyn watched her new friend with interest. She detected something familiar in him, because it was also something about herself. He was not fully present. Despite his gaiety, despite the energy in his quick steps around the table, she saw that a piece of him seemed to be missing, left behind somewhere.

Others from time to time also noticed his preoccupation. Hugh Fiorato, of the NYCB, observed, "Balanchine was something of a mystic. Often, he would say, for instance, 'I spoke to Tchaikovsky this morning, and he said he would help us.' I remember when we first did *The Nutcracker*, at curtain time opening night none of the costumes for the second act had arrived from Karinska. It seemed as if we would have to end the performance at intermission. But Balanchine said, 'Don't worry. I spoke to Tchaikovsky

Karen Hagestad Cacy

and they'll be here.' Sure enough, the costumes began drifting in. Dancers dressed in the hallways and rushed onstage."

George approached the star. "Miss Monroe . . ."

"Marilyn . . ."

"Marilyn, how are you finding my little party? Is okay?"

"I noticed what you are wearing – the western shirt and string tie. You rather resemble a New Mexico rancher tonight."

"I am one hundred percent American! I love wild west. Cowboy movies. Science fiction. You and your country have fully adopted me from my Russia."

"Do you miss it?"

"Do I miss what, my dear?"

"Russia."

"Ah. Yes. Russia. There is only the beautiful one, the one in my mind. The Georgian countryside. Yes, many things beautiful. Today, we have Communists with their bread lines. In Russia, today, everyone fails, no one wins. Terrible."

George Balanchine

Marilyn said, "You know my husband was accused by Congress of being a Communist sympathizer. They black-listed him."

"Must fight. Always must fight. Nothing comes easy."

Marilyn answered him in kind. "You know something . . . when you're a failure in Hollywood – that's like starving to death outside a banquet hall with the smells of filet mignon driving you crazy."

"My dear, you are not failure. You're special woman. You are poet, yes?"

"Yes. However, did you know that?"

Balanchine patted her hand gently.

"I know. I know."

---

marilyn monroe, through her own eyes:
"Life – /I am of both of your directions/ Life (crossed out)/ Somehow remaining hanging downward/ the most/ but strong as a cobweb in the /wind – I exist more with the cold glistening frost. / But my beaded rays have the colors I've/ seen in a painting –/ ah life they/ have cheated you."

Karen Hagestad Cacy

Chapter Twenty-Eight
Poulet braise au champagne
Buckwheat Kasha
St. Julien Bordeaux

Truman took a short break from the table. When he returned, Marilyn lightly brushed his sleeve.

"You have something white on your sleeve. There, all gone," she noted.

"What?!"

"No worries. I don't think anyone noticed it."

Truman said, "Who are you, my mother?"

Marilyn pouted. "Now, Truman. Don't go all cranky on me. After all, you are my date tonight. Be good to a girl, will ya'?"

Pamela rescued her. "Marilyn. We haven't had a chance to talk. I need a smoke. Want to join me?"

The two women left the table briefly and leaned over Balanchine's patio railing looking out at one of the most beautiful cities on earth.

Pamela began. "Paris is more beautiful, you know. But still, there's something about the energy here in New York. I have missed America."

---

marilyn monroe, through others' eyes:
"After dinner, we went into the bar to shoot craps. When (John) Huston gave Marilyn the dice, she asked: 'What should I shoot for John?' His answer: 'Don't think, honey, just throw. That's the story of your life. Don't think – do it.'"

K a r e n   H a g e s t a d   C a c y

"You're from England, aren't you? I was there filming *The Prince and the Showgirl,* with Sir Laurence Olivier."

"My former husband was Winston Churchill's son, actually."

Marilyn appeared momentarily confused. "Winston . . .?"

"Winston Churchill. You know . . . World War Two?"

Marilyn laughed. She was beginning to feel the effects of too many drinks, but she could still make jokes: "Gotcha!"

"So, you were joking. You knew."

"I knew. And I know. Everyone thinks if you're blonde with a pretty figure, there must not be anything upstairs."

Most people who met Monroe underestimated her, believed the persona she presented to the public was the real one. They often made that assumption at their own peril. Photographer Philippe Halsman said of her "I saw the amazing phenomenon of Hollywood being outsmarted by a girl whom it characterized as a dumb blonde."

Pamela said, "Listen, I have experienced the same sort of thing. Possibly, not as much as yourself. Still, men often underestimate me."

"What do you do about it?"

"That's an interesting question. I'll have to think about that."

The two women smoke in silence, then Pamela continued.

A Recipe from Mr. B's Kitchen

Buckwheat Kasha

Entree Side Dish

1 cup whole grain buckwheat groats

1 egg, lightly beaten

2 cups chicken consomme

½ stick butter (4 tablespoons)

salt and pepper to taste

George Balanchine and Mourka

Directions:

In heavy skillet with no butter, toast buckwheat groats over a medium flame. Add egg stirring constantly for 5 minutes. Pour in consommé. When all liquid has evaporated, stir in butter, and add salt and pepper. The kasha may be kept warm in a low oven.

Yield: Serves 4 – 6

"I move in with them."

"That's your solution?"

"I redecorate their homes. I spend their money. I listen carefully to their business deals. I learn how they make their money. They say I am an English courtesan. To all appearances, I suppose they could be right. But no one sees the other side of it."

"That you know what you're doing. That you're taking your own advantage."

"Yes, dear. Exactly. If the world chooses to shut you out, worm your way back in."

Marilyn answered her: "Oh, I know a thing or two about worming my way in. In the early years in Hollywood, there was this man, I'll call him, Mr. Sylvester, because that was his name. Mr. Sylvester. I'll never forget when I read for him. He says, 'Try one of the long speeches.' Then he interrupts my reading, "Would you please raise your dress a few inches?' So, I lifted the hem above me knee and kept on reading. "'A little higher, please," he says. I lifted the hem to my thighs without missing a word of the speech. 'A little higher,' Mr. Sylvester said again. For some time afterward, his words haunted me as I had heard the true voice of Hollywood – 'Higher, higher, higher.'

Pamela listened intently to her story. Marilyn appreciated her attention. Other women usually avoided her, Isak Dinesen and Alice Roosevelt Longworth being two exceptions – the actress hit it off with each of them right away. Tonight, standing in for Arthur, in the company of interesting people, she began to feel almost normal.

Truman approached them. "Everything all right over here?" he asked.

What a curious question. Marilyn nodded her head. He performed a somersault and returned to the table.

Pamela continued their conversation. "We all noticed you were late arriving. Do you have business here in the City?"

Marilyn was a bit taken aback by her question.

"I live in the City. And, of course, also in Connecticut with my husband. I am often late, I'm afraid. I told Lee I was simply unable to be on time. So, he says to me, "Well, be early then.""

"Lee?"

"Strasberg. You know, Lee Strasberg."

"Oh yes, The Actor's Studio. We were expecting your husband this evening. Of course, it's wonderful you were able to come in his place. But I'm sure everyone's been wondering . . ."

"He's finishing a writing project. When he gets into his work . . ."

"How does that make you feel?"

"What do you mean?"

The cobra struck.

"He's been married before, hasn't he, dear? He's quite an attractive man in that East Coast sort of way. I can see what you see in him, dear. But do you really know what he's up to tonight?" Marilyn's defenses shot up. What did this woman want? She appeared friendly at first, but now, like so many others before her, Pamela simply was seeking personal information. They'd only just met. They were having an interesting conversation.

And now, this.

She heard, but chose to ignore, Pamela's final remark as she turned on her heel.

"I never leave my men alone. Relationships require constant attention, my dear."

In an instant, Marilyn joined "The Ladies Who Lunch," signing up with the opposing team.

Her feelings were hurt. Normally, she didn't allow people to get close to her on brief acquaintance. Her invisible star shield went back up. But not before Pamela's remark managed to re-open an old hurt: Her own mother never told her she was pretty. All mothers should tell daughters they are pretty, even if they are not, she thought.

Marilyn quickly tasted the Bordeaux that was poured in her absence. Diana Vreeland gave her a knowing look as she said to Pat Buckley, loudly enough for Pamela to overhear:

"She wore so many diamonds . . .of course, she was famous for getting money out of the men who went out with her."

Pamela re-took her seat. Then Diana winked at Marilyn and added, "Naturally, you all know I was speaking of Peggy Hopkins."

Pat Buckley piled on, her voice dripping with sarcasm: "Because no one else would fit that description."

Marilyn, for the first time in her life, felt the comfort of female camaraderie. Pat and Diana had just tacitly welcomed her into their little sorority. She belonged, if only for one dinner party. It felt good. She reached over and took Truman's hand and held it. Just then, she caught Balanchine's eye. He, too, was watching out for her, but in a pleasant fatherly sort of way.

For Marilyn, it was an evening like no other.

That left Pamela out in the cold again. She rarely got on with other women. Now she could add one more member of the female species to her growing list of 'womanies.' Pamela Digby Churchill was a shallow woman of substance. With the benefit of a gentle-woman's up-bringing at her command she chose to pursue powerful men, to catch ahold of their well-tailored coat-tails rather than take her own responsibility. In that view, she was a rather typical woman of the fifties, orbiting their men.

Oddly, the woman she'd just tangled with was her polar opposite. The so-called 'trailer trash' movie star, behind the scenes, read the world's great literature, wrote poetry, and sought acceptance from New York's literary intelligentsia. Instead of chasing after men to support her, she constantly sought peace and quiet to think and make sense of her life and art.

Pamela had had enough of the party. She wasn't interested in yet another course of heavy food. And it was clear 'the women,' now including La Monroe, were lined up against her. Her last remaining avenue of interest was the wealthy one, the Israeli Russian Pseudo-Englishman. The trouble was, he was crude and vulgar, using his vast wealth to buy whatever he wanted.

---

marilyn monroe, through the eyes of ella fitzgerald:
"I owe Marilyn Monroe a real debt. It was because of her that I played the Mocambo. She personally called the owner and told him she wanted me booked immediately and if he would do it she would take a front table every night. . . . after that, I never had to play a small jazz club again. She was an unusual woman – a little ahead of her times. And she didn't know it."

She recognized the arrogance of power when she saw it. Maxwell was used to having his own way. Always. By his own admission, his interests bordered on the criminal, probably even on the world of international espionage. As she entertained these thoughts, she was startled to hear Pat Buckley speaking about her own powerful husband.

"Great men have their moments, I can tell you. A certain Christmas Eve with Bill in the Caribbean comes to mind. Everything was perfect. I bought and wrapped presents, placing them around a Christmas tree on the boat. I'd strung up little twinkly lights. Drinks were served. A tape of Christmas songs was playing. The boat was anchored in the most charming, lovely, beautiful, protected cove in the entire Caribbean. Everything was perfect."

Karen Hagestad Cacy

She paused to take a sound check on her audience.

"You see where this is going?"

"But then Bill suddenly decided it would be even more perfect if we up-anchored and moved across the way to a different cove. I said, 'Bill, just leave it.' But leaving it was not Bill's way. So off we went. And of course, a sudden squall hit, drenching us all, washing the gifts overboard, shorting out the Christmas lights, knocking over the tree. Then we went aground. So, there we were in the dark at a forty-five-degree angle atop a sandbar in a rainstorm, on Christmas Eve."

"Enough said!"

There was a brief lull in the conversation. The Duke could be heard speaking to his wife.

"I do hope there's a German wine served with the cheese course. They do such a terribly good job. It's nice to support them in everything, even wines. Ah! Wie überlegen alles was Deutsch ist– die Kultur, die Musik, das Essen, die Sprache. Und dieser Wein. Er ist Genuss pur. Ein Zeichen von hoher Zivilisation!" *("Ah! How superior are all things German -- the culture, the music, the food, the language. And this wine. It is pure enjoyment. A sign of a high civilization!")*

The Duchess replied, "You're just an old Nazi at heart, aren't you, darling?

Everyone at the table heard their remarks.

Including "Bobbie" Maxwell.

truman capote and the duke and duchess of windsor, through the eyes of anthony hale:

"Le Boeuf sur le Toit was where everybody went late, late at night after other people's dinners and balls and parties. Truman was involved in everything. Le Boeuf was in full force: the Windsor's and Jimmy Donahue . . . it was very, very snappy. There was always a cabaret with somebody singing and playing the piano. I think the duchess even sang at one point."

Karen Hagestad Cacy

Karen Hagestad Cacy

Chapter Twenty-Nine
German Rieslings

George quickly signaled Rene and Andy to move his guests from the table to the outdoor living room area Beaton assembled for the evening. Oriental rugs covered the terrace; large pillows were strewn around; a couch and several armchairs were provided with extra small blankets for warmth in case of an evening chill. Lights from several large lanterns flickered, reflecting off tall silver urns filled with long-stemmed white roses. Beaton's creation resembled a modern Garden of Eden. There even was a gigantic bowl of fruit positioned on a low table.

Noting Maxwell's mounting anger at the Windsor's remarks, George invited him inside to view paintings on loan from the Metropolitan Museum of Art for the night. He spoke to him in his native Russian to help calm him. While he removed the Czech from outside, servers laid out silver platters, with large hunks of cheese, white linen napkins and small plates, and fresh wine glasses.

---

george balanchine, through the eyes of allegra kent:
"Balanchine once explained the end of *La Somnambula* : 'Very simple. Poet gets better. Marries Somnambulist. They move to Scarsdale. Have nice house and five children. She cooks those awful heavy quiches.'"

With Maxwell safely closeted inside, Andy quickly introduced the cheese course and the Rieslings he'd selected, as Rene moved among the guests, filling their glasses.

"Riesling is 'the true king' of the German wine grapes. Indeed, in no other wine growing area on earth does Riesling reach such heights of quality and sheer deliciousness as it does in Germany."

The Duke said, "I quite knew that."

Karen Hagestad Cacy

Truman did a quick goose step, "Heil Hitler!"

Cecil grabbed him by the elbow and steered him away. "Not here, Truman. Dial it back a bit, dear."

Andy nervously cleared his throat and continued his presentation.

"These German wines are also unique in that the grapes are picked at many levels of ripeness and maturity, allowing the wine makers to produce Rieslings ranging from dry, Kabinett, to medium-dry, Spatlese, to sweet, Auslese, to super sweet, Beeren and Trockenbeerenauslese and Eiswein. There is a style of German Riesling for every palate. I've assembled the four varieties here for you to taste."

The Duke whispered, "Und dieser Wein. Er ist Genuss pur." *(And this wine! It is pure enjoyment!)*

Inside, George served Maxwell a glass of iced Vodka from his personal stock as the large man continued to fume about the Duke: "Boltoona yazeek do dobra ne dovedyawt!" *("A fool's tongue runs before his feet!")*

Ignoring the comment, Balanchine instead steered Maxwell towards a priceless oil painting of a snowy Siberian steppe. "Smotreetya, Bob. Artelnee Beaton, loochye keepeet." *("Look at this, Bob. With Beaton, a thousand things are possible.")*

Maxwell listened politely to George's presentation. He knew he was trying to defuse the situation. Then he rejoined the others. Walking to the center of the group, he raised his glass: "Russian Vodka! Always the best choice! Na Zdorovyeh!"

The Duke began to rise out of his chair, but his wife's firm grip on his arm kept him in check.

"Yes, darling. I know. I'll be your good boy."

Karen Hagestad Cacy

The others, in the interest of harmony, raised their glasses to Maxwell's toast. Every gathering has some sort of disagreement. So long as everyone remembers their manners . . .

With a flourish, George solicitously placed a napkin across Pamela's lap as though he were a waiter in a fancy restaurant. Next, he carefully prepared her a plate of cheeses, pate, and pickled egg.

"For you, Pamela. Enjoy. I chose these cheeses with you in mind. To welcome you with a taste of America."

Pamela asked him, "Tell me some things I need to learn about the ballet, director. What are some of your memories?"

The host was slurring his words and his accent was growing thicker. As he answered Pamela's question, his thoughts seemed to come in waves of memory, one after another. Diana moved closer so she could hear him.

". . . first impression of every single dancer. Each one like different animal. Barbara Walczak was porcupine. Tanny, Nicky and Maria were little monkeys, the best animal to be, the kind that can move and do anything . . . For my ballets, legs must be high. If hip is up or not, doesn't matter. I want to see the leg go up quickly. Some teachers ask, 'But, Mr. Balanchine, what about placement?' I tell them, 'When I say 'placement,' if you fall over you have no placement.'"

Diana asked, "I've heard that when you create a new ballet, you work quickly. Is that true?"

"Yes. Stravinsky and I work together. Once, we were working on sad scene. So, he ask Maria Tallchief, 'Maria! How long take to die?' . . . She fall to floor . . . Stravinsky began snapping his fingers – snap, snap, snap, snap – I think was four counts. 'That is enough,' he decided. 'Now you are dead.' And he put those counts into the score. We agreed: No one should pad a part. . . You see, was exact. . . ."

Diana said, "Editing is not just in magazines. I consider that editing should be in everything—thoughts, friendship, life. Everything in life is

Karen Hagestad Cacy

editing. And now, we see it also in choreography. Fred Astaire had a spareness . . ."

At the mention of Astaire, George's face lit up. "Favorite American dancer. He dance with no effort. No effort."

Diana said, "Yes, Astaire. In my view, the line and silhouette of the twentieth century started with the Ballets Russes, the only avant-garde I've ever known. It all had to do with line. Everybody had the line."

George joined Marilyn who was sitting by herself near the shrubbery. "Now my dear, we sit together."

Marilyn took his arm. Without a word, they both stared out at the city lights.

Eventually, George spoke.

"Must forgive. Rene thought this dinner would help. The hospital rooms . . . her pain . . . instead, create a happy little dinner . . ."

"It's not working, is it?" Marilyn said.

"No complaining."

---

george balanchine, through the eyes of tamara toumanova:
"I think Balanchine lived in his own world. I don't think many people really realized his sensitivity. . . . he was a solitary person, very much apart."

He moved his hands the same way he did in class when he was explaining a particular dance move to one of his ballerinas.

"Put the foot just so. . . raise the leg highest level . . . pain is no excuse . . ."

"But George, you are talking about physical pain. Emotional pain is another matter. Here, hold my hand. Let's be pals."

George stroked the top of her hand.
"Pals. Yes."

After a while, he offered, "We are by ourselves. Yes?"

Marilyn asked, "When did it start, this pain?"

"Very cold in Russia. I practiced and practiced my music. Have you read Dostoevski? Do you know Raskolnikov in Crime and Punishment? For me, Russian soul."

"I lived in foster homes. Nobody wanted me. I went to the movies all day long to get away from everything."

Tanaquil Le Clercq

"Sometimes, Tanny can't lift fingers. Horrid. I thought she might go insane. I told her, "This is our first five-year plan, this is our second,' and got her to accept the situation. Sometimes I can't . . . I can't . . ."

---

george balanchine, through the eyes of constance clausen:
"Since I lived on the West Side, I would run into Balanchine on the street for years . . . and he would say, 'Now, have you read the Russians?' He would give me lists – Dostoevski, Tolstoy, Gogol."

Marilyn put her arms around him. Both of them held on for dear life. For themselves. For each other. Finally, for Tanny, in her isolation.

Karen Hagestad Cacy

Meanwhile across the terrace, Diana was holding forth.

"You know Bruce Chatwin, don't you Truman? We were having dinner with Bruce Chatwin, and so I asked him, 'What are you writing about, Bruce?'

"He tells me, 'Wales, Diana.'"

"Naturally . . . you know me . . . I was beginning to imagine the whole thing."

"'Whales?!,' I asked."

"'Blue whales, Sperm whales!! THE WHITE WHALE!'"

"But Bruce says,

"'No, no, Diana! Wales! Welsh Wales! The country to the west of England.'"

"So, I said to him,

'Oh! Wales! I do know Wales. Little grey houses. Covered in roses. In the rain.'"

Truman said, "The letter 'H.'"

"What are you talking about, Truman?" asked Diana.

"The difference between 'Wales' and 'Whales' . . . the letter 'H.'"

"Oh."

Karen Hagestad Cacy

Karen Hagestad Cacy

Chapter Thirty
Royal Treatment

Cecil's liquor budget seemingly knew no bounds. Andy surprised the Duke with his favorite brandy, a seventy-five-year-old Forge de Sazerac. And George followed up with an Upmann cigar the shape and approximate size of a torpedo.

The pianist broke into a round of "Happy Birthday," as the guests settled indoors for dessert, coffee, and Brandy. Marilyn kicked off her shoes and snuggled onto Truman's lap.

Pat Buckley

Truman said, "I have some ooey-gooey, doll, if you want."

"What's ooey-gooey?"

"The stuff after the lipstick, to make your lips shine. I carry it with me everywhere. A girl can't be too prepared."

George stepped to the piano and announced a toast: "Friends, our dear friend and his lovely wife were married on May 4, 1937. I would like to offer a toast to them for a belated happy anniversary."

The guests rose and said in unison, "Here, here!"

The pianist began playing one of the couple's favorite songs. At the first notes, the Duke swept his bride onto her feet for a lively and loving dance.

"The bells are ringing, for me and my gal. The birds are singing, for me and my gal . . ."

Karen Hagestad Cacy

Everyone knew the words. Suddenly, the party livened up considerably. Beaton performed a quick two-step in a circle, and extended his hand to a smiling Pat. Truman grabbed ahold of Marilyn. Rather than take her by her hand, the diminutive author curiously caught ahold of her wrist. The actress didn't seem to mind. Friends are friends, no matter how they dance. George circled them with Mourka, his cat, seated atop his shoulders. At his command, Mourka jumped down and performed somersaults to the music, to everyone's delight. A ballet dancer with his dancing cat. How perfectly appropriate!

" . . . Everybody's been knowing, to a wedding they're going, and for weeks they've been sewing, Every Suzie and Sal . . ."

Pamela cut in on Pat to dance with Beaton, as Pat picked up Mourka and swung her around.

" . . . They're congregating, for me and my gal. The parson's waiting, for me and my gal. And sometime I'm going to build a little home for two, for three or four or more. In Loveland, for me and my gal."

As the song concluded, Renee carried out an elaborate birthday cake with lit candles.

The Duke stepped up. "I say, George, what a nice surprise."

"Make a wish, my darling," said the Duchess.

"I already have the girl of my dreams. And a wonderful life."

Truman, ever the gad-fly couldn't resist. "But you don't have everything! Wish for something real big, and I'll sprinkle fairy dust around you as you do."

The Duke beckoned to the Duchess. "Come help me, sweetheart. Truman has a point. Let's both make a wish. Ready?"

Karen Hagestad Cacy

With Truman flitting around the couple, the couple blew out the candles to much clapping and hilarity. Again, the pianist knew just what to play. Again, the Duke and Duchess danced around the room.

"Night and day, you are the one. Only you 'neath the moon or under the sun. Whether near to me or far. It's no matter, darling, where you are. I think of you, day and night."

The guests' brandy snifters were refilled. George dimmed the lights. Over in the corner, Diana, who worked all day and was growing tired, took a brief cat-nap. George gently placed a woolen throw across her legs.

Truman followed the Duke into the hall as he made his way to the bathroom.

"Psst. Your Highness. I have something to give you for your birthday. So, you really can be '*your highness,*' if you catch my drift."

Truman giggled. "Oops! Two double entendres in a single sentence!"

The Duke smiled as he accepted the small packet of white powder. "Ah, thank you, Truman. Is there enough here for my bride?"

"I have plenty. Enjoy yourselves. I know I am!"

As Truman turned around he bumped into Maxwell.

---

robert maxwell, through the eyes of israel's mossad:
"That Mossad file on Maxwell concluded with a paragraph extracted from a Department of Trade report on his methods: 'He is a man of great energy, drive and imagination, but unfortunately an apparent fixation as to his own abilities causes him to ignore the views of others if these are not compatible.'"

He was finding it difficult to mask his feelings about the man. "I suppose now you're going to want some too," he said uncharitably.

Karen Hagestad Cacy

"No need, my good man. I always bring my own."

Truman returned to the party as Maxwell waited impatiently in the hall for the Duke.

He blocked the Duke's way as he came out of the bathroom

Maxwell addressed him.

"Perhaps you've been wondering why I'm here tonight, Your Highness."

The Duke had no interest in the man or anything to do with him. He understood that George's company like other arts endeavors required its share of wealthy patrons. He assumed Maxwell's presence was part of some sort of a business arrangement. But the hall was narrow and he was trapped. He feigned an air of distant noblesse oblige routinely practiced by royalty the world over when finding themselves face to face with the 'hoi-polloi.'

"I'm sure George has invited only the finest people tonight. I regret that we have not had occasion to talk more this evening. You see, I am so enamored of my lady love, I tend to stay close to her at affairs."

"I say, did I hear you correctly earlier, do you really admire the Germans?"

---

the duke of windsor, through the eyes of major edward dudley "fruity" metcalfe:

"'I can't figger things out,' Metcalfe wrote to his wife on 22 October (1939). 'She [Wallis] & he [Edward] know every d---n thing. She will know whom I dined or lunched with or have spoken to & *even seen.* I believe she has spies out & they work well. Anyhow it's terrifying . . . I'm fed up with Paris & this war – whichever you like. I don't like my job . . .& I never feel secure & safe when working for HRH.'"

K a r e n   H a g e s t a d   C a c y

"I'm quite sure I don't know what you mean."

"We have learned many things about your aide-de-camp, Charles Eugene Bedaux. It seems this Frenchman may have spied for Germany here during the First World War. And, we know he was the one who opened doors in Nazi Germany for you and your wife during the Second World War. These facts cannot be overlooked."

"I'm quite sure I have no idea what you are saying. Who, exactly, are 'we'?"

George came to the Duke's rescue.

As they walked away, the Duke was agitated.

"A quite disagreeable man. Did you know him before tonight?"

George could see that the mood was shifting. His guests were falling apart before his eyes: Diana was asleep on his couch; The Jewish billionaire was stalking the Duke and Duchess in some sort of a drunken attempt to re-fight World War Two; Truman was snorting cocaine in the hallway and sharing his powder with anyone and everyone.

He answered the Duke. "So, sorry. Lincoln asked me to invite him. His wealth is in publishing, I'm told."

"And then some, my good man, and then some."

With that, the two returned to the party, determined to stay as far away from Maxwell as the room allowed.

Outside on the terrace, Marilyn's small body was struggling to make its peace between a prodigious quantity of dinner wine, the cocktails she'd downed earlier with Sam, and Truman's cocaine. Earlier, he approached her with his floral cloth bag filled with goodies: "Here, doll. Have some of Uncle Troo-man's fairy dust."

Karen Hagestad Cacy

Now, she found herself seated astride the penthouse balcony wall. She had no idea how she'd gotten up there. Her slim sheath was pulled revealingly above her thighs as she straddled the wall. To her left was a party in various stages of disarray. To her right, was a five story drop to a Manhattan street below. She felt dizzy. How could she get down?

Cecil was the first to spot her. He was known for his ability to hold his liquor and now he needed to be the designated rescuer of those who were impaired. He approached Marilyn carefully, so as not to frighten her.

"Here, here. Beautiful girl. How did you get up there? Never mind, Cecil will help you down."

He reached up for her, noticing in spite of himself, the star was naked beneath her tight sheath. As he held her, she wriggled down off the wall. In a corner, a second set of men's eyes had noticed Miss Monroe's state of undress. Ah, Maxwell thought, so she is a brunette. He made plans to advance for a closer look.

Beaton noticed Maxwell's wolfish stare and steered Marilyn inside to sit next to Pamela.

"Was that you up there on the wall? What will Arthur think when he hears. And, I can assure you with this crowd – Truman, Cecil, etcetera – he will hear." Pamela asked.

---

robert maxwell, through the eyes of others:

"Within 6 months, Maxwell had created an umbrella of companies. He even offered to service Bulgaria's foreign debt with a bank he created. He was the man with Midas touch who blew his golden trumpet and everybody danced to his tune. Fawned upon by president and commoner alike, offered anything he liked – a car, a mansion, even a king's palace – provided with anyone he liked – an actress, a dancer from a nightclub, even a pretty housekeeper who had briefly taken his fancy –Robert Maxwell was indeed the undisputed ruler of Bulgaria and in many ways beyond it, the first authentic tycoon of the Eastern Bloc."

Pat recognized the tell-tale signs of drug use going on around her. It made little difference that the party included some of "The Best People." They could be naughty as quickly as all the lower 'minions' living under less stellar circumstances. She crossed the room to rouse her friend from her nap.

"Come on, 'Trixie.' Time to go. Things seem to be getting a bit out of hand."

Rousing herself from her cat-nap, Diana answered her, "What? And miss all this? Not in a million!"

With Diana's pronouncement, the Ladies Who Lunch signed on for the full cruise.

'Beg pardon: Is this the ship to Bermuda?'

Truman carefully placed several cushions on the floor near the piano. Taking Marilyn's hand, he helped her down beside him.

"It's my fault, Holly. My fault. You are a delicate flower and my fairy dust was too much for you. Now, listen to me. I want to tell you something: "If you want something badly enough, you'll get it, whatever it is. You've got to really want it, and concentrate on it for twenty-four hours a day, but if you do, you'll get it. I have never found that to be untrue."

---

fruity metcalfe, through the eyes of diana vreeland:
"'He didn't do very much in life. I once asked him, 'Fruity, what do you do in the morning?' 'I dress.' 'Well, so do I.' 'Well, they put out my ties and so forth and I have to choose.'"

Chapter Thirty-One
"She murdered her husband."

George's guests appeared to be mellowing after the incident on the balcony. The pianist continued to play an array of popular tunes he'd ordered particularly to entertain the Windsor's. The host continued to float around the room, overhearing snatches of conversation.

The Duchess was filling Cecil in about Jimmy Donahue.

"Naturally, that name rarely passes my lips after our incident in Switzerland. A terrible, usurping of a person, if ever I knew one! But, since it's you, dear Cecil, I don't mind sharing."

Cecil said, "All I know is he uses the most expensive call-boys, with his unlimited cash. Did you know he stages elaborate orgies during his mother's absences in Palm Beach?"

"I have no doubt! It was in 1952 -- I remember the date because David had food poisoning -- Jimmy visited Barbara Hutton in San Francisco. He took her to the Beige Room which is a gay club . . ."

Cecil finished her sentence, " . . . with female impersonators. Yes, I've been there."

"Yes, well, Barbara heard the boys were doing a send-up of herself and Doris Duke. Naturally, she was interested. The skit had the two women riding in a limousine across America, when they stop at a service station to use the bathroom. Barbara goes first, but returns to warn Doris there is no toilet paper. Doris rummages through her bag but finds no substitute."

"'You should have said something earlier, Dee-Dee,' remarks Barbara. 'If I'd known I would have saved you a traveler's cheque. I just used my last one.'"

Cecil knew more than he let on about Jimmy. One story that made its rounds through Manhattan's gay community happened after Jimmy's well-publicized split from the couple. The story was typical of Jimmy's sense of humor cloaked in privilege. Asked by a newspaper columnist about rumors of the split between him and the Windsor's, he quipped, "I've abdicated."

Later he was seen sauntering down Fifth Avenue with a young male companion. "Let me introduce you," he whooped, "to the boy who took the boy who took the girl who took the boy off the throne of Merry Old England."

Truman approached.

"Telling stories? Well, I have two. One's about who's been having those new animal shots at a clinic in Switzerland. The other's, about a certain Cardinal and what he did in Rome, of all towns! Which one d'ya want to hear first?"

Across the room, the Duke was talking with Pat.

"Now Edward, please tell me what went on at that party on Long Island."

"When Wallis danced with Bill Woodward? She's a terribly good dancer, you know."

"Yes, dear. But then Bill was shot later that night by his wife!"

"It's true. Mrs. George Baker gave us a party on Long Island. Bill Woodward and his wife, Ann, were there. Charming couple. Both into horses like us. We both danced with them. They returned home in Oyster Bay after the party. Ann said she was nervous that night because there'd been prowlers around. Early in the morning, the police answered a call from Ann and found her husband lying naked on the bedroom floor, shot in the face. They say Mrs. Woodward was convinced there was an intruder and she shot him."

Truman plopped himself down next to them, and announced, "Ann Woodward murdered her husband. End of story."

Pat said, "Well, that settles it!"

"Here's something. Did you know that Andy Warhol never goes to funerals? His thought is, 'They went uptown to Bloomingdale's and then never came back. They went shopping.'

With that news, Truman hopped over to Diana and Marilyn. No one interacted with Maxwell, who moved from one corner of the room to another.

"Want more fairy dust?"

Diana spoke up for Marilyn. "No, she does not, Truman. You, of all people should know that stuff doesn't mix well with wine."

"I saw my girl outside earlier. Feeling better now, doll?"

"She will in a while. Why don't you take a seat? You seem jumpy, Truman."

"I'll tell you about my early years with pot."

Diana rolled her eyes. "Yes, do, dear. We've been wondering all evening about your early years with pot." Marilyn was enjoying Diana's take on things. She found herself laughing as Truman launched into his story.

"That year I was trying to cut back on my drinking. So, a friend gave me a lot of pot, except I didn't know how to roll it. I called him back and said, 'Can you send somebody over?' So, he had someone come to my house over at the UN Plaza. I set him up in the living room with all this pot. He rolled a hundred joints. I gave him a one-joint tip and also gave him a pair of evening slippers especially made for me at Lobb's of London.'

Three days later, I called him back to see if his friend could come back over. He says to me, 'Truman, he already rolled a hundred joints. How could you smoke a hundred joints in three days?'

So, I told him, 'Well, I shared.'"

Marilyn stretched her bare legs out on the couch. Truman reached across and placed them across his lap.

"There now, comfy? Did I tell you if anything happens to me I want to be cremated and half my ashes in LA and half in NY so I can continue to be bi-coastal."

Across the room, Pamela was attempting to talk politics with Pat Buckley.

"Now, Pat, tell me about this House Un-American Activities Committee. Europe is watching all of this closely, I can tell you."

> *marilyn monroe, through the eyes of isak dinesen:*
> "It's not that she is pretty although, of course, she is almost incredibly pretty – but that she radiates at the same time unbounded vitality and a kind of unbelievable innocence. I have met the same in a lion cub that my native servants in Africa brought me. I would not keep her."

Pat, who got enough politics at home with her columnist husband, wasn't interested. She sighed.

"Oh, Pamela, anything but that!"

"What about Marilyn's husband? Wasn't he a target of the committee?"

"So, I've heard."

Pamela couldn't take a hint. She kept digging.

Karen Hagestad Cacy

"I've heard that marrying Marilyn actually took the pressure off of him in an odd way."

"I don't keep up with such things. I have no idea about any of that," Pat answered.

Pamela concluded, "The courts finally decided it was best not to imprison the husband of America's most glamorous and desirable woman."

Pat gave Pamela her best flat gaze and took a long drag off her cigarette before answering.

"Do tell."

Chapter Thirty-Two
"Not of Our Class, Darling"

Noticing George standing on his balcony, Truman hopped back up to join him.

"Nice party, George. You still seem sad, though."

"No. No. Not sad. Just . . .not . . . just . . ."

"Artists must keep busy. When I get the 'mean reds,' the only thing that helps, well, other than vodka and pot and fairy dust, naturally, is work. We need to create, you and me. That's how our kind fights the 'mean reds.'"

"Yes, I agree. That, and God. Must believe. Do you, Truman?"

"Do I what?"

"Believe."

"Oh, the God thing. He hasn't stopped by for dinner, if that's what you mean. Wouldn't it be lovely if he were queer?"

The Choreographer

"Who, Truman?"

"God!"

Truman and Jack continued to enjoy the expatriate life in Italy, spending the summer of 1953 in the village of Portofino. Truman's favorite diversion at this time was the company of his friend Cecil Beaton. Like Truman, Beaton was a man with an insatiable appetite for good gossip who had perfected the art of collecting the right friends. Their combined address books listed everyone of note in America, Europe and the rest of the globe. Beaton's visit to Portofino in August was a pleasant end to the summer.

George poured Truman a brandy, and handed it to him.

After a while, Truman continued.

"You know, George, here it is: People don't love me. I'm a freak. People don't love me. People are fascinated by me, but people don't love me. When I walk into a room, there's a shock on people's faces. I see it; they don't see how they look; I see how they look. That's why I'm so outrageous, so ridiculous, and so squeaking and so carrying on, to relieve them of the sudden embarrassment. I do something so outrageous that all they can do is laugh and then it's okay. I have to do that every time I walk into a room or meet somebody. Except, of course, tonight, where I know people. Well, except for Comrade Maxwell over there in the corner. He just hates me. I can tell."

George said, "Not good idea. Business deal. Lincoln Kirstein, looking out for company budget."

"Yes, we all thought that might be it."

George asked him, "Tell me, is good party?"

"Is very good party. But as someone who makes trouble for a living, I smell a rat."

"Shtaw?!" *(What?!)*

"You don't seem surprised at the way things have developed tonight, George. You can't kid a kidder. You can tell me – This is a Balanchine production; We're the cast. Yes?"

George Balanchine in his string tie

---

truman capote, through his own eyes:
"The only way people can hurt me is if I let them get close to me. And sometimes I meet people who aren't what they make themselves out to be. Then I get hurt. But I'm very careful about that now, about who I get close to."

Not speaking, George simply smiled. Slowly, he leaned against Truman and softly touched his brandy snifter against Truman's. There was a sharp clink as glass met glass and truth met reality.

Truman was rather pleased with himself. He liked to figure things out. It was his writer's brain that always analyzed the passing scene in real time.

To George, like a small boy bringing a new friend into his confidence, he offered, "You know what? I'm short, so I catch some things that others miss. For instance, Christopher Isherwood used to tinkle on the rug at parties."

Cecil, overhearing Truman's remark, made an attempt to change the subject, asking him about an American woman he'd met in Portofino.

"Know her, Truman?"

K a r e n   H a g e s t a d   C a c y

"Know her?! She's the most loathsome creature in America. I'm surprised they let her into Italy. She ought to be beheaded in a public auditorium with hundreds of thousands watching."

Truman was a professional observer of the wealthy. He adored being entertained by them. On the one hand, he loved the luxury and the chance to observe them. On the other hand, he was jealous of their riches and disapproving of their way of life. There wasn't enough cocaine and liquor in the world that could turn off his reporter's gaze.

Tonight, he had his eyes on four guests in particular: The Duke and Duchess, Maxwell, and Marilyn. They seemed a rather odd mixture George had brought together. Truman closely watched them interact with each other. He watched for chinks in the armor.

The voluptuous movie star seemed to be enchanting the mogul who was used to getting his way, particularly with beautiful women. Marilyn's wedding ring made no difference, especially now that he'd caught a glimpse of her real 'jewels' beneath her sheath-dress as she was perched on the balcony.

Marilyn's marriage was in trouble. Earlier, she'd told Truman. "I'm in a fucking prison and my jailer is named Arthur Miller . . . every morning he goes into that goddamn study of his, and I don't see him for hours and hours."

Truman knew, watching Maxwell ogle her all evening, the man had one thing on his mind. He wanted to rub his face against her breasts, drink in the perfume of her luminous skin, and send his stubby hands up her thighs after hidden treasure. The alcohol and drugs he consumed helped further the Czech's belief that such an expedition could be successful.

Who could blame the man? Artist, Franz Kline said of her, "She looked like, if you bit her, milk and honey would flow from her."

Even women appreciated her charms. Fellow film star, Natalie Wood, said of her, "When you look at Marilyn Monroe on the screen, you don't

Karen Hagestad Cacy

want anything bad to happen to her. You really care that she should be all right . . . happy."

Men who met her, and Maxwell was no exception, echoed Hollywood columnist, Sidney Skolsky: "She appeared kind and soft and helpless. Almost everyone wanted to help her. Marilyn's supposed helplessness was her greatest strength."

Tonight, "Bobbie" busied himself reading the star's mood. As a successful businessman, he had an uncanny ability to peer beneath the surface of his adversaries. With Marilyn, he sensed her unhappiness. Was it her marriage? Was there a chance for him?

What was it she'd confessed to Sam earlier?

That's right: She told her friend, "Starting tomorrow I will take care of myself for that's all I really have and as I see it now have ever had. Roxbury – I've tried to imagine spring all winter – it's here and I still feel hopeless. I think I hate it here because there is no love here anymore."

Maxwell would help her all right. And himself, for good measure.

Then there was the matter of Balanchine's Mystery Guest and his wife. The Windsor's wartime admiration for Adolph Hitler and his brutal regime was no secret. The couple's continued feelings were confirmed years later by Sir Oswald and Lady Mosley, who moved near the Windsor's in 1951, after they fled Britain.

Truman met the Mosley's at Beaton's Portofino house several years earlier. They were there with the Windsor's, and the four seemed to be very good friends. That's where he heard their startling story.

In May 1940, Winston Churchill, acting on the recommendation of Sir Robert Vansittart and Clement Attlee, imprisoned the Mosely's in London for activities that were considered inimical to the public safety under the provisions of the specially introduced Regulation 18B. They suffered privations in jail and later were released. But at the end of the war, Clement

K a r e n   H a g e s t a d   C a c y

Attlee was elected prime minister, and continued to make the couple's lives miserable.

Lady Mosley and her husband were forbidden the use of passports and eventually fled the country aboard a chartered yacht for Ireland. They later went to France where they became acquainted with the Windsor's. The Mosley's continued to feel Hitler was a genius and a potential savior of the twentieth century. They said the Windsor's shared their view. Adding spice to the political stew were stories to the effect that the Duchess of Windsor was herself a Jew.

The novelist knew that volatile chemical compositions always require a catalyst, a final ingredient to set off the final explosion. In tonight's case, it was the pianist. With the brandy warming him, the Duke began absent mindedly singing in German in a near-perfect accent. To his pleasant surprise, the pianist began accompanying him. He urged the player to sing along and soon Beaton's tsarist Russian setting was filled with the sounds of Germany.

Truman had been to many parties in the past where the Duke and Duchess sang and danced up a storm. But those parties all were in Europe. From a corner, he watched as the Duke happily belted out his favorite German songs.

He complained to Cecil: "Oh God! Not the singing again! The last time I was in Paris, he was in a party mood and sang to us in German and then in Spanish . . . then made some of us cluster near the piano and sing *'Alouette,'* and *'Frere Jacques.'* I thought we'd never make it out of there!"

Cecil answered, "Yes, he rather adores German music. He actually speaks the language quite well."

Cecil reached over and caught Truman's arm before it was fully raised in the Nazi salute.

"Cut it out. Not the time, dear."

It probably was the national anthem that really got things started.

Karen Hagestad Cacy

"Deutschland, Deutschland ber alles, ber alles in der Welt. Wenn es stehte zun Schutz und Trutze Brderlich zu sammen hlt. Von der Etsch bis an den Belt. Deutschland, Deutschland ber alles, ber alles in der Welt."

The Duchess noticed the storm clouds gathering before the Duke. She could hold her liquor. It was one of her better qualities. When David offered her some of Truman's cocaine earlier in the evening, she declined.

"We don't know where that's from, darling. Put it away."

She kept an eye on the large man with coal black eyes as he stalked the party. She noticed him on the terrace as Cecil rescued Marilyn. Maxwell's lustful glances at the star were becoming more obvious and troubling as the evening wore on. The Duchess was becoming increasingly uncomfortable with him and avoided further contact with the billionaire.

As usual during their twenty-seven years of marriage, the Duchess was on guard and in control. She watched her husband's diet, his speech, even his moods. When he began singing the German national anthem, she knew it was time to call a halt.

"David. That's enough singing, my darling. Come sit down and have some coffee."

"Yes, Peaches."

The Duchess nervously kept her watch going as the pianist rose to take a much-needed break. Maxwell approached the couple. Without saying a word, he continued on past them, roughly bumping into the Duchess on his way by. He leaned over the piano and grabbed the pianist's sheet music, tore it to shreds, and unceremoniously tossed the music aside.

The Duke reacted. "I say!"

Maxwell glared at the couple as he walked away.

The Duchess put her hand on the Duke's arm.

Karen Hagestad Cacy

"Shush. Please, David, let it go. He's not worth our notice. What were you thinking, singing those German songs? You really have no sense of your surroundings sometimes."

"No dear, you're right there. You are the one who notices things, not me."

"You mean, 'not Edward, my bull in the china shop.'"

"Did you say 'my bull'? I rather like the sound of that. I am 'your bull,' darling, that's for sure."

The Duchess watched closely as George and Cecil circled back to Maxwell, engaging him in conversation, being solicitous. The man who'd just rudely bumped into a woman known on four continents as *'The Duchess,'* who very nearly became the *Queen of England,* without so much as a 'by your leave.' Who did he think he was? Just some Czech Jew masquerading as an Englishman with a large bank account.

Not royalty.

Not like them.

Not elegant.

Not of our class, darling.

In due time, the angry man lit a cigar and made his way out onto the terrace alone. No one bothered to seek him out this time. No one wanted anything more to do with him. Fair to say, everyone wanted him gone. Eventually, the unsuspecting doe stepped over to the balcony wall for another look at New York's skyline. The prey was much too close to the hunter. Such a beautiful city, was her last thought.

When it happened, Marilyn reacted in slow motion. No, this can't be happening to me, she thought. Not here. With people, all around. Maxwell shoved her into the bushes and placed a meaty paw over her mouth. The other hand already was snaking its way inside her dress. As she reached out to grab the wall for balance, her hand landed instead between the man's newly bared legs: things were getting quickly out of hand. If this had happened to her at a Hollywood party, she would have been prepared for it. Known how to handle herself. But here, in New York, her defenses were down. As he pushed her down, she could feel the thorns of the rose bush scraping her back.

She opened her mouth to scream. She thought she was screaming. But in the beginning, no sound came out.

The Duchess was the first one to notice something wasn't right. The loud crash as a ceramic planter fell off its pedestal alerted everyone else to trouble on the balcony. By the time they reached her, Marilyn was screaming, but oddly, not to them. Instead, she was reciting one of her own poems, at the top of her lungs:

"Help Help
Help
I feel life coming closer
when all I want
is to die
Scream –

You began and ended in air

but where was the middle?"

---

marilyn monroe, through her own eyes:
"See you around, like never.'"

The Duchess, who hadn't left the security of her own regal circumference camped near the piano, now rose, and stomped outside. Assisted by Diana and Pat, she reached down to pull Marilyn to her feet.

She didn't know when she'd been so angry. She approached Maxwell, even as the others hung back, uncertain of what to do next. She stepped up to within inches of the towering man and glared up into his face.

The Baltimore divorcee temporarily recovered her American accent. Gone, for now, was the English lady nearly on the English throne.

"You are a disgusting man! All the money in the world cannot buy class. You are nothing but a rude, over-sexed peasant!"

But Maxwell wasn't quite finished. With his trousers still hanging loosely around his ankles, he lifted one leg and swung it first behind him, then, to everyone's horror, with full force into the Duchess's leg. Immediately, blood began spurting from the angry gash made by Maxwell's custom-made, steel-toed dress shoe.

Cecil and Truman, assisted by Rene, stepped up and grabbed Maxwell, and threw him back into the rose bush.

Cecil shouted at him, "Stay there! Don't move!"

Then, to himself, "Only back a month, and I'm acting a sodding banshee!"

With that, he ushered everyone else back inside, closing and locking the balcony

---

marilyn monroe, through her own eyes:
"It's a good saying though not so funny —what it stands for though – pain: 'If I had my life to live over, I'd live over a saloon.' . . . . It is rather a determination not to be overwhelmed . . .I feel as though it's all happening to someone right next to me. I'm close, I can feel it, I can hear it, but it isn't really me." Marilyn Monroe.

Karen Hagestad Cacy

Beaton closed the French doors, leaving Maxwell alone with his thoughts, four stories up.

Balanchine, strangely calm, all things considered, ordered that Rene call the police. Rene thought he detected a slight smile pass across his boss's face as he left the room. How very odd, he thought fleetingly, as he fetched iodine for the Duchess's leg. Even odder was Truman doing handstands in the corner, repeating, "I'm beside myself! I'm beside myself! I'm beside myself!"

George had a more pressing matter to attend to. He needed to call his business partner: Lincoln Kirstein, who'd returned to New York from war-ravaged Europe in 1946 and immediately hurled himself into building a national ballet company. Lincoln Kirstein, who, with George, organized Ballet Society in the latter part of 1946.

Lincoln, who, Balanchine once told an interviewer, ". . . hands you money and runs away before you can thank him."

Back in the kitchen, out of earshot from the others, George dialed the phone.

"George, it's four in the morning! What's going on? Is it Tanny?!"

"No. Not Tanny this time. It's party . . . probably we forget Maxwell funding our next production."

"Why's that?"

"Because he is locked outside on patio. He attacked the Duchess and tried to assault Marilyn Monroe."

"What?"

"I said, 'He attacked . . .'"

Lincoln was just waking up: "Yes, yes, yes, I heard what you said. Marilyn Monroe's there?!"

Balanchine didn't answer.

The two considered the situation in silence for a moment.

Finally, Lincoln's characteristic dry humor kicked in.

"I suppose, then, we should look for another patron."

Chapter Thirty-Three
Memories

Tanny should have been here, he thought later.

What a night!

George slept soundly after the party. The next day, as after his other opening nights, he scanned the papers for reviews. This time, however, he uncharacteristically skipped the Arts sections, making straight for the society columns. He laughed at the many distortions. So, that's how stories get started in the Village, he thought. Later on, he made his way north to Connecticut to offer Tanny the full, truthful report.

Tanaquil Le Clercq

George found his wife in good spirits and eager to hear all his news. He poured Tanny her afternoon tea as they settled in for story-time. He tried to give her a full report, leaving nothing out. He wanted to place her there in her beautiful garden for the evening.

"Cecil loved your roses, my dear, all in bloom, as if on cue, for the party. Of course, he matched them with still more in giant bouquets set all around."

Tanny loved to hear her husband speak. For years, his voice trained her to jump higher, spin faster, and finish more neatly. He was the master, she was his student. Her large, expressive eyes followed him as he acted out his guests' roles. He really was the most amazing ham, she thought.

Karen Hagestad Cacy

Then, "And that's why I have loved him so, and will always love him so, no matter what."

George loved telling Tanny about the party. Her adoring eyes for once lacked the pain of illness. Like himself, she liked to laugh. They were two clowns, stumbling through life together, adept in the fine art of pretending.

He began with his reactions.

"I've been thinking, my dear, the seeds of the party's demise were there from the beginning. Lincoln's Jewish billionaire, Maxwell, hates America and Germany, I'm afraid. Naturally, that put him up against David and Wallis."

". . . who were Nazi sympathizers during the war . . ."

"Yes. Apparently, Hitler held out the promise he would replace David to the English throne, had things gone his way . . ."

"But this man still will underwrite a ballet next year, yes?"

"No."

"So, it's true, there was a fight. I heard drugs were passed around."

"Things got out of hand when Truman started passing out cocaine in the back hallway. Several of them, including the Duke, were mixing Truman's so-called 'fairy dust' with the wines and other drinks all night."

"Cecil Beaton, too? Pamela Churchill? Arthur Miller?"

"Yes, yes. But listen, that reminds me -- Miller's wife, Marilyn Monroe, showed up in his place!"

"Marilyn Monroe, in our living room?!?"

"Da, da. The same. And she was in bad shape, poor dear. At one point, Cecil had to help her down from the balcony wall, where she'd crawled, poor thing."

George paused to prepare some sandwiches. As he did, Tanny could hear him still talking to himself. He thought she couldn't hear him. Often, she did.

"Lovely girl. Sad, sad girl. Sweet, really. But headed for trouble, I think. Headed for trouble."

Tanny, pretended not to understand when he returned to her. "Headed for trouble, you said?"

"Da. Da. The night slipped away from me. That's what I was thinking. But listen, let me tell you the happy parts. Diana Vreeland is such a story teller. You should have heard her, Tanny, telling us about her years in England. She told about being presented at court."

As he spoke, George cleverly mimicked each person's manner of speaking.

"Diana told us of the time she was presented at court. She said, 'That was something. It took hours and hours before you even got there. So, you took food and you took a flask. And you sat forever, because all the cars were held up in the Mall, with all of London looking in at you and saying 'Ere's to you, dearie!' and 'Cheerio, duckie!' and all that divine Cockney stuff.'"

George continued. "She has a delightful way of talking that's uniquely her own. She said, 'I remember curtsying to King George and Queen Mary; Now I happen to love curtsying. I was brought up British, don't forget!'"

Suddenly, George's expression darkened.

"What is it, George? What are you remembering?"

"Something else. She was admiring Cecil's decoration of our apartment, the tsarist Russian setting. Her words were . . . I will tell you . . . I will quote to you . . .she visited Russia once."

Karen Hagestad Cacy

She said they told her, 'We're not a royal country.'"

"Then she said, 'We're all exiles from something, but never to be able to go back to our country is something we don't know.' When she'd been in Russia for only forty-eight hours, she thought to herself: 'Of all the countries I've known, if it were my country not to be able to come back to this one would be the most terrible.' When she found herself walking through Red Square in the middle of the night, she said she felt like a child."

"She said it was light right up until about eleven-thirty, but it wasn't sun, it was light, the light behind the sky. She didn't think she'd like the midnight sun. She said what she loves is darkness – changing. She loved the golden onion domes and the beautiful skies. She loves medieval Russia. She said, 'Moscow is really my town.' She adores what she calls 'les Russes.' She calls them that out of habit, because of the Ballets Russes, because of Fokine, because of all the émigrés she used to see in London, Paris, Lausanne, and New York."

Edward Degas: The Dance Class

Tanny reacted to her husband's words. "Yes, she's right, of course. I know you carry that sadness with you. The sadness of leaving, I mean."

George hated taking delivery of sorrow perhaps more than anything else in life. Even with Tanny, he refused his feelings. Those were deep inside him, driving and even defining him. He began playing with Mourka, getting the cat to jump over his outstretched leg.

Tanny knew the signal. It meant they were now treading lightly again.

George adjusted Tanny's plaid lap robe, placed Mourka in her lap, and abruptly walked outside. Recalling Diana's kind words about his country, had the opposite of their intended effect. George steeled his resolve to continue his practice of walling off his feelings. Some things – exile from one's homeland, an ill wife – were too difficult to bear. Such things needed to be left solely to God.

With Balanchine's hard-won fatalism came a certain harshness towards others. As he told a dancer in his company, "Defy me and see what happens –you'll have to crawl back." Although he had an unassuming daily demeanor around the theater, people knew better than to express their feelings to him. Away from the theater, he loved to talk about science and the movies – anything but dancing.

Some called him Georgian and heartless. Lincoln Kirstein described the impresario as being Georgian like Stalin, even sinister. "He seems as soft as silk, but he's as tough as steel."

Tanaquil had a passing acquaintance with some of his demons. He told her, "When I was young in Russia in a way we were little wild animals. We were forced to bring ourselves up, to improvise our lives and that left its mark." For years, he had terrible nightmares and would call out in his sleep in an unfamiliar tongue, probably Georgian, his first language.

Tanny"

george balanchine, through the eyes of richard thomas:
"I loved watching Balanchine wheel and deal, and do all his things with all the dancers. Screw people, he obviously did, right and left, in all kinds of ways."

K a r e n   H a g e s t a d   C a c y

Balanchine, like most great men could be maddeningly judgmental and ego-driven. In private, he could have his knives out.

He said of John Cranko's choreography, "You know why that one die?" (Cranko had died young.) "Tchaikovsky up in heaven looked down and saw that ballet *'Eugene Onegin,'* and went to God and said 'Get that one!'"

He personally disliked Prokofiev and Rachmaninov.

Of Shostakovich, he said "a dreadful composer, he wrote like a peasant."

Of Bartok and Dvorak, "Horribly overrated."

Of Sibelius, "now nobody plays him; his music is a disaster."

Yet, many described Balanchine with affection.

"He was both cool and ardent, sad and full of fun, arrogant and modest, a towering genius who likes to . . . play solitaire. A real Russian personality. Face sharp, body is lean, flexible. Walks erect confidently, quickly but without rushing. That impossible Texan string tie dangles from his neck. He exudes elegance, energy, joy."

George Balanchine, the husband, eventually returned inside as though nothing had happened. He poured Tanny more tea, offered his small rye sandwiches, re-adjusted Tanny's cushions. He laughed as Tanny played with Mourka.

It was the start of summer of 1958: George Balanchine and Tanaquil Le Clercq, like so many others across the country fighting terrible illnesses, took their pleasures where they could. George gardened, fixed things around the house, played concerti on the piano, prepared dinner later on.

Karen Hagestad Cacy

But now with his party production over and ballet's off-season yawning before him, the great George Balanchine went back into his shell. Once again, he sat alone at night, staring into the darkness. God would step in. God brought him this far. Surely, He would take him all the way.

As if on cue, one day, George knew He had appeared and spoken to him through Rene, urging that misery be driven from the door in the form of a big, whooping party. A party like no other. A party designed to dance on graves, laugh at the devil, and banish human frailty.

Who could argue with God? Certainly, not George, one of his most devout believers.

George Balanchine, a man for our times, embraced and was a free spirit of the West. Yet beneath the can-do attitude and pixie smile, after the curtain rang down on successful opening nights, the Russian struggled with memories accumulated over an historic lifetime: the Russian Revolution, the Diaghilev years, the Cold War, the "Twist," the Space Age, the Wild West, Stravinsky, the Russian Orthodox Church, from a childhood marked by starvation and illness, to a life of acclaim, travel, celebrity and luxury -- all signaled the life of a remarkable, but surprisingly simple man who still liked to iron his own shirts.

As the sunset of his life approached, the Russian impresario often recalled with fondness a young girl of fourteen who kidded around, barking like a dog to amuse him, and whose body, before it broke down, performed the most amazing feats of grace and virtuosity. Tanaquil Le Clercq was an original Balanchine ballerina, an American phenomenon. A tile in the puzzle of American culture.

Certain events remain in our hearts and imagination for years afterwards.

Closing his eyes over the past, George Balanchine could still see Truman Capote performing handstands in his living room, crying, "I'm beside myself!" "I'm beside myself!" "I'm beside myself!" as the police and Interpol arrived.

Curtain

Truth Takes a Holiday

The Jack Paar Show
Wednesday, June 25, 1958
11:30 p.m.

Beginning in July 1957, Jack Paar hosted a successful television talk show bearing his name. At forty, the acerbic host was, by turns, genial, accusatory, and, on occasion, anarchistic. A week after Balanchine's party, following a variety of 'as-told-to' reports in the New York press, late night TV's favorite host was prepared to get to the bottom of things.

1Jack Paar

Announcer: "Here's Jack!"

(Studio applause)

"Good evening, everyone. You know, before you were seated tonight, something went on I want to mention. Phil here was busy arranging the cue cards, and I was reminded of once early on in my career when I was reading off of them for a commercial. We're on the air, the camera's rolling. So, I'm reading along:

'Do your hands sweat? Do you have insomnia? Do you sometimes have difficulty turning your head?'

And I stopped reading.

My producer said, 'Jack, what's wrong?'

I said, 'I have this disease.'

(Laughter)

Woody Allen

But to begin this evening, I want to bring on a new, young comedian. He's a young man who's caught on big everywhere but on this show. I want him to be bigger than I am even if he'll never be back. Ladies and Gentlemen, may I present to you Mr. Woody Allen.

(Applause)

Woody Allen: ". . . I was delightful. I told a joke. You would've loved me . . . I had a deep cavity and my dentist had sent me to a chiropodist . . . "

(Applause)

"That was very funny material, Woody."

"Thanks very much, Jack. You know four years ago, when I was here, nobody else would've had me on."

"Well, I was drinking at the time. Woody, meet Oscar Levant. The two of you should know each other."

Oscar: "The only reason I'm appearing is there were no more beds left in the sanitarium."

Jack: "What do you do for exercise, Oscar?'

Oscar: "I stumble, then I fall into a coma."
(Laughter)

Karen Hagestad Cacy

Oscar: "You have the most responsive audience since Adolph Hitler . . . the good old days."

Jack: "Ladies and Gentlemen, please join me in welcoming back an old friend, Truman Capote"

(Applause)

Oscar Levant

There is an awkward silence, as the four exchange looks. Truman removes his glasses and slowly cleans them.

Jack: "So. Anything new, Truman?"

Truman squints at Jack and replaces his glasses. With a flourish, he puts his handkerchief back in his pocket.

Jack: "You always bring a certain aura of danger with you."

Truman: "Because you never know what the hell I'm going to say next."

Jack: "You mean like recently, when you said, all actors are stupid?"

Truman: You're overstating it. What I said was, some actors are stupid."

Jack: "You have the chance to change that tonight. Is there anything you might want to add?"

Truman: "If you take yer chances, 'ya take yer chances."

Jack: "I have no idea what that means."

Truman: "I have my own little secrets."

Karen Hagestad Cacy

Jack: "Not too many, by this time."

Truman: "You'd be amazed. My life is so strange, it's not like anybody."

Jack: "Have you been drinking? I've heard you might be suffering from alcoholism."

Truman: "My God, alcohol is the least of it. That's the joker in the cards."

Truman turns sideways in his chair, and swings his short legs over the arm.

"There's never been anyone like me and after I'm gone there ain't going to be anyone like me again."

Jack: "Word has it you went to a pretty wild party last weekend. Why don't you tell us about that?"

Truman: "Well, which one do you mean? I go to so many."

Jack: "It's in all the papers, Truman. The one where all hell broke loose."

Truman: "Oh, I know the one. Yes, I was there."

(More silence.)

Jack: "This isn't going to be easy tonight, is it, Truman?"

Truman: "No, no. I'll tell you. Things started out quite nicely, actually."

Jack: "And then what happened?"

Truman: "There was wonderful food, wine, dancing . . ."

Oscar: "Dancing! Shocking!"

Truman: "Yes, and then later on, there were some German songs, and pretty soon, everyone began yelling 'Heil Hitler!' and marching all around."

Jack: "The war's been over for several years now, Truman."

Truman: ". . . followed by violence."

Jack: "At the party . . ."

Truman: "That's right. Women were attacked."

Jack: "What women?"

Truman: "Pretty much all of them. And, some of the men."

Jack: "But Truman, I thought you only went to parties with the best people."

Truman: "Well-ll . . . The best people are the most fun of anyone . . . especially when they've had a few too many."

Jack: "I heard Marilyn Monroe was there."

Truman: "The police showed up . . . and Interpol."

Woody: "Interpol? Not the KGB?!"

Truman: "I think one of the guests may have been a spy, though.

Jack: "Are there any spies in your book, Truman?"

Truman: "How's that again?"

Jack: "In your book, *'Breakfast at Tiffany's.'*"

Truman: "Oh. My book. I was wondering when we might get around to that."

Break for Commercial

ACKNOWLEDGEMENTS

The author gratefully acknowledges the usefulness of the following resources:

Karen Hagestad Cacy

GEORGE BALANCHINE

Balanchine: A Biography, by Bernard Taper, Times Books, 1984.

I Remember Balanchine: Recollections of the Ballet Master by Those Who Knew Him," by Francis Mason, Doubleday, 1991.

All in the Dances: A Brief Life of George Balanchine, by Terry Teachout, Harcourt, Inc., 2004.

The Ballet Maker: George Balanchine, by Robert Gottlieb, Harper Perennial/Eminent Lives, 2004.

The New York City Ballet, Text by Lincoln Kirstein, Photographs by Martha Swope and George Platt Lynes, Alfred A. Knopf, 1973.

Dance for a City: Fifty Years of The New York City Ballet, by Lynn Garafola and Eric Foner, 1999. Columbia University Press.

Balanchine's Ballerinas: Conversations with the Muses, by Robert Tracy with Sharon DeLano, Linden Press/Simon & Schuster, 1983.

Balanchine: A Biography, by Bernard Taper, Times Books, 1984.

Repertory In Review: Forty Years of the New York City Ballet, by Nancy Reynolds, with Introduction by Lincoln Kirstein, The Dial Press, New York, 1977.

Karen Hagestad Cacy

MARILYN MONROE

Marilyn Monroe, by Eve Arnold, Alfred A Knopf, 1987.

Fragments: Poems, Intimate Notes, Letters by Marilyn Monroe, edited by Stanley Buchtal and Bernard Comment, Farrar, Straus and Giroux, 2010.

Marilyn Monroe: Metamorphosis, by David Wills and Stephen Schmidt, Harper Collins, 2011.

My Story, by Marilyn Monroe with Ben Hecht, Taylor Trade, 2007.

The Genius and the Goddess, Arthur Miller & Marilyn Monroe, by Jeffrey Meyers, University of Illinois Press, 2009.

PAT BUCKLEY
Airborne: A Sentimental Journey," by William F. Buckley, Jr., Little, Brown and Company, 1970.

Miles Gone By, a literary autobiography, by William F. Buckley, Jr., Regnery Publishing, 2004.

Losing Mum and Pup, by Christopher Buckley, Twelve: Hatchett Book Group, 2009.

The New York Times Magazine, April 26, 2009, *"Growing Up the Only Child of Two Charismatic – and Complicated – Buckley's: Mum and Pup and Me,"* by Christopher Buckley.

DIANA VREELAND
D.V., by Diana Vreeland, Edited by George Plimpton and Christopher Hemphill, Alfred A. Knopf, 1984.

Diana Vreeland Bazaar Years: Why Don't You?, by John Esten, Universe Publishing, 2001.

Karen Hagestad Cacy

Diana Vreeland: The Eye Has To Travel, by Lisa Immordino Vreeland, Abrams, New York.

Allure, by Diana Vreeland with Christopher Hemphill and Forward by Marc Jacobs, Chronicle Books, San Francisco 1980.

THE DUKE AND DUCHESS OF WINDSOR
The Windsor Story, by J. Bryan III and Charles J.V. Murphy, William Morrow and Company, Inc., New York, 1979.

The Duchess of Windsor: The Secret Life, by Charles Higham, McGraw-Hill Book Company, 1988.

PAMELA CHURCHILL
Life of the Party: The Biography of Pamela Digby Churchill Hayward Harriman, by Christopher Ogden, Little, Brown & Company, 1994.

CECIL BEATON
The Unexpurgated Beaton: The Cecil Beaton Diaries As He Wrote Them, 1970-1980, Introduction by Hugo Vickers, Alfred A. Knopf, New York, 2003.

ROBERT MAXWELL
Robert Maxwell, Israel's Superspy: The Life and Murder of a Media Mogul, by Gordon Thomas and Martin Dillon, Carroll and Graf Publishers, 2002.

Karen Hagestad Cacy

OTHER SOURCES

The Richard Burton Diaries, edited by Chris Williams, Yale University Press, 2012.

The Way We Lived Then: Recollections of a Well-Known Name Dropper, by Dominick Dunne, Crown Publishers, 1999.

Among the Porcupines, A Memoir, by Carol Matthau, Ballantine Books, 1992.

Hellraisers: The Life and Inebriated Times of Richard Burton, Richard Harris, Peter O'Toole, and Oliver Reed, by Robert Sellers, Thomas Dunne Books, St. Martin's Press, 2008.

The Grand Surprise: The Journals of Leo Lerman, Stephen Pascal, Alfred A. Knopf, 2007.

Title Page

"A dinner invitation, once accepted, is a sacred obligation. If you die before the dinner takes place, your executor must attend": Ward McAllister, New York socialite of the late 1800s.

Author's Preface

"Everyone is ga-ga on names today. That's why the paparazzi have taken over. People can't get over other people.": Diana Vreeland.
Allure, by Diana Vreeland with Christopher Hemphill and Forward by Marc Jacobs, Chronicle Books, San Francisco 1980, 24.

"What I do is assemble ingredients – it is like opening an icebox door and you look inside to see what you have stored away – and then I select, combine, and hope that the results will be appetizing.": George Balanchine.

Balanchine's Ballerinas: Conversations with the Muses, by Robert Tracy with Sharon DeLano, Linden Press/Simon & Schuster, 1983, ll.

The Best People

"The Duchess's money had to be crisp – either new from the bank or ironed by a servant. When the last guest arrived (at a party) the butler notified the Duchess in her room. She then appeared at the top of the stairs, like a queen, always exquisitely dressed . . . guests nibbled on five pounds of caviar. The Duchess kept a tiny gold pencil beside her plate and a discreet notepad. She might write a word or two during the course of the meal, such as 'Try truffles with this dish next time' or 'Salt in soup?'": Charlene Bry.

The Duchess of Windsor, The Secret Life, by Charles Higham, John Wiley & Sons, Inc., 1988, 413.

"I'm beside myself! I'm beside myself!": Truman Capote.

Truman Capote: In Which Various Friends, Enemies, Acquaintances, and Detractors Recall His Turbulent Career, by George Plimpton, Doubleday, Anchor Books edition published by arrangement with Nan A. Talese/Doubleday, 1997, 148.

"The eligible prince married the divorcee and surrendered his chance to bring the English throne into disrepute. Noel Coward said that a statue should be erected to Mrs. Simpson on every village green in the land, because in extracting Edward she had saved the nation from disaster.":
Noel Coward.
Source, unknown.

"At one party Burton, quite sloshed, told the Duchess, 'You are, without any question, the most vulgar woman I've ever met.' Hours later he picked her up and swung her round to such an extent that Liz thought he might drop and kill her.":
Richard Burton.

Karen Hagestad Cacy

Hellraisers: The Life and Inebriated Times of Richard Burton, Richard Harris, Peter O'Toole, and Oliver Reed, by Robert Sellers, Thomas Dunne Books, St. Martin's Press, 2008, 131.

Chapter One
George Balanchine

"A dancer's life must be the most exciting thing in the world – and the most excruciating. But, to have performed one arc of the arm, one moment of beauty, one something . . .": Diana Vreeland

Allure, by Diana Vreeland with Christopher Hemphill and Forward by Marc Jacobs, Chronicle Books, San Francisco 1980, 197.

"Diaghilev and his Ballets Russes had an enormous impact on fashion. The first great twentieth-century couturier, Paul Poiret, got many of his ideas from Diaghilev.": Diana Vreeland.

Diana Vreeland: The Eye Has To Travel, by Lisa Immordino Vreeland, Abrams, New York, 19.

"The best, of course, was Tanaquil Le Clercq. . . . She could dance to anything. She danced to music, not to counts. I remember when she caught polio in Denmark. She had just danced the last movement of Western Symphony. I came up and put my scarf around her, she was so wringing wet. The next morning, she couldn't get up. That was the end. It was really a very tragic moment for the New York City Ballet.": Leon Barzin.

Balanchine's Ballerinas: Conversations with the Muses, by Robert Tracy with Sharon DeLano, Linden Press/Simon & Schuster, 1983.

"His Russian Easter party was always the main festivity of the year. His Russian friends would gather at the apartment

Karen Hagestad Cacy

to dine right after midnight services. The next day another party would be held for Americans, non-Orthodox, and other friends. For these Easter celebrations, he always prepared his most lavish board – roasts, ptarmigans, fish in aspic, specially prepared horseradish and garnishes, Salade Oliviere, and, of course, the traditional pascha and kulitch, which contain all the rich ingredients and exotic tastes one dreams of during Lent: sweet butter by the pound, mounds of sugar, vanilla beans, saffron, cardamom, pressed almonds, raisins."
Source, unknown.

"Tanny Le-Clercq was magnificent as Choleric . . . Have you ever seen the great blue crane in flight? They are magnificent birds with long necks and long legs . . . Tanny's movement reminded me of that crane": Mary Ellen Moylan.
Balanchine's Ballerinas: Conversations with the Muses, by Robert Tracy with Sharon DeLano, Linden Press/Simon & Schuster, 1983.

Chapter Two
Marilyn Monroe
"God gave her everything. She does two things beautifully: she walks and she stands still": Billy Wilder.
Marilyn Monroe, by Eve Arnold, Alfred A Knopf, 1987, 17.

"Her skin was translucent, white, luminous. Up close around the periphery of her face, there was a dusting of faint down. This light fuzz trapped light and caused an aureole to form, giving her a faint glow on film.": Eve Arnold, photographer.
Marilyn Monroe, by Eve Arnold, Alfred A Knopf, 1987, 26.

"Joining a chorus of admirers, Sammy Davis, Jr. added, 'She hangs like a bat in men's minds.'": Sammy Davis, Jr.
Marilyn Monroe, by Eve Arnold, Alfred A Knopf, 1987, page 35.

"In 1956 Marilyn was much in the news. She had married Arthur Miller, she had formed a company with Milton Greene to produce her own films and she had contracted to make The Prince and the Showgirl with Laurence Olivier. . . . The unlikely combination of the intellectual playwright and the sexpot movie star who was, for the most part, identified in people's minds with the role of the dumb blonde that she played in many films, captured the imagination of the world press.": Eve Arnold, photographer.
Marilyn Monroe, by Eve Arnold, Alfred A. Knopf, 1987, 66.

"Life – I am of both of your directions/Life (crossed out)/Somehow remaining hanging downward/the most/but strong as a cobweb in the /wind – I exist more with the cold glistening frost. But my beaded rays have the colors I've/seen in a painting – ah life they/have cheated you.": Marilyn Monroe.
My Story, by Marilyn Monroe with Ben Hecht, Taylor Trade, 2007.

"You call to mind the bouquet of fireworks display, eliciting from your awed spectators an open-mouthed chorus of wondrous 'Oohs' and 'Ah's.' You are as spectacular as the silvery shower of a Vesuvius fountain; you have rocketed from obscurity to become our post war sex symbol—the pin-up girl of an age. And whatever press agentry or manufactured illusion may have lit the fuse, it is your own weird genius that has sustained your flight.": Cecil Beaton

Marilyn Monroe, by Eve Arnold, Alfred A. Knopf, 1987, 31.
"There was this secret in me – acting. It was like being in jail and looking at a door that said 'This Way Out.'": Marilyn Monroe.
My Story, by Marilyn Monroe with Ben Hecht, Taylor Trade, 2007.

" . . . she married her college education"

Karen Hagestad Cacy

Source, unknown.

"She has the extraordinarily cunning gift of being able to suggest one minute that she is the naughtiest little thing and the next minute that she is beautifully dumb and innocent.": Sir Laurence Olivier.
The Genius and the Goddess, Arthur Miller & Marilyn Monroe, by Jeffrey Meyers, University of Illinois Press, 2009, 161.

"Maybe all one can do is hope to end up with the right regrets.": Arthur Miller.
Vogue Magazine, August 2013, 86.

"While it's nice to be included in people's fantasies, you also like to be accepted for your own sake. . . . I'll think I have a few wonderful friends and all of a sudden, oh, here it comes. They do a lot of things. They talk about you in the press, to their friends, tell stories and you know, it's disappointing.": Marilyn Monroe.
Source, unknown.

"Of course, it does depend on the people, but sometimes I'm invited places to kind of brighten up a dinner table like a musician who'll play the piano after dinner, and I know they're not really invited for yourself. (sic) You're just an ornament." : Marilyn Monroe.
Source, unknown.

"If she wanted to go to school, she should go to railroad engineering school and learn to run on time.": Billy Wilder.
The Genius and the Goddess, Arthur Miller & Marilyn Monroe, by Jeffrey Meyers, University of Illinois Press, 2009, 57.
"You know, ma'am, if you lost some weight, put on a little makeup and combed your hair, you would look exactly like Marilyn Monroe.": Marilyn Monroe.
Source, unknown.

K a r e n   H a g e s t a d   C a c y

"For years, I dreamed I was Bernhardt. Either I was Salome, or I was some Polish tart . . . I was terribly dramatic. I mean, I was never not Bernhardt.": Diana Vreeland.
Allure, by Diana Vreeland with Christopher Hemphill and Forward by Marc Jacobs, Chronicle Books, San Francisco 1980, 104.

"She was already late . . . At eleven in the morning she wore a black velvet gown with straps the width of spaghetti strands . . . When I complimented her on the way she looked, she winked at me in the mirror and said 'Just watch me.' . . .First Marilyn appeared with Olivier, Rattigan and Milton Greene. They were on a balcony and below them were the press. Slowly Marilyn and Olivier came down the stairs and were engulfed by the crowd of friendly professionals. . . . At first, Sir Laurence gravely and seriously answered. Then Marilyn settled in, removed her coat, leaned forwards – and broke one of her thinner-than-thin straps. Suddenly the atmosphere changed – she made it fun: laughter was heard, a safety pin was offered and the press conference was hers.": Eve Arnold, photographer.
Marilyn, by Eve Arnold, Alfred A. Knopf, 1987, 66-69.

Chapter Three
Cecil Beaton

"The Duke of Windsor has never really liked me, you know. We never got on well. And his face! His face is what happens to a person whose life has no purpose. His face shows his empty life. Tragic, actually: He rather resembles a mad terrier, haunted one moment, then with a flick of the hand he laughs fecklessly": Cecil Beaton.
The Unexpurgated Beaton: The Cecil Beaton Diaries As He Wrote Them, 1970-1980, Introduction by Hugo Vickers, Alfred A. Knopf, 2002, 130.

Karen Hagestad Cacy

"Actually, Wallis has been a good friend to me, I like her. She is a good friend to all her friends. There is no malice in her. There is nothing dislikeable. She is just not of the degree that has reason to be around the Throne": Cecil Beaton.
The Unexpurgated Beaton: The Cecil Beaton Diaries As He Wrote Them, 1970-1980, Introduction by Hugo Vickers, Alfred A. Knopf, 2002, 316.

(Leo Lerman) *"served what he called 'nasty wine,' old biscuits and cheddar cheese."*
Truman Capote: In Which Various Friends, Enemies, Acquaintances, and Detractors Recall His Turbulent Career, by George Plimpton, Doubleday, Anchor Books edition published by arrangement with Nan A. Talese/Doubleday, 1997, 45.

"Mr. Capote, what do you think of Mr. Beaton?" "Well . . . out of the middle classes of England it's rather curious to get such an exotic flower.": David Bailey
Allure, by Diana Vreeland with Christopher Hemphill and Forward by Marc Jacobs, Chronicle Books, San Francisco 1980, 116.

"Edna Ferber, a frequent guest, thought the rule ridiculous, observing that guests were getting together to eat, not to mate": Phyllis Cerf Wagner.
Truman Capote: In Which Various Friends, Enemies, Acquaintances, and Detractors Recall His Turbulent Career, by George Plimpton, Doubleday, Anchor Books edition published by arrangement with Nan A. Talese/Doubleday, 1997, 43.

"The ballet master liked science fiction (he was ecstatic about the creation of a new American space agency,) TV westerns, and American ice cream. He wore bright pearl buttoned shirts, black string ties, a gambler's plaid vest and frontier pants."
Source, unknown.

"Michael Redgrave's problem is he's in love with himself but he's not sure if it's reciprocated.": Sir Anthony Quayle, British actor.
The Richard Burton Diaries, by Richard Burton, edited by Chris Williams, Yale University Press, 2012, 314.

"True good manners are a lot like charm. You either have them or you don't. You cannot teach people these things. While manners may seem to be a question of opening and closing doors and holding chairs and standing up when a lady comes into the room, etcetera, it really has more to do with acting with a sort of indefinably unobtrusive grace.": Richard Burton
The Richard Burton Diaries, by Richard Burton, edited by Chris Williams, Yale University Press, 2012, 553.

"I think no one really knows Mr. Balanchine. He is a mystery. I am comfortable with Balanchine because I never did something wrong to him. He has an elephant's memory if you do something wrong to him.": Felia Doubrovska.
Balanchine's Ballerinas: Conversations with the Muses, by Robert Tracy with Sharon DeLano, Linden Press/Simon & Schuster, 1983, 44.

Chapter Four
The Duke of Windsor

"David, come here a moment." "Just a second, darling. I have something on my mind." "On your what?" "I know darling, I haven't much of a mind.": Duchess of Windsor.
The Windsor Story, by J. Bryan III and Charles J.V. Murphy, William Morrow & Company, Inc., 1979, 555.

"Don't be so full of curiosity.": The Duchess of Windsor.
The Unexpurgated Beaton: The Cecil Beaton Diaries As He Wrote Them, 1970-1980, Introduction by Hugo Vickers, Alfred A. Knopf, 2002, 132.

Karen Hagestad Cacy

"The former Prince cut palace food purchases by two-thirds, and was served salads, fruit, and small cuts of meat. His and Wallis's only indulgence was a delicious Scandinavian dessert called rodgrod, made of crushed raspberries, red currants and rice."
Source, unknown.

"Almost childlike from a distance, the duke's face was puckered and deeply lined from too much exposure to the tropical sun on the couple's many travels.": Cecil Beaton.
The Unexpurgated Beaton: The Cecil Beaton Diaries As He Wrote Them, 1970-1980, Introduction by Hugo Vickers, Alfred A. Knopf, 2002.

"The Windsor's annual rat trail was always the same: Palm Beach, NYC, Paris, Biarritz, Cote d'Azur, Paris and back to NYC.": Charles Higham.
The Duchess of Windsor: The Secret Life, by Charles Higham, McGraw-Hill Book Company, 1988, 375.

"Why must you always have something hot in your mouth?": Duchess of Windsor.
The Windsor Story, by J. Bryan III and Charles J.V. Murphy, William Morrow & Company, Inc., 1979, 547.

"She had an enormous feather in her hair which got into everything, the soup, the gravy, the ice cream, and at every vivacious turn of her head it smacked Guy sharply in the eyes or the mouth . . .": Richard Burton.
The Private World of the Duke and Duchess of Windsor, by Hugo Vickers, Harrods Publishing, 1995, 225.

"At the cocktail hour, the wait staff was dressed impeccably and carried silver trays offering such delicacies as large grapes hollowed out and filled with cream cheese, bacon bits fried in brown sugar, cabbage leaf pieces with shrimps or prawns attached to them by picks, fried mussels, and

Karen Hagestad Cacy

chipolata sausages. Dinner was served in the couple's blue chinoiserie dining room at two round tables set for eight. There were silver and gold monogrammed cigarette boxes and cut-glass finger bowls. Favored as main courses were roast partridge, Chicken Maryland, grouse, and faux filets, and for dessert, dark chocolate cake called Sacher torte.": Charles Higham.
The Duchess of Windsor: The Secret Life, by Charles Higham, McGraw-Hill Book Company, 1988.

"Dinner parties at the chateau were small, but formal, and done with great style. Two cloths were put on for evening meals. The first layer was a cloth of gold, the second was fine Brussels lace. The effect was beautiful; The gold shone through under the glistening light of the candelabra. The monogrammed china and silver were of the highest quality. An individual menu was written out in copperplate for each guest and placed on a tine silver rest in from of him or her. The fowl were brought to the table "dressed" (with their feathers on) so everyone could see and feel them, then they were cooked and served.": Charles Higham
The Duchess of Windsor: The Secret Life," by Charles Higham, McGraw-Hill Book Company, 1988, 202.

"Forty five minutes of drinking before dinner is quite enough!": Duchess of Windsor.
The Windsor Story, by J. Bryan III and Charles J.V. Murphy, William Morrow & Company, Inc., 1979, 537.

"But one mustn't be too obvious about it. It's disconcerting to find a grimacing countenance suddenly turning in your direction, its robot-like action saying in effect, 'Here's the fish, and here am I.'": Duchess of Windsor.
The Windsor Story, by J. Bryan III and Charles J.V. Murphy, William Morrow & Company, Inc., 1979, 537.

"I got a gal in Baltimo', Streetcars run right by her do.'
Old American song.

"Among the guests who did show up were Hugh Lloyd Thomas, first secretary of the British Embassy in Paris, Lady (Walford) Selby, Walter Monckton, Fruity and Alexandra Metcalfe, the Eugene Rothschilds, George Allen, and Dudley Forwood.": Charles Higham.
The Duchess of Windsor, The Secret Life, John Wiley & Sons, Inc., 1988, 215.

"Helena Normanton of The New York Times boldly asked Wallis about her Nazi connections. . . Dudley Forwood, was approached by several reporters, one of whom asked, "Do you think the duke has fucked Mrs.Simpson yet?": Charles Higham.
The Duchess of Windsor, The Secret   Life,   by   Charles Higham, John Wiley & Sons, Inc., 1988, 217.

"Wallis would not be referred to as 'Her Royal Highness' following the wedding": Charles Higham.
The Duchess of Windsor, The Secret   Life,   by   Charles Higham, John Wiley & Sons, Inc., 1988, 214.

"What a smug, stinking lot my relations are and you've never seen such a seedy worn out bunch of old hags most of them have become.": Duke of Windsor.
The Duchess of Windsor, The Secret Life, by Charles Higham, John Wiley & Sons, Inc., 1988, 203.

"God's curses be on the heads of those English bitches who dare to insult you . . .get back at all those swine in England and make them realize how disgustingly and unsportingly they have behaved.": Duke of Windsor.
The Duchess of Windsor, The Secret Life, John Wiley & Sons, Inc., 1988, 203.

"The Duke and I sang the Welsh National Anthem in atrocious harmony. I referred disloyally to the Queen as

Karen Hagestad Cacy

'her dumpy majesty' and neither the Duke or Duchess seemed to mind.": Richard Burton.

The Richard Burton Diaries, edited by Chris Williams, Yale University Press, 2012, 157.

"Somerset Maugham," (in a card game with the Duchess), *"asked her why, holding three kings, she failed to support his bid of one no-trump. 'My kings don't take tricks,' she told him. 'They only abdicate.'":* Somerset Maugham.

The Windsor Story, by J. Bryan III and Charles J.V. Murphy, William Morrow & Company, Inc., 1979, 349.

Cecil Beaton thought their homes to be excessive. He disapproved of the use of war medallions, bamboo chairs, and gimmicky poufs.": Charles Higham.

The Duchess of Windsor, The Secret Life, by Charles Higham, John Wiley & Sons, Inc., 1988, 389.

"In her early years in England, Lady Mendl taught Wallis to tone down her personality to suit British requirements. She encouraged her to speak in a softer, more southern drawl instead of in harsh accents and to dress very simply, to accentuate the angular lines of her figure.": Cecil Beaton.

The Duchess of Windsor, The Secret Life, by Charles Higham, John Wiley & Sons, Inc., 1988, 101.

"Privately, I found the language pompous – heavy with references to 'my people' and 'my realm.'": The Duke of Windsor.

The Windsor Story, by J. Bryan III and Charles J.V. Murphy, William Morrow & Company, Inc., 1979, 181.

"We Georgians are not Russians in culture, not at all. We are Mediterranean people, like Italians.": George Balanchine.

Balanchine: A Biography, by Bernard Taper, Times Books, 1984, 25.

Karen Hagestad Cacy

"Elegance is refusal.": Diana Vreeland.
Allure, by Diana Vreeland with Christopher Hemphill and Forward by Marc Jacobs, Chronicle Books, San Francisco 1980, 203.

"You have delighted us long enough." Jane Austen.
Source, unknown.

I thought he'd never go. Too boring. He talked of absolutely nothing but himself the whole time.": Duchess of Windsor.
The Windsor Story, by J. Bryan III and Charles J.V. Murphy, William Morrow & Company, Inc., 1979, 566-567.

"At times his parents humiliated him to the point where he actually burst into tears. . . . 'I'm fed up. I've taken all I can stand . . .I want no more of this princing! I want to be an ordinary person. I must have a life of my own.'": Freda Dudley Ward.
The Windsor Story, by J. Bryan III and Charles J.V. Murphy, William Morrow & Company, Inc., 1979, 69.

"I like giving parties; I like dressing up.": Duchess of Windsor.
The Windsor Story, by J. Bryan III and Charles J.V. Murphy, William Morrow & Company, Inc., 1979, 534.

"What were the King's real motives? Was he so abjectly in love that he could not face reigning without Wallis Simpson at his side? Did he want to be King at all? Or had he wanted to escape and found in the marriage issue a convenient bolt-hole? Was it perhaps the Government who wanted to rid Britain of their King for reasons quite unconnected with the marriage?": Hugo Vickers.
The Private World of the Duke and Duchess of Windsor, by Hugo Vickers, Harrods Publishing, 1995, 29.

Chapter Five

Karen Hagestad Cacy

George Balanchine

(Typical Windsor guest list of the time): *"The company included the British Ambassador and Ambassadress to the Quai d'Orsay; Prince and Princess Dmitri Romanoff (the former Lady Milbanke,) and his cousin Prince Yussupoff, who had conspired in the assassination of Rasputin (and was married to Czar Nicholas II's niece, Princess Irina); Cyrus Sulzberger of the New York Times, and his Greek wife, Marina; Count and Countess Czernin, of the Austrian aristocracy; Margaret Biddle, who had been maneuvering for an appointment to the American Embassy; the Philippe de Rothschilds; the Supreme Commander in Europe, Gen. Alfred M. Gruenther, USA, and his wife, Helene, editor and publisher of Elle; etc."*
The Windsor Story, by J. Bryan III and Charles J.V. Murphy, William Morrow & Company, Inc., 1979, 535.

(Speaking of the Kennedys): *"Out of a litter of nine, there's almost bound to be one good pup.":* Duchess of Windsor.
The Windsor Story, by J. Bryan III and Charles J.V. Murphy, William Morrow & Company, Inc., 1979, 536.

(George Balanchine): *"enjoyed cooking and working around outside as usual. He built a little tool house and had various projects. He was very informal, always going around with his shirt off, working, getting the sun, digging around at the roses and cutting the grass.":* Pat Wilde.
The Ballet Maker: George Balanchine, by Robert Gottlieb, Harper Perennial/Eminent Lives, 2004, 142.

"Everybody is in love with Balanchine in a way, because he teaches and works with love. . . I look at him . . .as an inevitable force – like I would look at lightening, at Niagara Falls, at Mount Vesuvius, at cosmic events": Ruthanna Boris.
Balanchine's Ballerinas: Conversations with the Muses, by Robert Tracy with Sharon DeLano, Linden Press/Simon & Schuster, 1983, 53.

Chapter Six
Diana Vreeland

"I want this place to look like a garden, but a garden in Hell.": Diana Vreeland.
The Unexpurgated Beaton: The Cecil Beaton Diaries As He Wrote Them, 1970-1980, Introduction by Hugo Vickers, Alfred A. Knopf, 2002, 175.

"Why Don't You have a yellow satin bed entirely quilted in butterflies? . . .Why Don't You rinse your blond child's hair in dead champagne to keep its gold, as they do in France? . . .The bikini is the most important thing since the atom bomb. . . If they've got long arms, long legs and a long neck, everything else kind of falls into place.": Diana Vreeland.
Diana Vreeland Bazaar Years: Why Don't You? by John Esten, Universe Publishing, 2001.

"The eye has to travel.": **Diana Vreeland**
Allure, by Diana Vreeland with Christopher Hemphill and Foreward by Marc Jacobs, Chronicle Books, San Francisco 1980, 13; also, *Diana Vreeland: The Eye Has To Travel,* by Lisa Immordino Vreeland, Abrams, New York.

"The bikini is the most important thing since the atom bomb. / These girls . . . If they've got long arms, long legs and a long neck, everything else kind of falls into place": Diana Vreeland.
Source, unknown.

"Red is the great clarifier – bright, cleansing, and revealing. It makes all colors beautiful. I can't imagine becoming bored with red – it would be like becoming bored with the person you love.": Diana Vreeland.

Diana Vreeland: The Eye Has To Travel, by Lisa Immordino Vreeland, Abrams, New York, 47.

"Oh, I know how to handle these boys. You just get tougher than they are.": Diana Vreeland.
Source, unknown.

"'What is the name of that designer who hates me so?' 'Legion,' was the response.": Diana Vreeland.
Diana Vreeland: The Eye Has To Travel, by Lisa Immordino Vreeland, Abrams, New York, 33.

"'The next morning, they found the Peruvian army waiting, absolutely furious, and pointing to the ground. It was covered with mountain lion tracks.'": Model, Mirabella.
Source, unknown.

". . . I got the full effect of her freshness. Her brain was ticking over with extraordinary quickness and clarity. She was in a rare confidential mood and . . . even has ideas of coming to England to live, and asked me to find out how much it cost me to keep the London house.": Cecil Beaton.
The Unexpurgated Beaton: The Cecil Beaton Diaries As He Wrote Them, 1970-1980, Introduction by Hugo Vickers, Alfred A. Knopf, 2002, 200.

"Looking in the mirror is all right by me. I loathe narcissism, but I approve of vanity.": Diana Vreeland.
Allure, by Diana Vreeland with Christopher Hemphill and Forward by Marc Jacobs, Chronicle Books, San Francisco 1980, 56.

". . . she asked me to find a picture of Maria Callas she remembered clipping from an Italian paparazzi magazine . . . 'If eyes were bullets,' she said, . . . everyone in sight would be dead.'" : Christopher Hemphill.
Allure, by Diana Vreeland with Christopher Hemphill and Forward by Marc Jacobs, Chronicle Books, San Francisco 1980.

Karen Hagestad Cacy

"Once, during a rare conversational lapse, the (tape) machine turned itself off loudly . . . 'Poor little thing,' Mrs. Vreeland said sympathetically, 'it has a mind of its own – it gets bored. We mustn't let the splash drop! We must be amusing all the time!'": Christopher Hemphill.
Allure, by Diana Vreeland with Christopher Hemphill and Forward by Marc Jacobs, Chronicle Books, San Francisco 1980, 9.

Chapter Seven
Robert Maxwell

"Maxwell's empire was growing into one of the most powerful crime syndicates in the world, embracing the Russian Mafia, the crime families of Bulgaria, in NY and crime families of Japan and Hong Kong. One could say Maxwell was creating a global criminal network. He was a robber of the first order, setting in motion a chillingly effective structure of global criminals.": Gordon Thomas and Martin Dillon.
Robert Maxwell, Israel's Superspy: The Life and Murder of a Media Mogul, by Gordon Thomas and Martin Dillon, Carroll and Graf Publishers, 2002.

"During the war we had a whole routine going. I write jingles sometimes, and one day we were sitting in the Russian Tea Room and he said, 'Let us write the Russian Tea Roomba. I'll write the music and we'll make a lot of money for the company.' I loved that. We had fun.":
Ruthanna Boris.
Balanchine's Ballerinas: Conversations with the Muses, by Robert Tracy with Sharon DeLano, Linden Press/Simon & Schuster, 1983.

"To help keep it together, 'Balachivadze' played piano for silent films, and worked as a messenger boy and saddler's

assistant working for scraps of food. He walked miles to find peasants in the country with whom he could trade the salt he had saved for potatoes. ": Robert Gottlieb.
The Ballet Maker: George Balanchine, by Robert Gottlieb, Harper Perennial/Eminent Lives, 2004, 19.

"In that time, 'Balachivadze' even stole from government supplies. Had he been caught, he could have been executed. Cats were regularly caught, strangled and cooked. He recalled that "sometimes we were given horse feed." Horses dropped dead in the streets. Sometimes in the night people with knives took whatever they could. He remembered that at the time he had 30 boils.": Robert Gottlieb.
The Ballet Maker: George Balanchine, by Robert Gottlieb, Harper Perennial/Eminent Lives, 2004, 19.

"You know, I am really a dead man. I was supposed to die and I didn't, and so now everything I do is second chance.": George Balanchine.
The Ballet Maker: George Balanchine, by Robert Gottlieb, Harper Perennial/Eminent Lives, 2004, 58.

Karen Hagestad Cacy

Chapter Eight
Cecil Beaton

"Cecil really could call up anyone in the world. He couldn't call up royalty – they don't take telephone calls – but they'd call him. Everyone wanted to meet this extraordinary character and be photographed by him.":
Diana Vreeland.
Allure, by Diana Vreeland with Christopher Hemphill and Forward by Marc Jacobs, Chronicle Books, San Francisco 1980 116-117.

"I was only nineteen and I was so brilliant, so brilliant in those days!": Truman Capote
Source, unknown.

"Yesterday morning, Truman told me so many dreadful things about everybody. It's wonderful how Truman acquired (sic) bits of information and then passes them off as his own.": Leo Lerman.
The Grand Surprise: The Journals of Leo Lerman, Stephen Pascal, Alfred A. Knopf, 2007, 43, diary entry: March 11, 1947.

"Truman would describe everybody – Babe Paley, Slim Keith, Phyllis Cerf, Gloria – everything. He talked about the differences in the various social strata of that special New York City, where and how people were placed, who were the most elite and the richest, where they stood as hostesses, and how New York was really run.": Carol Matthau.
Among the Porcupines, A Memoir, Ballantine Books, 1992, 131.

Chapter Nine
Truman Capote

"I first met Truman at a cocktail party . . . he was sitting on a love seat with two or three other people, all facing different directions and talking. He was very quick – as I entered he looked up and said to the person sitting beside him, 'Yes, Paul Bowles is a very good writer.' They weren't talking about me at all, but he said it in such a way that I could hear. He was a consummate actor. He wrote all his roles and acted them out.": Paul Bowles.
Truman Capote: In Which Various Friends, Enemies, Acquaintances, and Detractors Recall His Turbulent Career, by George Plimpton, Doubleday, Anchor Books edition published by arrangement with Nan A. Talese/Doubleday, 1997, 237.

" . . . the young man's career 'was like a carefully planned military campaign.'": Cecil Beaton.

"Always write about what you know about. Don't write a book about how to care for your poodle. You don't have a poodle.": Truman Capote.

"We became friends immediately . . . His particular charm was an endless, non-explanation of anything.": Diana Vreeland.
Truman Capote: In Which Various Friends, Enemies, Acquaintances, and Detractors Recall His Turbulent Career, by George Plimpton, Doubleday, Anchor Books edition published by arrangement with Nan A. Talese/Doubleday, 1997, 47.

"Truman's eclectic treasures somehow remind you of the contents of a very astute little boy's pockets . . . (Truman was a) *"manipulative court jester . . . With his wit, shit-stirring and conniving ways, he was able to twist rich people around his finger. It was very important to him to feel that people preferred him to their husbands, wives or children. And quite often they did. They'd choose Truman*

Karen Hagestad Cacy

because he was so beguiling and then they'd become addicted to him.": John Richardson.

Truman Capote: In Which Various Friends, Enemies, Acquaintances, and Detractors Recall His Turbulent Career, by George Plimpton, Doubleday, Anchor Books edition published by arrangement with Nan A. Talese/Doubleday, 1997, 153.

"I immediately fell for him – it didn't take me five minutes to be won over completely as he did with everyone I ever saw him encounter. He had a charm that was ineffable. He exerted this charm freely.": John Huston

Truman Capote: In Which Various Friends, Enemies, Acquaintances, and Detractors Recall His Turbulent Career, by George Plimpton, Doubleday, Anchor Books edition published by arrangement with Nan A. Talese/Doubleday, 1997, 125.

"He would call someone on the phone: 'Beauty? Gorgeous? Adorable One? This is Troo-man. Do you want to have lunch?' He always came rehearsed. Someone who knew him said he would never just have lunch with you, he'd lined up things to tell you. He came loaded for bear. Always. Always had storied about who had had the latest shots at that clinic in Switzerland, or some scandalous gossip about some cardinal of the Catholic Church."
Source Unknown.

"He confided to Beaton that the only time he felt calm was when he took impromptu road trips in his beloved green Jaguar. Driving soothed him, as did motels, where he enjoyed sinking into a warm bathtub with a glass of scotch and a few sleeping pills."
Source Unknown.

"Truman was inspired to use the word 'swan' by . . . a nineteenth-century journal by Patrick Conway, who wrote that he had seen 'a gathering of swans, an aloof armada . . . their feathers floating away over the water like

the trailing hems of snowy ball-gowns' and was reminded of beautiful women.": Patrick Conway.
Source, unknown.

"My dear, women always have problems. Just tough it out. Consider yourself a very expensive personal secretary. Executive secretary. Just hang in there and take all the perks, go to all the parties, buy all the clothes, enjoy your life.": Truman Capote
Source, unknown.

"Always from the time I knew him . . .he was fascinated by society. When he was in Greenwich he knew people who were terribly boring, but he was interested in their houses and the way they lived. He was always fascinated by the intricacies of society.": Diana Vreeland.
Truman Capote: In Which Various Friends, Enemies, Acquaintances, and Detractors Recall His Turbulent Career, by George Plimpton, Doubleday, Anchor Books edition published by arrangement with Nan A. Talese/Doubleday, 1997, 29.

"The real difference between rich and regular people is that the rich serve such marvelous vegetables. Little fresh born things, scarcely out of the earth. Little baby corn, little baby peas.": Truman Capote
Source, unknown.

Plimpton, op.cit., 148.

"His friend, John Huston, once told him he was the only male he'd ever seen attired in a velvet suit."
Source, unknown.

" . . . Truman Capote and Babe Paley reportedly used to discuss moisturizers in Talmudic detail.": Christopher Buckley.
Losing Mum and Pup, by Christopher Buckley, Twelve: Hatchett Book Group, 2009, 67.

Karen Hagestad Cacy

Chapter Ten
Pat Buckley

"The mind boggles!"/ "I simply don't understand why the President just doesn't pass the bloody bill himself."/"Well, if you ask me, it's all too ridiculous for words."/"That woman is so stupid she ought to be caged."/"It is of an imbecility not to be credited.": Christopher Buckley.
Losing Mum and Pup, Twelve: Hatchett Book Group, 2009.

"Her author son, Christopher Buckley, lovingly described his mother's entrances to gatherings as being 'in full prevarication.'": **Christopher Buckley.**
Source, unknown.

"I'm just an Arab wife. When Bill says, 'Strike the tent,' I do.": Pat Buckley.
Losing Mum and Pup, by Christopher Buckley, Twelve: Hatchett Book Group, 2009, 147.

Bill Buckley traveled to her hometown of Vancouver, British Columbia to ask for her hand in marriage, Pat instructed him to wait downstairs in the foyer. Pat scrambled up the stairs and excitedly informed her mother of the purpose of their visit. Buckley overheard the entire conversation, at the conclusion of which could be heard the sounds of extended hysterical laughter. It seems the young Canadian socialite regularly brought young men home with the same story.: **Christopher Buckley.**
Source, unknown.

"If he comes through this thing alive, I'll kill him!": Pat Buckley.
"Airborne: A Sentimental Journey," by William F. Buckley, Jr., Little, Brown and Company, 1970, xiii.

"When Mum was in full prevarication, Pup would assume an expression somewhere between a Jack Benny stare and

the stoic grimace of a 13th-century saint being burned at the stake. He knew very well that King George VI and Queen Elizabeth did not routinely decamp at Shannon . . . Her fluent mendacity, combined with adamantine confidence, made her really indomitable. . . . She was really, really good at it. She would have made a fantastic spy. . . She was beautiful, theatrical, bright as a diamond, the wittiest woman I have ever known . . .": Christopher Buckley. *Losing Mum and Pup,* Twelve: Hatchett Book Group, 2009.

"My wife and Bill were fond of each other and enjoyed making each other laugh. . . In her omnivorous reading she had downed a heavy tome on Catholicism, and she asked him to clarify some abstruse point about Saint Paul and the founding of the church that seemed to her somehow self-contradictory. 'Well, the theological question becomes . . .' he began, but he seemed to get stuck. He backed up and started a whole new sentence and came up short again. Before he could start a third, his amused spouse said, 'Bill, you always like to try new things. Why not admit you don't know the answer?'": Dick Cavett. "Dick Cavett: Talk Show, by Dick Cavett, St. Martin's Griffin, 2010, 113.

"Now social lies are something else again. I don't mind if you say 'I can't dine tonight because I have a business dinner.' That's almost conventional, isn't it? I once had a marvelous Irish temporary maid whom I was absolutely impossible to. I made her tell lies – social lies – on the telephone by the hour. 'Madame has not returned from lunch . . .' 'Madam is taking a nap and cannot be disturbed . . .' And if I really didn't want to talk to someone, 'Madam is out of town.' After six months, she finally left me. And as she was walking out the door, she said, 'Goodbye, madam. And now I'm going straight.'": Diana Vreeland . *D.V.,* by Diana Vreeland, Edited by George Plimpton and Christopher Hemphill, Alfred A. Knopf, 1984, 159.

"The best raspberries, too, are the black ones, and they should be tiny – the tinier and the blacker, the better! Strawberries should be very big and should have very long stems attached so that you can pull them out easily. Yvonne, my maid, used to choose
them individually for me at Fraser-Morris. Very splendid. God knows what they cost nowadays. Once I asked how much they were apiece. Yvonne was shocked. 'Ask, Madame?' she said. 'Listen, Yvonne!' I said. Everybody asks. 'But madame . . .' So you mean to tell me, Yvonne, I said, that you'd walk into Harry Winston's to buy a tiara, and not ask? One asks! Truth is a hell of a big point with me!":*
Diana Vreeland.
D.V., by Diana Vreeland, Edited by George Plimpton and Christopher Hemphill, Alfred A. Knopf, 1984, 157.

"I think the greatest rogues are they who talk most of their honesty.": Anthony Trollope, nineteenth century novelist.

"He was very amusing. If you had him for dinner, an evening of talk, he had these glasses he'd bring along: a clear pair, a slightly shaded pair, and a really dark pair. It was quite apparent that he couldn't lie properly unless his eyes were covered. So he would change glasses. When they were really dark, you knew a huge exaggeration, a lie was coming. We called them the 'shades of truth.' The Dupont's have a house over there on Fishers Island, and when they gave a lunch, they sent over this massive boat for Truman. He was very pleased with himself. When he came back he said that 'there were one hundred for an outdoor lunch.' (Medium-shaded glasses.) 'there had been a young girl there, in her teens. Hundreds of gulls – it was the mating season – were circling around the dock. As lunch went on, this girl was dying to go down to the dock and look at the gulls. Everyone said, No, don't. They're very vicious at this time of year.' (Darker glasses.) 'Finally, she went with an umbrella to watch them, On the docks, the umbrella collapsed in the wind and the gulls tried to

Karen Hagestad Cacy

peck her eyes out.'   (Darkest, darkest shades.)": David Jackson.

Truman Capote: In Which Various Friends, Enemies, Acquaintances, and Detractors Recall His Turbulent Career, by George Plimpton, Doubleday, Anchor Books edition published by arrangement with Nan A. Talese/Doubleday, 1997. 142.

"And Bill said to me, 'Ducky, you look absolutely gorgeous. Where's the rest of the dress?' It was up to the kazoo!": Pat Buckley.

Losing Mum and Pup, by Christopher Buckley, Twelve: Hatchett Book Group, 2009, 205.

"She had very bad taste, but she was adorable.": English decorator, Keith Irvine.
Source, unknown.

"These ladies, Pat Buckley, Nan Kempner, and CZ Guest, were really comfortable in their own skin and that extended to their décor."   (Her style was) *"high camp boudoir."*: Decorator Todd Romano.
Source, unknown

"Even when Pup was despairing of her behavior ---as he did only occasionally – and sought refuge on the lecture circuit, or wherever, he would call her every night, trying reconciliation with, 'Hi, Duck.' 'Duck' was the formal, vous version of 'Ducky,' their term of affection for each other.": Christopher Buckley.

The New York Times Magazine, April 26, 2009, *"Growing Up the Only Child of Two Charismatic – and Complicated – Buckley's,"* by Christopher Buckley, 28.

Karen Hagestad Cacy

Chapter Eleven
"Piggy Bird"

"You must present foot to floor. /You get your heel forward so you could hold a martini on it./Do not step on bent knee, step on straight knee.": George Balanchine.
Source, unknown.

"One day she'd shown up with a bandage across her small nose. 'What happened?' he asked. Another dancer answered for her. 'She kicked herself.'"
Source, unknown.

"Life is so unlike theory.": Anthony Trollope, nineteenth century novelist.

"Tanaquil loved to dance, and I would dream that she was on stage and that I was excited about her dancing and was congratulating her. She had been so special. It was a tremendous loss to the company, to the shape of the company. I had been struck by her from the very beginning . . . We shared a dressing room, and I thought she was so intelligent, so sensitive, and talented. She had a real feeling of drama about her body, and ballets she felt comfortable in made her glow / "We pulled together very strongly when she got sick and Balanchine left to take care of her. I think most of us felt as if a parent had gone away for a long time. But we knew he would come home.": **Melissa Hayden.**
Source, unknown.

Hayden said, "We pulled together very strongly when she got sick and Balanchine left to take care of her. I think most of us felt as if a parent had gone away for a long time. But we knew he would come home.": **Melissa Hayden.**
Source, unknown.

Karen Hagestad Cacy

"Never angry in class or rehearsal, his soft voice would repeat what he wanted them to do. Sometimes he would need to repeat himself several times before a dancer got it. It was common for dancers to say it was because of Balanchine's quiet determination that they had the courage to attempt the near impossible."
Source, unknown.

"I make some steps for my friends. They are nice. Sometimes it's all right. But I will tell you what you have to do." (to be a good choreographer.) *"You have to be a very good dancer yourself. I didn't say famous, I said, good. You have to know how dancers feel. You will never know unless you have done it. Then you have to know music very well. Then you have to look everywhere, everything, all the time. Look at the grass in the concrete when it's broken, children and little dogs, and the ceiling and the roof. Your eye is camera and your brain is a file cabinet.":* **George Balanchine.**
Source, unknown.

"There were real water, cascading fountains, and huge shipwrecks . . . At the Imperial Theater, everything grand was possible because of the Imperial Treasury and the Tsar's commitment to the theater. Soldiers labored below stage to create stage miracles, and cheap labor was readily available, as was a vast children's corps de ballet.": **George Balanchine.**
Source, unknown.

"At the Imperial Theater, everything grand was possible because of the Imperial Treasury and the Tsar's commitment to the theater. Soldiers labored below stage to create stage miracles, and cheap labor was readily available, as was a vast children's corps de ballet.": George Balanchine.
Source, unknown.

Karen Hagestad Cacy

"I go to church but nobody knows.": George Balanchine.
Source, unknown.

"You know, those men in Tibet up in the Mountains. They sit nude in the cave and they drink only water through straw and they think very pure thoughts/You know, that is what I should become. I would be with them/But, unfortunately, I like butterflies.": George Balanchine.
Source, unknown.

"When my father died, we were sitting having coffee. And it was a bright, sunny day. Balanchine said 'You see, Tamartchka, Papa is not gone. The sun shines. He is here with you.'": Tamara Toumanova.
Source, unknown.

"Must believe. Must believe.": George Balanchine.
Source, unknown.

"I could never tell you how Balanchine creates; it would be like trying to hold running water/He had a sense of humor, and there was a feeling of camaraderie at rehearsals/In Balanchine's work the individuality of a dancer always comes into play.": Mary Ellen Moylan.
Balanchine's Ballerinas: Conversations with the Muses, by Robert Tracy with Sharon DeLano, Linden Press/Simon & Schuster, 1983.

Chapter Twelve
Pamela Churchill

"Everyone always talks about the rich men I have slept with, no one ever talks about the poor men I have slept with.": Pamela Churchill
Life of the Party: The Biography of Pamela Digby Churchill Hayward Harriman, by Christopher Ogden, Little, Brown & Company, 1994, 250.

You know when I was a student, Balanchine gave me some advice, He said, 'Don't ever get fat and don't ever get married.' /He would rather have his girls on stage than in the kitchen or nursery.": Mary Ellen Moylan.
Balanchine's Ballerinas: Conversations with the Muses, by Robert Tracy with Sharon DeLano, Linden Press/Simon & Schuster, 1983.

Chapter Thirteen
The Duchess of Windsor

The couple's one-time friend, Jimmy Donahue, heir to the Woolworth fortune, used to embarrass the footmen by making loud remarks about their genitals.
Source, unknown.

"We'll never be invited again to the Duke and Duchess of Windsor's soirees. And Thank God, he said fervently. Rarely have I been so stupendously bored.": Richard Burton.
The Richard Burton Diaries, edited by Chris Williams, Yale University Press, 2012, 223.

"Cafe society in Paris is downright trashy, a weird collection of social derelicts.": Cecil Beaton.
The Windsor Story, by J. Bryan III and Charles J.V. Murphy, William Morrow & Company, Inc., 1979, 576.

Karen Hagestad Cacy

"It is extraordinary how small the Duke and Duchess are. Two tiny figures like Toto and Nanette that you keep on the mantelpiece. Chipped around the edges. Something you keep in the front room for Sundays only. Marred Royalty.": Richard Burton.
The Richard Burton Diaries, edited by Chris Williams, Yale University Press, 2012.

"Her mouth was too big, her nose was too long, and her clenched teeth grin was almost grotesque. But her eyes and her hair were nice; so was her voice also. Her figure was trim though too thin to be exciting. She shone at parties – always full of vitality. She could dance up a storm and match drinks with anybody. She would hold forth to a group of people."
Source, unknown.

"What is the difference between a night on the beach at Coney Island and a night on the beach in Hollywood? Answer: At Coney, the girls lie on the beach and look at the stars. In Hollywood, the stars lie on the girls and look at the beach.": Duchess of Windsor.
Source, unknown.

"She played poker hard: One poker night we had a big pot going and Wallis suddenly jumped up and knocked the table over, and all the cards and chips fell on the floor. She said a cat had startled her by rubbing against her leg, but I think she saw she was going to lose the pot. As somebody said, 'She saw the kitty but not the cat.'"
Source, unknown.

"She was an awful little flirt."
Source, unknown.

"There's never been a blue like the blue of the Duke of Windsor's eyes. When I'd walk into the house in Neuilly, he'd be standing at the end of the hall. He always received

Karen Hagestad Cacy

you himself, which was terribly attractive, and he always had something funny and friendly to say to you while you disposed of your coat. But I'd see him standing there, and even in the light of the hall, which was quite dim, I could see that blue. It comes from being at sea. Sailors have it. I suppose it's in the family --- Queen Mary had it too, But he had an aura of blue around him. I mean what I say –it was an azure aura surrounding the face. Even in a black and white picture you can feel it.": Diana Vreeland.
D.V., by Diana Vreeland, Edited by George Plimpton and Christopher Hemphill, Alfred A. Knopf, 1984, 104-105.

"Edward! Who'll want to read about a boyhood as dull as yours? It's a waste of time!": Duchess of Windsor.
Source, unknown.

" . . . 'filthy French?'": The Duke of Windsor.
Source, unknown.

"The Eiffel Tower is huge and hideous; the French are gluttons; a certain French painting of a British naval review is frightful; the curator of a museum in the Marais is a senile idiot; Gerard Marais came to dinner and proved to be a bounder; a celebrated photographer talks nonsense; the Jardin d'Acclimation is a wretched sort of zoo.": Duke of Windsor, in his personal diary.
The Windsor Story, by J. Bryan III and Charles J.V. Murphy, William Morrow & Company, Inc., 1979, 571.

'Monster of Glamis.'": Duke of Windsor
Source, unknown.

(Truman) plans to start a 'Just Ducky' restaurant and serve duck-burgers, duck soup and duck dessert/he'd be the 'Go-Go Girl' in the Tar-Baby bar there: Cecil Beaton.
Source, unknown.

Karen Hagestad Cacy

(The Marquess of Bath) went through the whole war with a duck on a lead, praying for bombs to fall so that his duck would have a pond to swim in. He always had that duck, looking to the sky, both of them, and if they heard the crunch of a nearby bomb, the two would set off on the dead run to see if the bomb crater would fill up with water so the duck could swim.": Diana Vreeland.
D.V., by Diana Vreeland, Edited by George Plimpton and Christopher Hemphill, Alfred A. Knopf, 1984, 99.

"Pamela Churchill.   The queen of dinner parties and marrying well."
Source, unknown.

"George Balanchine is the man above all others in the world who can make those impressions and images visible. Like a diver, he plunges into the dark depths of music and comes back quietly with a pearl.": Richard Buckle.
Balanchine's Ballerinas: Conversations with the Muses, by Robert Tracy with Sharon DeLano, Linden Press/Simon & Schuster, 1983.

Chapter Fourteen
Arrivals

"Did you know I'm always having the most extraordinary conversations with taxicab drivers? They have views, I can tell you, on everything!": Diana Vreeland.
D.V., by Diana Vreeland, Edited by George Plimpton and Christopher Hemphill, Alfred A. Knopf, 1984, 141.

"My God, Rene, taxis are expensive! I should take a bus like the rest of the world. You can't picture it? Neither can my grandchildren. They tell a story about me: Nonnina – that's what they call me; it's Italian for 'little grandmother' – Nonnina took a bus with Grandpa once, and you know what

she said to him? 'Oh, look!   There are people here!'": Diana Vreeland
D.V., by Diana Vreeland, Edited by George Plimpton and Christopher Hemphill, Alfred A. Knopf, 1984, 88.

"Mrs. Vreeland speaks one-third of the time like a gangster, one-third of the time like the head of a multinational corporation. . . and the rest of the time like an emigre from one of the French-speaking pixie kingdoms.": Jonathan Lieberson ("*Empress of Fashion: Diana Vreeland,*" *Interview,* December 1980, 22.)
Diana Vreeland: The Eye Has To Travel, by Lisa Immordino Vreeland, Abrams, New York, 11.

"I had one foot in the door of a cab, the cab started to go and I was thrown back on my head and dragged along the ground . . .   And then the driver saw me, stopped the cab, and looked at me on the ground. 'Oh My God, what have I done?' he said. You started to move and I wasn't in the car. Why did you move? 'I have no idea.' Now listen, there is a mirror, but never mind. No bones are broken. No one's hurt. Let's get on with it.' So I got in the cab and the driver said to me, 'Lady I've got to tell you something, this is my first night out in the cab and you are the first person I've driven.' You've got to begin somewhere. Never look back, boy! Never look back. But still, you've got to look in the mirror to see if the person's in the car!'": Diana Vreeland.
D.V., by Diana Vreeland, Edited by George Plimpton and Christopher Hemphill, Alfred A. Knopf, 1984, 193.

"The year must have been 1930, because I remember Reed was here in New York on business that year and I was home alone in London. One night a friend was going to take me to dinner and to a movie at a divine movie house on Curzon Street where you called up to reserve tickets and where everybody knew everybody – it was rather chic to go, but it was important to be on time.   My friend was to pick me up at precisely eight o'clock.   Eight o'clock arrived.

Karen Hagestad Cacy

Then, eight-fifteen. I was standing in front of the fire downstairs, wondering. I couldn't believe it, because my friend was always extremely prompt, as all Englishmen were in those days. At ten minutes to nine, in walked a man who hadn't shaved since morning, whose tie was askew, whose collar was rumpled. You simply didn't see men like that at ten to nine in the evening in London. . . . he'd be clean as a whistle – and on time. 'Diana,' he said, 'I have just lived through the most terrible day of my life. At nine o'clock this morning, I was called to Buckingham Palace to meet the King and the Prince of Wales. I sat in the room with them, lunch was served, a bottle of wine was passed . . . we made conversation – stiffly. The man who was telling me. . . Fruity Metcalfe . . . was the Prince of Wales's aide-de-camp. You see he was invited to lunch with King George and the Prince as a sort of buffer. And Fruity told me that the Prince looked his father, the King, 'straight in the eye' and told him that never, under any circumstances, would he succeed him. Mrs. Simpson was not yet on the scene!": Diana Vreeland.
Diana Vreeland, Edited by George Plimpton and Christopher Hemphill, Alfred A. Knopf, 1984, 70-71.

"Now I think it's something around you like a perfume or like a scent. It's like memory . . . it pervades.": Diana Vreeland to Christopher Hemphill.
Allure, by Diana Vreeland with Christopher Hemphill and Forward by Marc Jacobs, Chronicle Books, San Francisco 1980, 11.

Karen Hagestad Cacy

Chapter Fifteen
Upstairs/Downstairs

"There's nothing wrong with your tie! For heaven's sake, let it alone.": Duchess of Windsor.
The Windsor Story, by J. Bryan III and Charles J.V. Murphy, William Morrow & Company, Inc., 1979, 548.

The Duke was fussy about trifles like the pudding knot of his tie and the set of the flower in his buttonhole. He tugged at the knot again and again. Tonight, he wore a Scottish plaid of the Black Watch – black and green kilts and a sort of white shirt – very smart.
Source, unknown.

" . . . the Duke's face is rather wizened, his teeth, yellow and crooked, and his gold hair is becoming rather parched./His face now begins to show the emptiness of life. It is too impertinent to be tragic . . . He looks like a mad terrier, haunted one moment, then with a flick of the hand is laughing fecklessly.": Cecil Beaton.
The Unexpurgated Beaton: The Cecil Beaton Diaries As He Wrote Them, 1970-1980, Introduction by Hugo Vickers, Alfred A. Knopf, 2002.

"that fat Scotch cook/ Loch Ness monster/fourteen carat beauty": Duke and Duchess of Windsor.
Source, unknown.

"Peaches!": The Duke of Windsor's pet name for the Duchess.

"The Duke's self-imposed rule was that he never took a drink before seven in the evening.": Hugo Vickers.
The Private World of the Duke and Duchess of Windsor, by Hugo Vickers, Harrods Publishing, 1995, 220.

Karen Hagestad Cacy

Chapter Sixteen
The Procrastinators: Robert Maxwell

"To establish his position, Maxwell had chosen to arrive deliberately late, an old trick of his. His guests had been waiting almost an hour before his car swept to a halt in front of the red carpet last rolled out for the visit of the late Yuri Andropov.": Gordon Thomas and Martin Dillon.
Robert Maxwell, Israel's Superspy: The Life and Murder of a Media Mogul, by Gordon Thomas and Martin Dillon, Carroll and Graf Publishers, 2002, 159.

". . . the Macmillan deal meant he had access to the company's charitable trust. He used it to spend lavishly on events in New York, paying large sums of money, sometimes as much as $100,000, for a seat at charitable functions attended by people he wanted to impress." Ibid, 171.

"As the Renault swept out of the airport gates, Maxwell delivered a familiar order to the chauffeur. 'Mettez le feu!' . . . The beacon symbolized for Maxwell another sign of his own importance: in his mind's eye it placed him among the heads of state who regularly flew into Le Bourget." Ibid, 157.

Ibid, 32.

Ibid.

Ibid, 175.

Karen Hagestad Cacy

Chapter Seventeen
The Procrastinators: Marilyn Monroe

"I just wanted to show this fascinating woman with her guard down, at work, at ease off stage, during joyous moments in her life and as she often was – alone.": Sam Shaw, photographer.

"Marilyn Monroe! She was a geisha. She was born to give pleasure, spent her whole life giving it – and knew no other way.": Diana Vreeland.
Allure, by Diana Vreeland with Christopher Hemphill and Forward by Marc Jacobs, Chronicle Books, San Francisco 1980, 142.

"She was astoundingly beautiful, without the trace of a line or wrinkle on her beguiling face. What fascinated me most was her evident inability to remain motionless. Whereas people normally move their arms and head in conversation, these gestures in Marilyn Monroe were reflected throughout her body, producing a delicately undulating effect like the movement of an almost calm sea. It seemed clear to me that it was something of which she was not conscious; it was as natural as breathing, and in no way an affected 'wriggle,' as some writers have suggested.": Marilyn Monroe.
Margot Fonteyn: Autobiography, by Margot Fonteyn, Alfred A. Knopf, 1976, 154.

"If you knew Garbo, if you'd ever been to a Garbo dinner, meaning you're three or five at the most . . . but don't let me go grand on you. I'm only talking about the way she holds her mouth when she's talking to you. I can't say what it is she does. If I could say it, I could do it myself.": Diana Vreeland.

Karen Hagestad Cacy

Allure, by Diana Vreeland with Christopher Hemphill and Forward by Marc Jacobs, Chronicle Books, San Francisco 1980, 33.

"She (Marilyn Monroe) *was very directed, a self- improver. Lots of lists and to do's. She wanted to play Shakespeare – Juliet and Lady Macbeth. Wanted to create a new production company with Marlon Brando."*
Source, unknown.

"After dinner, we went into the bar to shoot craps. When Huston gave Marilyn the dice, she asked: 'What should I shoot for John?' His answer: 'Don't think, honey, just throw. That's the story of your life. Don't think – do it.'":
John Huston.
Source, unknown.

Chapter Eighteen
Pamela Churchill

"His wife was undergoing an extended period of mourning and off with her sister when Pam moved in. A friend close to the Rothschild family at the time observed that 'Pamela always seemed to move in on people when wives were off duty.'"
Life of the Party: The Biography of Pamela Digby Churchill Hayward Harriman, by Christopher Ogden, Little, Brown & Company, 1994, 233.

". . . she brings me my drink and keeps quiet.": Elie de Rothschild.
Life of the Party: The Biography of Pamela Digby Churchill Hayward Harriman, by Christopher Ogden, Little, Brown & Company, 1994, 237.
"One dinner at our house when Gianni was not there, she kind of held the floor. But later she seemed to change her

Karen Hagestad Cacy

style and listen a great deal more. / At her own apartment, Pamela introduced guests individually by taking them by the arm, escorting them quickly around the room, whispering the name of each guest in their ear. She was an extremely deft and gracious hostess. She was very discreet and very considerate of the men she was with.": Marian Shaw.
Life of the Party: The Biography of Pamela Digby Churchill Hayward Harriman, by Christopher Ogden, Little, Brown & Company, 1994, 249.

"When Pamela met a man she adored, she just unconsciously assumed his identity, as if she were putting on a glove." Leonora Hornblow.
Life of the Party: The Biography of Pamela Digby Churchill Hayward Harriman, by Christopher Ogden, Little, Brown & Company, 1994, 190.

"There was nothing covert about Agnelli's long-standing relationship with Pamela. She lived openly in one of his houses, served as hostess at his parties, and was the happy recipient of extravagant gifts of jewelry, designed clothing, and money. But Agnelli could not be faithful to one woman, even to his mistress."
Source, unknown.

"Entertaining Pamela was expected when she crossed the Atlantic. After all, no one was a more hospitable host than she when American friends visited Paris. But Babe Paley did not like Pamela, whom she called 'that bitch,' and was not enthusiastic about this visit. Barbara Cushing Paley was Betsey Cushing Whitney's sister. Both Cushing girls were wary of a Pamela Churchill on the prowl, given her history with their husbands, Bill Paley and Jock Whitney, and their fears that she was coming around for another try. . . . That did not mean that they avoided each other; simply that everyone was careful.": Babe Paley.
Life of the Party: The Biography of Pamela Digby Churchill Hayward Harriman, by Christopher Ogden, Little, Brown & Company, 1994, 265.

Karen Hagestad Cacy

Chapter Nineteen
Cocktails at Eight. Dinner at Nine.

"His Russian Easter party was always the main festivity of the year. His Russian friends would gather at the apartment to dine right after midnight services. The next day another party would be held for Americans, non-Orthodox, and other friends. For these Easter celebrations he always prepared his most lavish board – roasts, ptarmigans, fish in aspic, specially prepared horseradish and garnishes, Salade Oliviere, and, of course, the traditional pascha and kulitch, which contain all the rich ingredients and exotic tastes one dreams of during Lent: sweet butter by the pound, mounds of sugar, vanilla beans, saffron, cardamom, pressed almonds, raisins."
Balanchine: A Biography, by Bernard Taper, Times Books, 1984, 243.

(The Duchess of Windsor's Ball) *"They then descended to the hotel where 1200 of NY's most glittering members of the Social Register waited. When the last guest arrived, the butler notified the Duchess in her room. She then appeared at the top of the stairs, like a queen, always exquisitely dressed. The stair case was lined with hundreds of orchids. The guests below nibbled on five pounds of caviar."*
Source, unknown.

George Balanchine's Recipe for Blini Hors d'Oeuvres.
Source, unknown.

"The Maison VEUVE AMBAL was founded in the heart of the Burgundy wine growing region. The estates are located in four different wine-growing regions and this diversity gives the rich and complex aromas that can be found in the Maison's wines. In fact, VEUVE AMBAL's Cremont de Bourgogne uses the special features of each Burgundy

wine-growing region like a painter uses a large palette of colors to enhance the qualities of his work.": Web Site VEUVE AMBAL Le Pre Neuf, 21200 Montagny, Le Beaune, France.

Chapter Twenty
Ten for Dinner

"By 1947, the duke was drinking heavily. The duke drank only gin; the duchess took only a Dubonnet or one of those nasty weak Vermouth tasting things."
Source, unknown.

Chapter Twenty-One
Blinis

"So, Jimmy said to his chauffeur, 'Where are we?' And the chauffeur responded, 'Lexington Avenue, Mr. James.' And Jimmy ordered him, 'Take me over to Fifth where I belong.'"
The Windsor Story, by J. Bryan III and Charles J.V. Murphy, William Morrow & Company, Inc., 1979, 499.

"As a gossiper, he had the fascination of a candied tarantula."
Source, unknown.

"Donahue walked into Cerutti's, that gay bar on Madison Avenue."
"The Duchess of Windsor: The Secret Life," by Charles Higham, McGraw-Hill Book Company, 1988, 371.

"All literature is gossip.'
Source, unknown.

Karen Hagestad Cacy

"Life is nothing more than a moderately good play with a badly written third act.": Truman Capote.
Source, unknown.

"So, Donahue took a number of sailors, soldiers, and marines to a party at his mother's apartment over on Fifth Avenue. They stripped one of the GI's, and began shaving off his body hair. They were using an old-fashioned open razor . . . Then Jimmy castrated the soldier. Everyone became hysterical, and the man was thrown into Jimmy's car, driven to the 59th Street Bridge, and tossed onto the sidewalk. Donahue was arrested but released when Mrs. Donahue paid the poor man, I hear, a quarter million dollars, to drop the charges." Truman Capote.
"The Duchess of Windsor: The Secret Life," by Charles Higham, McGraw-Hill Book Company, 1988, 371.

"The [William] Buckley's gave a celebration of Estee Lauder at Mortimer's, and all the gratin was in gushing attendance.": Leo Lerman.
The Grand Surprise: The Journals of Leo Lerman, Stephen Pascal, Alfred A. Knopf, 2007, 554, diary entry: October 14, 1985.

"The couple made no attempt to understand the French. Indeed they didn't like them. An American woman arriving in a storm at their Paris home complained, 'What a storm. This country of yours . . .' 'This is not my country!' the Duke snapped.": The Duke of Windsor.
The Windsor Story, by J. Bryan III and Charles J.V. Murphy, William Morrow & Company, Inc., 1979, 571.

"Unlike Wallis Warfield, Edward Albert Christian George Andrew Patrick David, the future King Edward VIII, had never known anything but the material security that goes with wealth and birth at the top. He was named Edward for his paternal grandfather, soon to become King Edward VII, and for the six King Edwards who had preceded him.

Karen Hagestad Cacy

Though Edward was the Prince's formal, official name, the name he signed, he was David to his family and intimate friends."
The Windsor Story, by J. Bryan III and Charles J.V. Murphy, William Morrow & Company, Inc., 1979, 55.

"Perhaps some of you would prefer smoked salmon. Two hands. Good. Waiter, two caviars, two smoked salmon. I recommend a melon next.' Those delicious little Charentais melons were in season. Then he moved to the entree: 'I recommend a double mutton chop, with souffle potatoes and fresh asparagus.'": The Duke of Windsor.
The Windsor Story, by J. Bryan III and Charles J.V. Murphy, William Morrow & Company, Inc., 1979, 575.

"Lettuce is divine, although I'm not sure it's really food. The consommé at Maxim's! That, to me, was food. It had every bone from every animal, every vegetable . . . it's the best nourishment in the world . . . Toast should be brown and black. Asparagus should be sexy and almost fluid . . . alligator pears can never be ripe enough – they should be black. What you throw in the garbage can, I eat!": Diana Vreeland.
D.V., by Diana Vreeland, Edited by George Plimpton and Christopher Hemphill, Alfred A. Knopf, 1984, 157.

""Cecil was a man of great elegance. Through vanity, he always ordered his clothes a size smaller than he required because it looked better."
The Unexpurgated Beaton: The Cecil Beaton Diaries As He Wrote Them, 1970-1980, Introduction by Hugo Vickers, Alfred A. Knopf, 2002, 7.

""He had been an outsider when young, and he thus developed the facility to observe, first with nose pressed up against the glass, and then from within."

The Unexpurgated Beaton: The Cecil Beaton Diaries As He Wrote Them, 1970-1980, Introduction by Hugo Vickers, Alfred A. Knopf, 2002, 8.

Chapter Twenty-Two
"Norma Jean"

"I am invariably late for appointments – sometimes as much as two hours. I've tried to change my ways but the things that make me late are too strong and too pleasing.": Marilyn Monroe.
Source, unknown.

"I arrived late, but I hope I have made up for it by staying for so long.": Pauline Rothschild, quoted by Cecil Beaton.
The Unexpurgated Beaton: The Cecil Beaton Diaries As He Wrote Them, 1970-1980, Introduction by Hugo Vickers, Alfred A. Knopf, 2002, 281.

"A sex symbol becomes a thing; I just hate to be a thing.":
Marilyn Monroe.
Source, unknown.

"As Marilyn made her entrance, a vision in white, she was approached from the opposite end of the shop by her arch-imitator Jayne Mansfield. As they passed, each stared fascinated at the other, then seemed to slither past – and one could imagine two sinuous snakes taking stock of each other. There were no darting tongues, but one imagined them.": Eve Arnold.
Marilyn Monroe, by Eve Arnold, Alfred A Knopf, 1987, 46.

"I've been on a calendar, but I've never been on time.":
Marilyn Monroe.
Source, unknown.

Karen Hagestad Cacy

"Goodbye, Norma Jean, Though I never knew you at all . . . And it seems to me you lived your life like a candle in the wind, Never knowing who to cling to when the rain set in . . ." : Elton John

Excerpt from a song at the funeral of Marilyn Monroe, composed and sung by Elton John.

"I saw her bodily – Marilyn – for the first time and I was struck as by an apparition in a fairy tale. Well, she's beautiful – anybody can notice this, and she represents a certain myth of what we call in France 'la femme eternelle.' On the other hand, there's something extremely alert and vivid in her, an intelligence. It's her personality, its a glance, it's something very tenuous, very vivid, that disappears quickly, that appears again. You see, it's all these elements of her beauty and also her intelligence . . . last night I had the pleasure of having dinner next to her and I saw that these things came fluidly all the time . . . all these amusing remarks, precise, pungent, direct. It was flowing all the time. It was almost a quality of naivete . . . and it was completely natural . . . she's very good that way; one has to be local to be universal.": Henri Cartier-Bresson, photo-journalist.

Marilyn Monroe, by Eve Arnold, Alfred A Knopf, 1987, 72-73.

"If I'd observed all the rules, I'd never have got anywhere.": Marilyn Monroe.

Source, unknown.

"Her imitators tried to recreate her walk, but they never even came close to that swivel of the hips that was her trademark. Like Chaplin, she built her film character around her walk. . . .as with everything else (the smile, the voice, the glow) she could turn on the undulating hips at will. . . . No wonder she often spoke of herself in the third person.": Eve Arnold.

Marilyn Monroe, by Eve Arnold, Alfred A Knopf, 1987, 17.

Karen Hagestad Cacy

Chapter Twenty-Three
The Man From the Bar

"And though it is much to be a nobleman, it is more to be a gentleman.": Anthony Trollope, nineteenth century novelist.

"Dogs never bite me; just humans.": Marilyn Monroe.
Source, unknown.

"You know, there was the flavor, the extravagance, the allure, the excitement, the passion, the smash, the clash, the crash . . . this (Diaghilev) *man smashed the atom! . . . His influence on Paris was complete.":* Diana Vreeland.
D.V., by Diana Vreeland, Edited by George Plimpton and Christopher Hemphill, Alfred A. Knopf, 1984, 13-14.

" . . . my parents were racy, pleasure-loving, gala, good-looking Parisians who were part of the whole transition between the Edwardian era and the modern world . . . Money didn't seem to be of any importance to them . . . because of the life they led with fascinating people and events. All kinds of marvelous people came to the house – Diaghilev was very impressive. He had a streak of white hair and a streak of black hair and he put on his hat in the most marvelous way. I remember him very clearly.": Diana Vreeland.
D.V., by Diana Vreeland, Edited by George Plimpton and Christopher Hemphill, Alfred A. Knopf, 1984, 11-12.

"I once heard her talk in her ordinary voice, which was quite unattractive. So, she invented this appealing baby voice.": George Cukor, Director *"Something's Got To Give."*

"Sometimes I've been to a party where no one spoke to me a whole evening. The men, frightened by their wives or sweeties, would give me a wide berth. And the ladies would gang up in a corner to discuss my dangerous character.": Marilyn Monroe.

Karen Hagestad Cacy

My Story, by Marilyn Monroe, with Ben Hecht, Taylor Trade, 2007.

"Stas Radziwill (Prince Stanislas Radziwill (1914-76), Polish nobleman) sits silent throughout dinner party in South of France. Mrs. Kellock, rich American, turns to Stas and says, 'Do you realize you have not addressed one word to me the whole evening?' Stas replies, 'When I sit next to women like you, my best friend is potato.'": Prince Stanislas Radziwill.
The Unexpurgated Beaton: The Cecil Beaton Diaries As He Wrote Them, 1970-1980, Introduction by Hugo Vickers, Alfred A. Knopf, 2002, 375.

Chapter Twenty-Four
Politics Start at the Water's Edge

"Americans! I do not like them. I do not like their principles; I do not like their manners, I do not like their opinions.": Anthony Trollope, nineteenth century novelist.

"Here in New York, every man worships the dollar, and is down before his shrine from morning to night.": Anthony Trollope, nineteenth century novelist.

"Mind you, this took place in 1948. Miss Barney's circle was not limited to lesbians . . . though certainly all the more presentable dykes in town were on hand. Sometimes she had rather curious or unexpected people . . . but it was always very proper . . . talk about this concert or that concert, or so-and-so's paintings, or 'Alice has a fabulous new recipe for eggs.'"
Source, unknown.

"Miss Barney's circle was not limited to lesbians . . . though certainly all the more presentable dykes in town were on hand. . . . Sometimes she had rather curious or unexpected people – the publisher of Bottegh Oscure. Marguerite

Karen Hagestad Cacy

Caetani, Peggy Guggenheim, Djuna Barnes (they always spoke of her as the redheaded bohemian,) but it was always very proper . . . talk about this concert or that concert, or so-and-so's paintings, or 'Alice has a fabulous new recipe for eggs.' The only shocking thing I ever remember was when Carl Van Vechten came for tea and peed on the sofa by mistake. Everybody said, 'Oh-oh, wait a minute,' and then they turned, and down the line Esther Murphy, with the same problem, was peeing on her sofa.": Truman Capote.
Truman Capote: In Which Various Friends, Enemies, Acquaintances, and Detractors Recall His Turbulent Career, by George Plimpton, Doubleday, Anchor Books edition published by arrangement with Nan A. Talese/Doubleday, 1997, 85.

" . . . the Loel Guinnesses visited me and Jack in Verbier in Switzerland for dinner: I made the perfect dinner for them at our house and we had the perfect wine and the house was beautiful. Everything was perfection. Suddenly, Jack looked at Loel Guinness and said 'What the fuck are you doing here, you big fat Nazi?' After that there's nothing you can do. You can't excuse yourself. You can't excuse him. You just have to sit there and die. Can you believe he would do that? No, my dears, I can tell you, separate them at once.": Truman Capote.
Truman Capote: In Which Various Friends, Enemies, Acquaintances, and Detractors Recall His Turbulent Career, by George Plimpton, Doubleday, Anchor Books edition published by arrangement with Nan A. Talese/Doubleday, 1997, 97.

"It was more café society than gratin, mixed with 'newspaper celebrities.'": Cecil Beaton.
Source, unknown.

"When I was a child, I learned that the best way to keep out of trouble was by never complaining or asking for anything. Most of the families had children of their own, and I knew they always came first. They wore the colored dresses and

Karen Hagestad Cacy

owned whatever toys there were, and they were the ones who were believed,": Marilyn Monroe.
My Story, by Marilyn Monroe with Ben Hecht, Taylor Trade, 2007.

" . . . in Hollywood important people can't stand to be invited someplace that isn't full of other important people. They don't mind a few un-famous people being present because they make good listeners. But if a star or a studio chief or any other great movie personages find themselves sitting among a lot of nobodies, they get frightened as if somebody was trying to demote them.: Marilyn Monroe.
My Story, by Marilyn Monroe with Ben Hecht, Taylor Trade, 2007.

Chapter Twenty-Five
Places, Everyone!

" . . . seated in Outer Hebrides!": **Cecil Beaton.**
Source, unknown.

"The only real elegance is in the mind; if you've got that, the rest really comes from it. What I'm talking about is general conversation. Country-house stuff. I adore someone who has the attention of the whole table. Too much these days there's this ritual at dinner of talking to the person on your right and then turning to your left. And people are much too keen on even-steven numbers at dinner ." ". . . Of course, it helps if there's some preposterousness in the air . . . something outrageous or memorable. Greta Garbo always brought a spark that ignited everyone around the table. A great gusher of language. Garbo never called anyone by their first name. 'Mrs. Vreeeelanddd.' Everyone called her 'Miss G.' . . . I learned everything in England. I learned English!": Diana Vreeland.

D.V., by Diana Vreeland, Edited by George Plimpton and Christopher Hemphill, Alfred A. Knopf, 1984.

"The only real elegance is in the mind; if you've got that, the rest really comes from it. What I'm talking about is general conversation. Country-house stuff. I adore someone who has the attention of the whole table. Too much these days there's this ritual at dinner of talking to the person on your right and then turning to your left. And people are much too keen on even-steven numbers at dinner .": Diana Vreeland. Source, unknown.

". . . Of course, it helps if there's some preposterousness in the air . . . something outrageous or memorable. Greta Garbo always brought a spark that ignited everyone around the table. A great gusher of language. Garbo never called anyone by their first name. 'Mrs. Vreeeelanddd.' Everyone called her 'Miss G.' . . . I learned everything in England. I learned English!": Diana Vreeland. Source, unknown.

(Leo Lerman complaining to Diana Vreeland, and her response): *"Anxiety like a distant ship, very far off. What is it? It rises like a miasma from my deep feeling that I am not working enough to earn my pay. All those years of unceasing work, and now – shreds."* (Lerman) *"Listen, buster, you must get used to leisure*!"(Vreeland): Leo Lerman. *The Grand Surprise: The Journals of Leo Lerman,* Stephen Pascal, Alfred A. Knopf, 2007, 511, diary entry: August 11, 1984.

Chapter Twenty-Six
Slow Borschok, Fast Company

"Chefs are curiously color blind," replied the Duchess. "Leave them to their own devices, and you may end up with an all-rose dinner – Crème Portugaise, Saumon Poche with Sauce Cardinal, Jambon with Sauce Hongroise, and Bombe

Marie-Louise. But whatever else might appear on the menu, it should not be soup. One of my firmest rules is 'Don't start a dinner with soup. It's an uninteresting liquid that gets you nowhere.'": The Duchess of Windsor.
Source, unknown.

"It was she (Mrs. Simpson) *who gave the chef and butler their orders; and as she directed the flow of conversation, the King visibly rejoiced; he was like a soloist waiting confidently for the conductor's nod. An observer described the scene to the writer Geoffrey Bocca: the King 'watched her happily as she laughed, joked, talked, spread her strong expressive hands in acute, sharply defined gestures. Then the King would be restored to his old bouncy self.'"*
The Windsor Story, by J. Bryan III and Charles J.V. Murphy, William Morrow & Company, Inc., 1979, 185.

"I recall during the war . . .do you know my friend Ray Goetz? The most amusing man who ever lived. He was married to Irene Bordoni. He was big in the theatre. He brought over that divine Spanish singer, Raquel Meuller, who sang 'Who Will Buy Me Violets?' Anyway once during the war, I said to him, 'Oh Ray!' Isn't it awful about the war?' He turned. He looked at me for just a minute – just a split second – and asked, 'What war?' And with that, he walked right past me like a shadow.": Diana Vreeland.
Source, unknown.

"He was very religious, his faith so deep that normal troubles of existence never touched him. He was absolutely sure that God was on his side. Politically, he was of the almost extinct species –a monarchist. He loved pomp and crowns and never forgot that as a young boy he was presented to the Tsar after one of the performances of the Mariinsky theater . . . His hatred of the Soviet Union was maniacal.": Tamara Geva.
Source, unknown.

Karen Hagestad Cacy

" . . . my husband was punished like a small boy who gets a spanking every day of his life for a single transgression. There was the matter of the monarchy's lack of dignity toward my husband. It occurred to me how ridiculous it is to go on behind a family-designed, government-manufactured curtain of asbestos that protects the British Commonwealth from dangerous us . . . This man, with his unparalleled knowledge, trained in the affairs of State . . . was first given an insignificant military post. Eventually, he was 'put out of harm's way' with an appointment of little consequence – the Governorship of the Bahamas.":   The Duchess of Windsor.
Source, unknown.

(Jerry Zipkin) *"He's as queer as a two-dollar bill. His face is the shape of a bidet* . . . (Sinatra) *was an artist* . . . (the Stones) *are just entertainers . . . Venice is like eating an entire box of chocolate liqueurs in one go . . . that one's about as sexy as a pissing toad . . . he carries a whip for self-flagellation . . ."*: Truman Capote.
Source, unknown.

(Jimmy Donahue) *" . . . a friend called Jimmy a Manhattan Caligula."*
1957, Source, unknown.

(Hostesses often received instructions that when they issued invitations to the Duke and Duchess, Jimmy should be included as well.) *"Can my naughty boy come too?" the Duchess playfully wrote, more than once."*: The Duchess of Windsor.
Source, unknown.

Noel Coward met Capote in Portofino and had a frank discussion with him on the Windsor-Donahue-Windsor triangle: "I like Jimmy," Coward said. "He's an insane camp, but fun. And I like the Duchess; she's the fag-hag to end all – but that's what makes her likeable. The Duke, however, well, he pretends not to hate me. He does, though.

Because I'm queer and he's queer but, unlike him, I don't pretend not to be. Anyway, the fag-hag must be enjoying it. Here she's got a royal queen to sleep with and a rich one to hump.": Noel Coward.
1951, Source, unknown.

"At one of his parties . . . he set Princess Ghislaine de Polignac up with a handsome other guest. She complained to Jimmy and he said to her 'Oh chou-chou, I'm sorry. I told him you were a transvestite.'": Jimmy Donovan.
Source, unknown.

"Once, he was bored by leisurely service in Mexico, so he bellowed at the proprietor: 'Just tell me the name of your country and I'll instruct the State Department to stop your foreign aid.'": Jimmy Donovan.
Source, unknown.

" . . . what he said about the Duchess after their falling out: 'She married a king but she screwed a queen.'": Jimmy Donovan.
Source, unknown.

"When Stravinsky came to live in America, George had an apartment on East Fifty-Seventh Street. . . .He had been quite strapped financially, but he was going to give a dinner for Stravinsky. George said to me, 'When Stravinsky comes, it'll be easier for me if you are here.' Socially he was quite gauche, and of course in this case he was worshipful. Besides having cooked all day and bought the most expensive things, he found two bottles of wine he couldn't possibly afford. When Stravinsky appeared George said, 'Now we have lovely wine.' 'What for?' Stravinsky replied. 'I always bring my own, because nobody at the moment can offer me what I drink.' George was crestfallen; he had spent practically a month's salary on those two bottles.": Lucia Davidova.
Source, unknown.

Karen Hagestad Cacy

" . . . Jimmy, for Wallis, was a last throw of the dice. Count Jean de Baglion, gay, plump, wickedly funny and exceptionally clever, was reported to have provided the Duchess and Jimmy with his apartment. Jimmy's apparent homosexuality shielded the couple from revelations in the press. The Duchess rationalized their 'friendship' by saying she could relate very easily to him because they both were Southerners, even though there was a generation gap. He played the piano, he could tell jokes, he was so witty. Duchess had lunches with Jimmy at the Mediterranee and dinners at the Relais des Porquerolles. When asked, the Duchess reportedly said, "I married David for better or for worse, but not for lunch.": The Duchess of Windsor.
Source, unknown.

"Well, when I have to be somewhere for dinner at eight o'clock, I will lie in the bathtub for an hour or longer. Eight o'clock will come and go and I still remain in the tub. I keep pouring perfumes into the water and letting the water run out and refilling the tub with fresh water. . . . Sometimes I know the truth of what I'm doing. It isn't Marilyn Monroe in the tub but Norma Jean. I'm giving Norma Jean a treat. She used to bathe in water used by six or eight other people. Now she can bathe in water as clean and transparent as a pane of glass. . . . . People are waiting for me. People are eager to see me. I'm wanted. And I remember the years I was unwanted. All the hundreds of times nobody wanted to see the little servant girl, Norma Jean – not even her mother. I feel a queer satisfaction in punishing the people who are wanting me now. But it's not them I'm really punishing. It's the long ago people who didn't want Norma Jean.": Marilyn Monroe.
My Story, by Marilyn Monroe with Ben Hecht, Taylor Trade, 2007.

"I went out and looked in the hall. My mother was on her feet. She was screaming and laughing. They took her away

Karen Hagestad Cacy

to Norwalk Mental Hospital. . . . It was where my mother's father and grandmother had been taken when they started screaming and laughing. / The thought of having a baby stood my hair on end. I could see it only as myself: another Norma Jean in an orphanage.": Marilyn Monroe.
My Story, by Marilyn Monroe with Ben Hecht, Taylor Trade, 2007.

"Small as a child, he looked like no other male adult I'd ever seen. His head was big and handsome, and his butterscotch hair was cut in bangs. Willowy and delicate above the waist, he was, below, as strong and chunky as a Shetland pony.": John Malcolm Brinnin.
Truman Capote: In Which Various Friends, Enemies, Acquaintances, and Detractors Recall His Turbulent Career, by George Plimpton, Doubleday, Anchor Books edition published by arrangement with Nan A. Talese/Doubleday, 1997, 58.

"Truman's in the middle of a story and hears: 'For Christ's sake! Wherever I go I hear that American faggoty pansy voice! Can't I ever get away from you guys?' Truman bristled and got up: 'Just you shut up! Wherever you go you cause fights and trouble . . . fights and trouble . . . Just you shut up! Don't wreck people's lives. Stop calling people faggots.' Then Truman resumes the story calmly.": Karl Bissinger.
Truman Capote: In Which Various Friends, Enemies, Acquaintances, and Detractors Recall His Turbulent Career, by George Plimpton, Doubleday, Anchor Books edition published by arrangement with Nan A. Talese/Doubleday, 1997, 90.

"But there was something wouldn't let me go back to the world of Norma Jean. It wasn't ambition or a wish to be rich and famous . . . There was a thing in me like a craziness that wouldn't let up. It kept speaking to me, not in words abut in colors – scarlet and gold and shining white, greens, blues. They were the colors I used to dream about in my childhood when I tried to hide from the dull, unloving world

Karen Hagestad Cacy

in which the orphanage slave, Norma Jean, existed.": **Marilyn Monroe.**
Source, unknown.

Chapter Twenty-Seven
Sole Bonne Femme

"Anyway, this woman's neighbor at the table, a South American, emptied his largest wineglass and concealed it in his lap, under the tablecloth. She was mystified until a moment later he put it back beside his other glasses, full."
Source, unknown.

"'Cecil, why is it that you are so loathsome in London and yet so delightful in the country?' ": **Cecil Beaton recounting a question by Michael Pitt-Rivers.**
The Unexpurgated Beaton: The Cecil Beaton Diaries As He Wrote Them, 1970-1980, Introduction by Hugo Vickers, Alfred A. Knopf, 2002.

". . . but I'm reading the most divine scandal . . . I'm going to send you this wonderful African pornography . . . Fame is only good for one thing – they will cash your check in a small town . . . I don't care what anybody says about me as long as it isn't true.": **Truman Capote.**
Various sources.

"I went up to Queen Mary and kissed her on both hands and then on both cheeks. She was as cold as ice. When I approached my brother, now King George VI, he completely broke down. So, I said to him, 'Buck up, Bertie. God save the King!'": **The Duke of Windsor.**
Source, unknown.

"Balanchine was something of a mystic. Often, he would say, for instance, 'I spoke to Tchaikovsky this morning, and

Karen Hagestad Cacy

he said he would help us.' I remember when we first did The Nutcracker, at curtain opening night none of the costumes for the second act had arrived from Karinska. It seemed as if we would have to end the performance at intermission. But Balanchine said, 'Don't worry. I spoke to Tchaikovsky and they'll be here.' Sure enough, the costumes began drifting in. Dancers dressed in the hallways and rushed onstage.": Hugh Fiorato.

I Remember Balanchine: Recollections of the Ballet Master by Those Who Knew Him," by Francis Mason, Doubleday, 1991.

Life – /I am of both of your directions/ Life (crossed out)/ Somehow remaining hanging downward/ the most/ but strong as a cobweb in the /wind – I exist more with the cold glistening frost. / But my beaded rays have the colors I've/ seen in a painting –/ ah life they/ have cheated you.: Marilyn Monroe.

Source, unknown.

Chapter Twenty-Eight
Poulet braise au champagne
Buckwheat Kasha
St. Julien Bordeaux

"After dinner, we went into the bar to shoot craps. When (John) Huston gave Marilyn the dice, she asked: 'What should I shoot for John?' His answer: 'Don't think, honey, just throw. That's the story of your life. Don't think – do it.'": John Huston.

Source, unknown.

"I saw the amazing phenomenon of Hollywood being outsmarted by a girl whom it characterized as a dumb blonde.": Philippe Halsman.

Source, unknown.

Karen Hagestad Cacy

"There was this man, I'll call him, Mr. Sylvester, because that was his name. Mr. Sylvester. I'll never forget when I read for him. He says, 'Try one of the long speeches.' Then he interrupts my reading, "Would you please raise your dress a few inches?' So, I lifted the hem above me knee and kept on reading. '"A little higher, please," he says. I lifted the hem to my thighs without missing a word of the speech. 'A little higher,' Mr. Sylvester said again. For some time afterward, his words haunted me as I had heard the true voice of Hollywood – 'Higher, higher, higher.'": Marilyn Monroe.
Source, unknown.

"I told Lee I was simply unable to be on time. So, he says to me, 'Well, be early then.'": *Marilyn Monroe.*
Source, unknown.

(Her own mother never told her she was pretty.)
"All mothers should tell daughters they are pretty, even if they are not.": Marilyn Monroe.
Source, unknown.

"She wore so many diamonds . . .of course, she was famous for getting money out of the men who went out with her." I was speaking of Peggy Hopkins.": Diana Vreeland.
Source, unknown.

"I owe Marilyn Monroe a real debt. It was because of her that I played the Mocambo. She personally called the owner and told him she wanted me booked immediately and if he would do it she would take a front table every night. . . . after that, I never had to play a small jazz club again. She was an unusual woman – a little ahead of her times. And she didn't know it.": Ella Fitzgerald.

"Great men have their moments, I can tell you. A certain Christmas Eve with Bill in the Caribbean comes to mind.

Karen Hagestad Cacy

Everything was perfect. I bought and wrapped presents, placing them around a Christmas tree on the boat. I'd strung up little twinkly lights. Drinks were served. A tape of Christmas songs was playing. The boat was anchored in the most charming, lovely, beautiful, protected cove in the entire Caribbean. Everything was perfect." "But then Bill suddenly decided it would be even more perfect if we up-anchored and moved across the way to a different cove. I said, 'Bill, just leave it.' But leaving it was not Bill's way. So off we went. And of course, a sudden squall hit, drenching us all, washing the gifts overboard, shorting out the Christmas lights, knocking over the tree. Then we went aground. So, there we were in the dark at a forty-five degree angle atop a sandbar in a rainstorm, on Christmas Eve.":
Pat Buckley.
Losing Mum and Pup, by Christopher Buckley, Twelve: Hatchett Book Group, 2009, 119.

"Le Boeuf sur le Toit was where everybody went late, late at night after other people's dinners and balls and parties. Truman was involved in everything. Le Boeuf was in full force: the Windsor's and Jimmy Donahue . . . it was very, very snappy. There was always a cabaret with somebody singing and playing the piano. I think the duchess even sang at one point."
Source, unknown.

Chapter Twenty-Nine
German Rieslings

"Riesling is 'the true king' of the German wine grapes. Indeed, in no other wine growing area on earth does Riesling reach such heights of quality and sheer deliciousness as it does in Germany."
"German wines are also unique in that the grapes are picked at many levels of ripeness and maturity, allowing the wine makers to produce Rieslings ranging from dry,

Karen Hagestad Cacy

(Kabinett,) to medium-dry (Spatlese,) to sweet (Auslese,) to super sweet (Beeren and Trockenbeerenauslese and Eiswein.) There is a style of German Riesling for every palate.": Web Page: Morrell, "Fine Wines of Germany."
One Rockefeller Plaza, New York, NY 10020.

"Balanchine always said that he remembered the first impression of every single dancer. . . . He also used to kid around that dancers were different animals. He could be very wicked. I remember I was a porcupine. My friend Barbara Milberg who was very beautiful was a delicious mushroom. Tanny and Nicky and Maria were little monkeys – the best animal to be, the kind that can move and do anything. He had animals for everything.": Barbara Walczak.
I Remember Balanchine: Recollections of the Ballet Master by Those Who Knew Him," by Francis Mason, Doubleday, 1991.

"'Maria! How long it will take you to die?' . . . I began to fall to the floor . . . Stravinsky began snapping his fingers – snap, snap, snap, snap – I think it was four counts. 'That is enough,' he decided. 'Now you are dead.' And he put those counts into the score. No one was allowed to pad a part. Again, you see, it was exact.": Maria Tallchief.
I Remember Balanchine: Recollections of the Ballet Master by Those Who Knew Him," by Francis Mason, Doubleday, 1991.

"Balanchine once explained the end of La Somnambula by saying 'Very simple. Poet gets better. Marries Somnambulist. They move to Scarsdale. Have nice house and five children. She cooks those awful heavy quiches.'": Allegra Kent.
I Remember Balanchine: Recollections of the Ballet Master by Those Who Knew Him," by Francis Mason, Doubleday, 1991.

"I think Balanchine lived in his own world. I don't think many people really realized his sensitivity. . . . he was a solitary person, very much apart.": Tamara Toumanova.
Source, unknown.

"Since I lived on the West Side, I would run into Balanchine on the street for years . . . and he would say, 'Now, have you read the Russians?' He would give me lists – Dostoevski, Tolstoy, Gogol.": Constance Clausen.
Source, unknown.

"I lived in foster homes. Nobody wanted me. I went to the movies all day long to get away from everything.": Marilyn Monroe.
Source, unknown.

"Tanny couldn't even lift her fingers. It was horrid. Balanchine really saved her from insanity. He made what he called a five-year plan for her. He said, 'This is our first five-year plan, this is our second,' and got her to accept the situation. Then he couldn't continue, and it was very tough on him.": Natalie Molostwoff.
Source, unknown.

Dinner with Bruce Chatwin – 'What are you writing about, Bruce?' 'Wales, Diana.' 'Whales?! Blue whales, Sperrrm whales!! THE WHITE WHALE!' 'No, no, Diana! Wales! Welsh Wales! The country to the west of England.' 'Oh! Wales! I do know Wales. Little grey houses. Covered in roses. In the rain.'": Diana Vreeland.
D.V., by Diana Vreeland, Edited by George Plimpton and Christopher Hemphill, Alfred A. Knopf, 1984.

"Maharajahs and maharanis, the Czar and the Czarina, the Kaiser and the Kaiserin . . . and Queen Mary and King George V! She passed by for just a few minutes, but to this day I would recognize her as I recognize you.": Diana Vreeland.
D.V., by Diana Vreeland, Edited by George Plimpton and Christopher Hemphill, Alfred A. Knopf, 1984, 19.

Chapter Thirty
Royal Treatment

'ooey-gooey': Truman Capote's term for lip gloss.
Source, unknown.

"the Duke's favorite brandy, a seventy-five-year-old Forge de Sazerac, accompanied by an Upmann cigar the shape and approximate size of a torpedo."
The Windsor Story, by J. Bryan III and Charles J.V. Murphy, William Morrow & Company, Inc., 1979, 539.

"That Mossad file on Maxwell concluded with a paragraph extracted from a Department of Trade report on his methods: 'He is a man of great energy, drive and imagination, but unfortunately an apparent fixation as to his own abilities causes him to ignore the views of others if these are not compatible.'"
Robert Maxwell, Israel's Superspy: The Life and Murder of a Media Mogul, by Gordon Thomas and Martin Dillon, Carroll and Graf Publishers, 2002, 12.

"'I can't figger things out,' Metcalfe wrote to his wife on 22 October (1939). 'She [Wallis] & he [Edward] know every d---n thing. She will know whom I dined or lunched with or have spoken to & even seen. I believe she has spies out & they work well. Anyhow it's terrifying . . . I'm fed up with Paris & this war – whichever you like. I don't like my job . . . & I never feel secure & safe when working for HRH.'":
Major Edward Dudley "Fruity" Metcalfe.
Hidden Agenda: How the Duke of Windsor Betrayed the Allies, by Martin Allen, Macmillan, 2000, 153.

Charles Eugene Bedaux may have spied for Germany during the First World War, and was the one who opened doors in Nazi Germany for the Windsor's during the Second World War.
Source, unknown.

Karen Hagestad Cacy

"Within 6 months, Maxwell had created an umbrella of companies. He even offered to service Bulgaria's foreign debt with a bank he created. He was the man with Midas touch who blew his golden trumpet and everybody danced to his tune. Fawned upon by president and commoner alike, offered anything he liked – a car, a mansion, even a king's palace – provided with anyone he liked – an actress, a dancer from a nightclub, even a pretty housekeeper who had briefly taken his fancy –Robert Maxwell was indeed the undisputed ruler of Bulgaria and in many ways beyond it, the first authentic tycoon of the Eastern Bloc."
Robert Maxwell, Israel's Superspy: The Life and Murder of a Media Mogul, by Gordon Thomas and Martin Dillon, Carroll and Graf Publishers, 2002.

"If you want something badly enough, you'll get it, whatever it is. You've got to really want it, and concentrate on it for twenty-four hours a day, but if you do, you'll get it. I have never found that to be untrue.": Truman Capote.
Source, unknown.

"'He didn't do very much in life. I once asked him, 'Fruity, what do you do in the morning?' 'I dress.' 'Well, so do I.' 'Well, they put out my ties and so forth and I have to choose.'": Diana Vreeland.
D.V., by Diana Vreeland, Edited by George Plimpton and Christopher Hemphill, Alfred A. Knopf, 1984, 71.

Chapter Thirty-One
"She murdered her husband."

"By 1947, when he met the Windsor's, New York playboy Jimmy Donahue was as notorious in society as his father had been. Despite the fact that press agents organized numerous women for his as well-publicized dates, he remained exclusively interested in men. With unlimited

Karen Hagestad Cacy

cash, he could afford the most expensive call-boys; he staged elaborate orgies during his mother's absences in Palm Beach."
Source, unknown.

While the Duchess was absorbed with the Duke's food poisoning in 1952, Jimmy went to stay with Barbara Hutton in rented house at Hillsborough (SF). Freed from the courtly constraints of escorting the Windsor's around, he and Barbara took themselves off to the Beige Room, a gay club which featured female impersonators. Barbara had been told that one of the transvestite acts was a send-up of herself and the other richest woman in the world, Doris Duke. The women were portrayed traveling across America in the back of a limousine when they stop at a service station to visit the bathroom. Barbara goes first but on her return warns there is no toilet paper. Doris, desperate, rummages through her bag but finds no substitute. "You should have said something earlier, Dee-Dee," remarks Barbara. "If I'd known I would have saved you a traveller's cheque. I just used my last one."
Source, unknown.

"Asked by a newspaper columnist about the rumors that there had been a split between him and the Windsor's, he quipped, 'I've abdicated.' Later he was seen sauntering down Fifth Avenue with a young male companion. 'Let me introduce you,' he whooped, 'to the boy who took the boy who took the girl who took the boy off the throne of Merry Old England.'"
Source, unknown.

"He would call someone: 'Beauty? Gorgeous? Adorable One? This is Truman, do you want to have lunch?' He always came rehearsed. He would never just have lunch with you, he'd lined up things to tell you. He came loaded for bear. Always. Always had storied about who had had the latest shots at that clinic in Switzerland, or some

Karen Hagestad Cacy

scandalous gossip about some cardinal of the Catholic Church."
Source, unknown.

"In January 1955, the Windsor's visited President Eisenhower at the White House. In October Mrs. George Baker gave a party for the Windsor's at her elaborate home at Locust Valley, Long Island. Fifty-eight guests attended for a banquet and dancing. Among the guests were two recent acquaintances of the duchess, the wealthy and handsome 35-year old sportsman and horse race owner William Woodward, Jr., and his wife Ann. Wallis very much liked Woodward's mother, the still glamorous and fascinating former Elsie Ogden Cryder. The Woodward's left the party at I am returning to their home at Oyster Bay. . The Windsor's, who were staying with Mrs. Baker, were advised of the shooting that night, Wallis had even danced with Bill Woodward at the party. The duke shared Woodward's interest in horses and they had enjoyed their meetings socially over the previous months. Wallis as questioned twice by the police. The Windsor's were asked about the killing wherever they went. They decided wisely not to get involved, and made no attempt to contact Ann, though they remained in close touch with Mrs. Baker and with Elsie Woodward on the matter."
Source, unknown.

"Many refused to believe Ann's version of the story. The most persistent skeptic was Capote who thought her guilty of murder. (his later book outlined this and he was spurned by society, on whom his whole life hinged; the Windsor's later after the book would be as angry with him as everyone else. Not now though.)"
Source, unknown.

"Did you know that Andy Warhol never goes to funerals? His thought is, 'They went uptown to Bloomingdale's and

Karen Hagestad Cacy

then never came back. They went shopping.'": **Truman Capote.**
Source, unknown.

"That year he had stayed away from too much drinking, too much cocaine, though he was smoking a lot of pot. Somebody gave him a lot of pot but he didn't know how to roll it. He said 'Can you send somebody over?' So, I asked a friend of mine if he would mind going over to roll some joints for Truman. This friend went over to the UN Plaza. Truman greeted him and set him up in the living room with all this pot. He rolled a hundred joints and then he thought he'd had it. Truman gave him a one-joint tip and also gave him a pair of evening slippers which he said were his, "especially made for me at Lobb's of London." . . .Within 3 days, Truman called me back to say 'Could you send this friend of yours back to roll some more joints?' 'Truman, he told me he rolled a hundred joints. How could you smoke a hundred joints in three days?' He said, 'Well, I shared.'":
Truman Capote.
Source, unknown.

Did I tell you if anything happens to me I want to be cremated and half my ashes in LA and half in NY so I can continue to be bi-coastal.": **Truman Capote.**
Source, unknown.

"It's not that she is pretty although, of course, she is almost incredibly pretty – but that she radiates at the same time unbounded vitality and a kind of unbelievable innocence. I have met the same in a lion cub that my native servants in Africa brought me. I would not keep her." : Isak Dinesen.
The Genius and the Goddess, Arthur Miller & Marilyn Monroe, by Jeffrey Meyers, University of Illinois Press, 2009, 175.

"But the intensely romantic and highly publicized marriage greatly enhanced his image and actually took the pressure off Miller. The courts finally decided it was best not to

Karen Hagestad Cacy

imprison the husband of America's most glamorous and desirable woman."

The Genius and the Goddess, Arthur Miller & Marilyn Monroe, by Jeffrey Meyers, University of Illinois Press, 2009, 149.

Chapter Thirty-Two
"Not of Our Class, Darling"

"Truman and Jack continued to enjoy the expatriate life in Italy, spending the summer of 1953 in the village of Portofino. Truman's favorite diversion at this time was the company of his friend Cecil Beaton. Like Truman, Beaton was a man with an insatiable appetite for good gossip who had perfected the art of collecting the right friends. Their combined address books listed everyone of note in America, Europe and the rest of the globe. Beaton's visit to Portofino in August was a pleasant end to the summer."
Source, unknown.

"People don't love me. I'm a freak. People don't love me. People are fascinated by me, but people don't love me. When I walk into a room, there's a shock on people's faces. I see it; they don't see how they look; I see how they look. Why I'm so outrageous, so ridiculous and so squeaking and so carrying on is simply to relieve them of the sudden embarrassment. I do something so outrageous that all they can do is laugh and then it's okay. I have to do that every time I walk into a room or meet somebody." You never "The only way people can hurt me is if I let them get close to me. And sometimes I meet people who aren't what they make themselves out to be. Then I get hurt. But I'm very careful about that now, about who I get close to.": Truman Capote.
Source, unknown.

"The only way people can hurt me is if I let them get close to me. And sometimes I meet people who aren't what they make themselves out to be. Then I get hurt. But I'm very

Karen Hagestad Cacy

careful about that now, about who I get close to.": **Truman Capote.**
Source, unknown.

"Christopher Isherwood used to tinkle on the rug at parties."
Source, unknown.

"Truman was a professional observer of the wealthy. He adored being entertained by them. On the one hand, he loved the luxury and the chance to observe them. On the other hand, he was jealous of their riches and disapproving of their way of life."
Source, unknown.

"I'm in a fucking prison and my jailer is named Arthur Miller . . . every morning he goes into that goddamn study of his, and I don't see him for hours and hours.": **Marilyn Monroe.**
My Story, by Marilyn Monroe with Ben Hecht, Taylor Trade, 2007.

"She looked like, if you bit her, milk and honey would flow from her.": **Artist, Franz Kline.**
Source, unknown.

"When you look at Marilyn Monroe on the screen, you don't want anything bad to happen to her. You really care that she should be all right . . . happy.": **Natalie Wood.**
Source, unknown.

"She appeared kind and soft and helpless. Almost everyone wanted to help her. Marilyn's supposed helplessness was her greatest strength.": **Sydney Skolsky.**
Source, unknown.

"Starting tomorrow I will take care of myself for that's all I really have and as I see it now have ever had. Roxbury – I've tried to imagine spring all winter – it's here and I still

feel hopeless. I think I hate it here because there is no love here anymore.": **Marilyn Monroe.**
My Story, by Marilyn Monroe with Ben Hecht, Taylor Trade, 2007.

"In May 1940, Winston Churchill, acting on the recommendation of Sir Robert Vansittart and Clement Attlee, imprisoned the Mosely's in London for activities that were considered inimical to the public safety under the provisions of the specially introduced Regulation 18B. They suffered privations in jail and later were released. But at the end of the war, Clement Attlee was elected prime minister, and continued to make the couple's lives miserable."
"The Duchess of Windsor: The Secret Life," by Charles Higham, McGraw-Hill Book Company, 1988.

"Lady Mosley and her husband were forbidden the use of passports and eventually fled the country aboard a chartered yacht for Ireland. They later went to France where they became acquainted with the Windsor's. The Mosley's continued to feel Hitler was a genius and a potential savior of the twentieth century. They said the Windsor's shared their view. Adding spice to the political stew were stories to the effect that the Duchess of Windsor was herself a Jew."
"The Duchess of Windsor: The Secret Life," by Charles Higham, McGraw-Hill Book Company, 1988.

"See you around, like n'ever.'": **Marilyn Monroe.**

"Help Help
Help
I feel life coming closer
when all I want
is to die
Scream –
You began and ended in air

K a r e n   H a g e s t a d   C a c y

but where was the middle?": Marilyn Monroe.
The Genius and the Goddess, Arthur Miller & Marilyn Monroe, by Jeffrey Meyers, University of Illinois Press, 2009, 56, and

"It's a good saying though not so funny –what it stands for though – pain: 'If I had my life to live over, I'd live over a saloon.' . . . . It is rather a determination not to be overwhelmed . . .I feel as though it's all happening to someone right next to me. I'm close, I can feel it, I can hear it, but it isn't really me." **Marilyn Monroe.**
My Story, by Marilyn Monroe with Ben Hecht, Taylor Trade, 2007.

"I'm beside myself! I'm beside myself! I'm beside myself!": **Truman Capote.**

(Lincoln Kirstein) *". . . hands you money and runs away before you can thank him.":* **George Balanchine.**
Source, unknown.

"How can Kirstein be a director of a ballet company? He took some ballet lessons from me and he can't get his feet off the floor.": **Mikhail Fokine.**
Source, unknown.
"I lunched with Lincoln, who was vituperative and 'honest fellers' about almost everyone . . . 'Nora's finished,' he said. 'Diana (Adams) is the comer. Balanchine adores her. Her arms get better, says Balanchine. . . . Jerry (Robbins) is a shit – a mean spirited, opportunist little bastard. Gore (Vidal)'s horrible . . .' So he went on, gaily demolishing." : **Leo Lerman.**
The Grand Surprise: The Journals of Leo Lerman, Stephen Pascal, Alfred A. Knopf, 2007.

Karen Hagestad Cacy

Chapter Thirty-Three
Memories

"That was something. It took hours and hours before you even got there. So, you took food and you took a flask. And you sat forever, because all the cars were held up in the Mall, with all of London looking in at you and saying 'Ere's to you, dearie!' and 'Cheerio, duckie!' and all that divine Cockney stuff. . . .I remember curtsying to King George and Queen Mary; Now I happen to love curtsying. I was brought up British, don't forget! . . . 'We're not a royal country.'. .We're all exiles from something, but never to be able to go back to our country is something we don't know. . . . Of all the countries I've known, if it were my country not to be able to come back to this one would be the most terrible.' When she found herself walking through Red Square in the middle of the night, she said she felt like a child." 'It was light right up until about eleven-thirty, but it wasn't sun, it was light, the light behind the sky.' She didn't think she'd like the midnight sun. She said what she loves is darkness – changing. She loved the golden onion domes and the beautiful skies. She loves medieval Russia. She said, 'Moscow is really my town.' She adores what she calls 'les russes.' She calls them that out of habit, because of the Ballets Russes, because of Fokine, because of all the émigrés she used to see in London, Paris, Lausanne, and New York.":* Diana Vreeland.

D.V., by Diana Vreeland, Edited by George Plimpton and Christopher Hemphill, Alfred A. Knopf, 1984.

"Defy me and see what happens –you'll have to crawl back.": George Balanchine.
Source, unknown.

"(Balanchine) is 'Georgian like Stalin, even sinister. He seems as soft as silk, but he's as tough as steel.": Lincoln Kirstein.
Source, unknown.

Karen Hagestad Cacy

"I loved watching Balanchine wheel and deal, and do all his things with all the dancers. Screw people, he obviously did, right and left, in all kinds of ways.": **Richard Thomas.**
Source, unknown.

"When I was young in Russia in a way we were little wild animals. We were forced to bring ourselves up, to improvise our lives and that left its mark.": **George Balanchine.**
Source, unknown.

(John Cranko's choreography): *"You know why that one die?"* (Cranko had died young.) *"Tchaikovsky up in heaven looked down and saw that ballet 'Eugene Onegin,' and went to God and said 'Get that one!'"* (Shostakovich) *"a dreadful composer, he wrote like a peasant."* (Bartok and Dvorak) *"Horribly overrated."* (Sibelius) *"now nobody plays him; his music is a disaster.":* **George Balanchine.**
Source, unknown.

"He was both cool and ardent, sad and full of fun, arrogant and modest, a towering genius who likes to . . . play solitaire. A real Russian personality. Face sharp, body is lean, flexible. Walks erect confidently, quickly but without rushing. That impossible Texan string tie dangles from his neck. He exudes elegance, energy, joy."
Source, unknown.

"Balanchine was Georgian, exactly the same countryside Stalin came from. In a very mild way, he had that tendency of character. He liked to be in his own place and what he says goes.": **Igor Youskevitch.**
Source, unknown.

Truth Takes a Holiday
From various taped Jack Paar television shows:

. . . I was reminded of once early on in my career when I was reading off of them for a commercial. We're on the air, the camera's rolling. So, I'm reading along: 'Do your hands sweat? Do you have insomnia? Do you sometimes have difficulty turning your head?' And I stopped reading. My producer said, 'Jack, what's wrong?' I said, 'I have this disease.': Jack Paar.

He's a young man who's caught on big everywhere but on this show. I want him to be bigger than I am even if he'll never be back. Ladies and Gentlemen, may I present to you Mr. Woody Allen.: Jack Paar.

" . . . I was delightful. I told a joke. You would've loved me. . . . I had a deep cavity and my dentist had sent me to a chiropodist . . . ": Woody Allen.

"Thanks very much, Jack. You know four years ago when I was here, nobody else would've had me on.": Oscar Levant.

"Well, I was drinking at the time.": Jack Paar.

"The only reason I'm appearing is there were no more beds left in the sanitarium.": Oscar Levant.

"What do you do for exercise, Oscar?": Jack Paar.

"I stumble, then I fall into a coma . . . You have the most responsive audience since Adolph Hitler . . . the good old days.": Oscar Levant.

"You always bring a certain aura of danger with you.": Jack Paar.

"Because you never know what the hell I'm going to say next.": Truman Capote.

(. . . when you said, all actors are stupid) . . . "You're overstating it. What I said was, some actors are stupid.": Truman Capote.

"If you take yer chances, 'ya take yer chances.. . I have my own little secrets. . . " Truman Capote.
"Not too many by this time.": Jack Paar.

"You'd be amazed. My life is so strange it's not like anybody.": Truman Capote.

" . . . you might be suffering from alcoholism.": Jack Paar.

"My God, alcohol is the least of it. That's the joker in the cards. . . There's never been anyone like me and after I'm gone there ain't going to be anyone like me again.": Truman Capote.

Author's Notes
George Balanchine, "Mr. B," America's premier dance impresario: im.pre.sa.rio\n, [It, fr. Impresa undertaking, fr. Imprendere to undertake fr. (assumed) VL imprehendere-- more ar EMPRISE](1746) I: the promoter, manager, or conductor of an opera or concert company 2: one who puts on or sponsors an entertainment:
Webster's Ninth New Collegiate Dictionary, Merriam-Webster, Inc., 1990.

"Ballet is a riddle of means and ends . . . It is as if the performer and spectator come together to hold in their hands a bird with a broken wing. The creature can be felt to stir, to struggle for freedom. Its life responds to human warmth; its wing might brush your cheek as it flies away": Gelsey Kirkland.

Karen Hagestad Cacy

Dancing on my Grave, by Gelsey Kirkland with Greg Lawrence, Berkley Book, 1986, 81 but why means large honor was once write Les of art as a it is a top aide to Ruelle you are our chimney will worldwide, are buying in lower slope of July oh PPG are all the radio layer closes in you-know.

"I call her (Suzanne Farrell) 'pussy-cat fish,' because the cat was cheetah, for speed, and the fish was dolphin, for intelligence.": George Balanchine.
Source, unknown.

Karen Hagestad Cacy is also the author of the novels,

- ✓ Death by President
- ✓ Return to Ismailia
- ✓ Summer at Pebble Beach

Her other credits include:

- ✓ SAY UNCLE! a two-act play
- ✓ SAY UNCLE! a screenplay
- ✓ "Dinner at Mr. B's," a three-act play

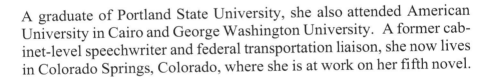

A graduate of Portland State University, she also attended American University in Cairo and George Washington University. A former cabinet-level speechwriter and federal transportation liaison, she now lives in Colorado Springs, Colorado, where she is at work on her fifth novel.

Contact: cacykarenhagestad@yahoo.com

Made in the USA
Columbia, SC
05 April 2021

35596194R00178